FIGHTING
DIRTY

JUNE HAMPSON

First published in Great Britain in 2011 by Orion Books,
an imprint of The Orion Publishing Group Ltd
Orion House, 5 Upper Saint Martin's Lane
London WC2H 9EA

An Hachette UK Company

1 3 5 7 9 10 8 6 4 2

A CIP catalogue record for this book
is available from the British Library.

ISBN (Hardback) 978 0 7528 9736 3
ISBN (Trade Paperback) 978 0 7528 9737 0

Typeset by Deltatype Ltd, Birkenhead, Merseyside

Printed in Great Britain by Clays Ltd, St Ives plc

The Orion Publishing Group's policy is to use papers
that are natural, renewable and recyclable products and
made from wood grown in sustainable forests. The logging
and manufacturing processes are expected to conform to
the environmental regulations of the country of origin.

www.orionbooks.co.uk

This book is for my readers and my students

You cannot step into the same river,
for other waters are continually flowing in.
Heraclitus, ca. 500BC

Acknowledgements

Thank you Juliet, Sara and Natalie.
Orion has a special crew working magic.

PROLOGUE

The hand around his throat tightened. Paulie wrenched at the powerful arm but the grip was rigid. It was difficult for him to breathe and all his power seemed to be draining away. Then the boy shoved his thumb into Paulie's eye. This sudden further pain gave him the strength to buck and he slithered through the boy's grip, but then the boy's palm connected with Paulie's chin. He registered the salty taste of fresh blood and knew he'd bitten through his tongue. Blood dripped from Paulie's mouth and his knees buckled.

He was falling ...

The man named Heinz yelled above the jeering crowd, 'Git up, you little bastard, I got a lot of money ridin' on you!'

Paulie, naked, slippery with his own blood and sweat, squatted on the floor. Standing in the corner of the room was the well kitted-out Jamie Lane who was often at the fights but who rarely spoke. Suddenly a mighty kick bounced Paulie back against the bars of the cage surrounding them and the other boy, red-haired and muscular, aimed a further kick that connected with Paulie's shoulder. When Paulie tried to raise his neck the boy took a few fighter's dancing steps, then with a light leap in the air landed both his feet on Paulie's skull.

Too late to fend off the kicking attack, Paulie lay there, a rushing sound in his head. He put up his hand and cupped his ear then saw the blood that had trickled on to his fingers.

The noise from the crowd seemed muffled. He curled himself into a foetal position and lay there, unmoving. He felt confused and broken, like a doll that's been stamped on. Then he saw Heinz pushing through the people and the cage door was unlocked.

Despite the noise and pain, Paulie's spirits rose.

'Bout over,' the blond man yelled, his tone decisive. More booing erupted from the crowd crammed in the stinking basement. Stamping feet caused the smell of sweat and filth to swirl like fog. Despite the egg cartons pinned to the ceiling and walls to absorb the sound, the noise was tumultuous.

Through blurry eyes, Paulie saw Jamie Lane turn away, pulling up the collar of his leather jacket as he did so. Heinz raised the redhead's arm, pronouncing him the winner. Still dancing about, the boy looked triumphant. His freckled body was pale except where Paulie's teeth and fists had left bloodied marks.

Paulie roused himself and shook his head to restore his failing eyesight and scrambled brain. After a while the buzzing in his skull stopped. Bare feet on his head had hurt, but not as much as an opponent wearing boots would have done.

'Pay the fuckers!' Heinz yelled into the fifty-odd crowd who were still calling out and protesting about the shortness of the fight. Paulie's eyes alighted on the beefy man guarding the door. Heinz yelled again, 'Then get all the bastards out!'

Heinz snarled at the redhead, 'Get fuckin' dressed then push off. You'll get your money later.' His face peered into Paulie's. Paulie could smell his tangy aftershave and it made his stomach heave. 'You'll be as right as rain tomorrow.'

The red-haired boy disappeared and Paulie sat, still in the cage, getting his wind back. He watched the last punter collect his winnings from the beefy bloke then exit through the paint-peeled front door – and then there were only the four of them: Jamie Lane, Heinz, Beefy, and himself.

Paulie felt a little better now and wiped away the blood on his arms, making the skin smeary with the red grime. He noted with satisfaction that there was dirty blood belonging to the redhead beneath his nails.

'What's it to be this time for their wages?' Beefy nodded towards Paulie. 'Second-hand BMX bikes or Atari consoles? Or money? We done all right tonight.' He locked and bolted the door.

'We'd have done better if that little shit had won.' Jamie Lane gestured towards Paulie while still keeping his eyes on the money Beefy was counting.

'He's tired.' Heinz was smiling.

'He's a fuckin' kid. They don't get tired, wanker!' Jamie snapped. He tucked the roll of notes handed to him by Beefy in his inside pocket and approached Paulie.

'Get up,' he said.

Paulie crawled out of the cage to freedom. Every bone in his body was aflame. 'Me 'ead hurts,' he mumbled.

'And my fuckin' 'eart 'urts where it pains me most, an' that's in me bleedin' wallet.'

Paulie knew he'd disappointed Jamie Lane. He tried to excuse himself.

'I don't feel well.' The vision of the man swam, melting into two people then back again to a single figure.

'You looks like you've gone ten rounds with fuckin' Muhammad Ali, not a kid your own age,' said Beefy.

Paulie felt a rush of something sliding and put a hand to his ear. It came away covered in bright red, wet blood. He looked at it as though it didn't belong to him.

'Don't you worry about that, mate, it 'appens sometimes. You'll get used to it,' Heinz said dismissively. Perhaps it didn't matter, thought Paulie. Perhaps the man was for once telling the truth. After all, he supposed the man saw far more blood at the dog fights that he organised.

Jamie Lane stared at him for a few moments before walking to the front door and announcing, 'I'm off.'

When the door closed, Paulie looked expectantly at Heinz.

'Can I be paid now, before I goes home?'

'You expect to be paid for losing me money, do you? You'll get something, lad. An' I knows I can trust you not to squeal about these fights. You'll be dead meat if it comes back to me that you been shoutin' your mouth off. Keep your trap shut an' you'll get a bit extra. But you gotta give to get, you know? Stand up and follow me.'

Paulie knew what was coming next and his heart fell. He badly wanted to cry but knew he daren't show this man his true feelings. Of course he'd keep his mouth shut. Not just about the fighting but about the other stuff. If anyone at school found out about it they'd make his life a misery by calling him names. The fact he could fight his way out of trouble meant nothing. He'd never be able to shake off the label they'd stick on him. Heinz had him by the short and curlies.

Somewhere, close by, a transistor was playing 'Chariots of Fire' by Vangelis. Paulie liked that music.

Gloom descended over him again. He couldn't see a way to rid himself of Heinz, or how to stop doing the other stuff he hated, and he needed the money.

He was just glad that, unlike some of the other boys who fought in Chestnut House, his mother and his nan hadn't been there to see him lose. It must be a terrible thing to hear your family shout and stamp and yell at you to finish off your opponent.

Heinz sat down on a stool and once more Paulie obediently fell to his knees. The blond man unzipped his fly and eleven-year-old Paulie's head, as usual, bent forward.

CHAPTER 1

'Be careful what you wish for, you might just get it.'

Daisy Lane looked into the slate-grey eyes of her lover, eyes that had been replicated in their three-year-old daughter. She creased her forehead with disbelief at his words then tentatively asked, 'You'd really take my Jamie back to London for a while, Roy?'

The radio was playing 'Apache'. The music gave the hallway a welcoming feel. Daisy automatically pulled the cashmere scarf from Roy's neck and looped it over the stair rail. He slid out of his black wool overcoat and slung it after the neckpiece.

The gangster put his big hand on her shoulder. His eyes scoured her face.

'He's a fuckin' head case, Dais, so you've got to let me 'ave full rein.'

'I needs you to keep an eye on him, not beat him to death if he upsets you.'

She shrugged off his hand, but still he looked intently at her.

'He upsets you right enough. 'Ave you looked in the mirror lately, girl?'

Daisy knew she'd lost weight, lost her sparkle; knew her hair wasn't the shiny blonde she'd once been proud of. Worry and hard work were taking their toll and there were times when she felt she was losing control of situations she had sailed through in the past. She needed to gather together her thoughts, her life and her health before the disintegration of her family finally spiralled out of control.

Even if it meant Roy Kemp taking her beloved eighteen-year-old son away with him.

'I'm just tired.' She put her arms around Roy and nuzzled her face into the hollow of his neck. The fresh scent of Imperial Leather soap comforted her. She said carefully, 'Jamie has money an' I don't know where he gets it from. When I ask he just shrugs his shoulders. I'm not bleedin' stupid, Roy. Jamie's up to something.'

'Dais, do you always think the worst?'

'With my Jamie I do. If he's out from under me feet, I'll 'ave more time to spend with Gypsy.' She looked at Roy, the villain it seemed she'd been tied to for most of her life. She knew him and loved him, and he would always be a part of her.

Years ago he'd told her he'd look after her boys. He'd been like a father to Eddie, but Jamie had been aloof and ignored Roy's offer of friendship. Perhaps it was now time for Jamie to leave the nest and find out what life was like outside the family unit.

'He'll jump at the idea of being in the Smoke, always says Gosport's a dead an' alive hole.' Daisy stepped back then ran her fingers through her limp hair. 'Besides, I need to work. And between you and me, I enjoy bein' behind the bar down at the White Swan, sometimes I even forget me troubles ...'

'You sure it ain't the attention of the blokes makes you forget?'

She thought how funny it was that after all these years his nearness could still make her go weak at the knees, even when he was upset, as now. Grabbing hold of her arm, he said,

'You don't need to work at all, especially not in a poxy pub in Gosport. Why won't you let me take care of you?'

The same old argument, thought Daisy. Why wouldn't he realise once and for all that she needed her independence?

'The White Swan's not poxy.' She could feel the heat of his hand on her skin. 'And neither is Gosport. It's my home! An' I earn my living here.'

Roy gave a huge sigh that seemed to deflate his big frame. He stepped back, letting go of her and shaking his head with just a hint of a smile turning up the corners of his generous lips, and Daisy was reminded of why he only had to snap his fingers and half the tarts in London flocked to his side. Whatever had he seen in her, only five foot three in her bare feet, and with eyes some said were like those of the film star Joan Collins but which she thought were too large for her thin face. She marvelled that all those years ago Roy had wanted her, and that he still hankered after her.

'Anyway, I don't need you to give me money. I can work to keep me own family, thank you very much!'

She knew he wouldn't continue with this argument so she gave it her parting shot. 'I been working all me life and I'll continue until the bleedin' daisies flower above me grave!'

A great rumble of laughter filled the hall and followed Roy as he ambled down to the kitchen.

He pulled out the bench from beneath the table and sat down heavily. 'But I can buy Gyp and you a few presents from time to time?'

'Yes. And you'll find Jamie will take everything you offer.'

Daisy went to the kettle and plugged it in. Then she set about taking mugs from the cupboard.

Roy said, 'I'm glad at last you've stopped seein' that boy through rose-coloured spectacles ...'

Tears filled her eyes. 'I don't want him to end up in prison. He wants someone to need him, Roy.'

'He's got plenty of people to care about him, or he did 'ave before he did the dirty on 'em all. Even his own brother don't want to know 'im … And how's it going to work out with both of them working for me?'

'Which is the point I'm *making*, Roy. You treats my Eddie like he's your own son. It'd be nice if you could do the same for Jamie.' Daisy slapped a plate of Bourbon biscuits down on the scrubbed wooden table so hard two fell off the edge of the plate. Roy put out a hand to stop them sliding to the floor.

'Eddie's a good boy,' he said. 'So 'e's in prison for killin' a bloke, but he didn't do that for his own gain, remember, he did it to save your life, Daisy.'

'I know that! And Eddie's not a boy any longer, he's twenty-one.' Daisy stood in front of Roy with her hands on her hips. She thought about that night when notorious murderer Gaetano Maxi had tried to kill her and Eddie had knifed him to save her. Five years in prison was his punishment. Even to think about her Eddie inside made Daisy's heart ache, but she knew life had to go on. 'Enough about Eddie, he'll be out soon,' she said. 'And I'm glad you're willing to give Jamie a chance to make something of his life. Just make sure he doesn't get shot on the streets of London like that bloke Stephen Waldorf.'

Roy's face was impassive as he said, 'The coppers thought Waldorf was that escaped prisoner, David Martin.'

'Yes, and a good way to start nineteen eighty-three. His family will always remember this as the year the coppers made a bleedin' mistake. Just you look after my boy!'

Roy's long legs were stretched out in front of him. He was dressed as usual in a suit and a silk shirt. His Italian leather shoes looked soft and comfortable. While the tea stewed she pulled out a chair opposite him, sat down and gave him a smile.

He picked up one of her hands and said, 'I'm a gangster and Jamie's father's a police DCI and yet it's me you want to look after him?' His face was suddenly grey, and she saw he was tired, too.

'His father's not interested in him, you know that. Not now Vinnie's set up home again with his ex-wife.' Daisy felt suddenly ashamed at the sadness in her voice. 'Besides, I know you won't have him doin' anythin' you won't want Eddie to be involved in. He'll be safe with you.'

The radio was now playing 'Tainted Love'. The music was so low, Daisy could hear the clock ticking.

'When Eddie gets out of prison he'll turn to me, Daisy. Him and Jamie hate the sight of each other. What'll Eddie think?'

'You'll soon 'ave Jamie eatin' out of your hand, and – who knows – my two sons might even make up their differences. Besides, who's the boss of your fuckin' empire? Not you by the sound of it!'

A shadow crossed Roy's face. His grip on her hand tightened and she could see his thoughts were taking a different direction.

'Jamie's not been hurting my Gyp? He might seem to care for her but he's a heavy 'anded bastard where females is concerned. Is that why you need a break from him? Tell me the truth, Dais.'

Daisy jumped up from the chair, freeing her hand from his and reeling away from him. 'How could you even think such a thing? Jamie loves Gypsy. He wouldn't hurt or let anyone else hurt a hair on that little girl's head. Take back those 'orrible words, Roy Kemp! Jamie idolises your child. He loves her as much as he loves me and sometimes I think we're the only two people he really cares about!'

'Come 'ere.' Roy had risen and he pulled her into his arms. She slid close, feeling the contours of his body. It was as natural as sliding her feet into her comfortable slippers. 'I'm sorry, Dais.' His voice wavered. 'It's just that Jamie 'asn't got a very good track record with young girls, has 'e?'

'I've sorted that.' Another of Jamie's messes left for her to clear up. A tragedy that had produced her first grandchild.

For a moment, there was silence, only the fast beating of her heart.

It was then and only then that she allowed herself to cry, her face buried in his shirt. She felt his arms tighten about her. His lips brushed her hair.

'I've got a nasty feelin' I'm goin' to get a lot more than I bargained for,' Roy said, his lips lowered to her ear. She lifted her face and her eyes met his.

'Let's go to bed,' she said.

He pulled away from her. 'You don't have to thank me that way.'

'Ever considered I might *want* to go to bed with you, Roy Kemp?'

He smiled down at her and she felt as though a large dark cloud had suddenly lifted.

'You can twist me round your fuckin' little finger,' he said. He kissed her lightly on her nose then, yanking out his shirt front, squinted at it. Daisy saw his eyes held laughter as he said, 'An' look what you done to me new clobber.'

'Just as well you keeps a spare in me wardrobe then, ain't it?'

Daisy took his hand and pulled him from the kitchen towards the hallway. At the bottom of the stairs, he paused.

'We're letting a pot of your good tea go to waste,' he said.

Daisy put out her hand and touched the bulge in his trousers.

'Bugger the tea. This mustn't go to waste,' she said.

He laughed. 'What you goin' to do to me, Daisy Lane?'

'Whatever I bleedin' wants, I 'ope,' she said, leading him upstairs.

CHAPTER 2

Eddie touched his sore face. The scar would run through his left eyebrow to his hairline.

He turned the page of the book he was trying to read then gave up. He couldn't follow the simple storyline with so much on his mind. The clanking of Winchester Prison's steel doors and the rattling of keys, mixed with the shouting of the other cons, was getting on his nerves. Even the disinfectant in the mopped-down cells seemed to be choking him.

'You were lucky that fucker didn't get your eye.'

Eddie rose and chucked his novel on the bed, clapping his hand on his mate's shoulder. 'Too fuckin' right, Ginge,' he replied, a little too brightly.

'At least it won't spoil your chances with the birds, Eddie Lane,' Ginge said. Eddie turned away.

There was only one woman for him even though he hadn't allowed his cousin, Summer, a visit during the time he'd been inside. He wanted to see her, longed to see her, to touch her red-gold hair and smell the womanly scent of her. But not like this. Not with him shut up like a bleedin' animal. She was in his thoughts from the moment he opened his eyes to the time the lights went out.

Eddie looked at Ginge. His bright red hair stood up like a cock's comb and his teeth, though brilliantly white, were like tombstones in his wide mouth. He also had a body so thin that with his bright hair he looked like a Swan Vesta.

'You only got a few more weeks to go. Even with the move to the open, that'll soon pass.' Ginge was rolling cigarettes, the skinniest fags that Eddie had ever seen. Ginge said they made the tobacco last longer.

'What about you, mate? You're out soon after me,' said Eddie, smiling at his friend. Ginge was a forger and he specialised in passports – or had, until a mush fleeing to Spain and picked up at Gatwick had spilled the beans on him. Ginge was always cheerful. Eddie liked that about him. He could have ended up sharing a cell with a thug, Dogface for example. He shuddered. 'What you doin' when you get out?' he asked.

'Same old, same old,' said Ginge. 'Ain't you pleased to be 'aving a change of scenery soon? I've 'eard Ford is a doddle.'

Eddie had a flashback to the governor's office. Him standing there like a six-year-old at school. Oak bookcases surrounding the dreary room and the furniture like someone's granny had left it on the tip. He remembered the radio softly playing 'I Love Rock and Roll' and smiled at the odd choice of music the governor preferred. Eddie had thought he'd be an opera lover.

'You're being transferred to an open prison not far from Arundel in Sussex. You've not served a long sentence but this is to allow you to become acclimatised to a life without bars. We don't want you leaving our care institutionalised.' The governor had started pacing the room over the threadbare carpet. He stopped suddenly and stared hard at Eddie. 'It's come to my attention that you've been taking advantage of the career opportunities we run here. I don't ever want to see a clever bloke like you back in this nick again, or indeed any other prison.'

What the governor didn't realise was that Eddie's draughtsmanship would enable him to make accurate layouts for jobs. He needed to be sure at the planning stages that no errors would be found in the premise's measurements.

There was no answer Eddie could give to the governor except, 'Thank you, sir.' He knew once the big boys had made a decision to remove him to Ford there was no going back. Nor did he want there to be. The sooner he got away from Dogface the better.

Eddie's hand strayed to his face once more. Yes, he was lucky. Dogface had been aiming for his throat.

Previously Eddie had kept himself to himself and had had very little trouble with the other prisoners. Then Dogface had recently rolled in from the Verne in Dorset.

Eddie had been in the canteen, sat at a table eating the slop they served for dinner and minding his own business when Dogface slipped up behind him and thrust forward a sharpened knife. Eddie had seen the glint of the steel and ducked. He'd saved his throat but the bastard had cut into his forehead.

'What the—?' Eddie had shouted, twisting to Dogface and his two henchmen. The table, screwed to the floor, didn't move but most of the food containers overturned when Dogface's fist hit the surface. Within seconds the ancient parquet flooring was awash with greasy food and drink.

Eddie knew he mustn't lose his temper.

The other cons were getting agitated and the smell of anger and revenge was in the air.

Even as the blood dripped down his face, Eddie stayed calm.

When the screws came running, he stood out of Dogface's reach while his henchmen held him back.

The officer discovered no fight.

Eddie was composed enough to say, 'I slipped and banged

me forehead on the table. This kind man was trying to help me up.' He waved his hand to Dogface, who was scowling but silent.

'So this knife belongs to you?' The screw held out the normally blunt kitchen knife sharpened to a fine point by being honed on the cell wall. Eddie could see blood on it. His blood.

'No, sir, that's not my knife. I reckon that one got into the cutlery drawer by mistake.' He turned to the hapless Dogface then looked at the crowd of cons. 'That's not one of our dinner knives, is it?' The prisoners shook their heads and murmured, 'No, we ain't never seen that knife before.'

Ginge said, 'I ain't 'alf glad I didn't get that knife. Could 'ave cut me mouth on that.'

Eddie had wiped blood that was dripping down his face from his wound and said to Dogface, 'Thank you for your help. If I can return the favour ...'

'Get that fuckin' mess cleared up,' broke in the screw and turned away.

Dogface stepped towards him and bent forward. Eddie could smell his foetid breath as the man said, 'I runs this place now. You might be Roy Kemp's little blue-eyed boy but it don't mean shit in 'ere. I'm gonna get you. You'll be scared of every corner in case I'm waitin' there.'

Eddie knew then that Roy's favours to him, the radio, the extra meals, decent trainers, all paid for by bribing the screws, had been noticed by Dogface. Eddie had never really thought that his gifts from Roy Kemp would instil jealousy in the other cons.

Back in the cell, with his face cleaned up, Ginge had said to him, 'I don't know 'ow you kept your 'ands off him.'

Eddie sighed. 'That was his intention. And if I *had* hit 'im,

I'd have lost me remission. I couldn't play Dogface's game, could I?'

Dogface had inferred he was being kept by Kemp. There wasn't any use reminding the cons that Roy was like a father to him, but it did rankle him that he was on Roy's payroll and not pulling his weight.

'Do many of the cons reckon I ponce off London's biggest gangster?'

Ginge turned his head away.

'Tell me the truth, you owe me that.'

Ginge nodded. 'Take no notice. Any one of 'em would shit themselves to be in your shoes. It ain't as though you couldn't teach 'em all a bleedin' lesson if you wanted.'

'Too right. But it's more important to me to get out of this place,' Eddie replied.

''Course it is,' said Ginge.

'Remember when Dogface first arrived, I never expected him to come at me in the kitchen with the tin opener after he'd sliced open a big tin of peas,' said Eddie. 'I tried for ages to find out how I pissed him off without doing a bleedin' thing.'

Ginge started laughing and lit one of his smokes. The end of the cigarette flared until the empty paper burned. The smell of the match was acrid.

'I never seen no one move as quick as you. That can lid was in your hands quick as a wink, and there was Dogface losing the tip of 'is ear when you swung out with it.'

'Bastard deserved that,' Eddie said softly. 'I'll give him his due, he never squealed on me.'

'I reckon that bloke always 'as to be top dog,' said Ginge. Eddie began to laugh and after a few moments Ginge realised what he'd said. 'Top dog – that's funny, ain't it?'

Eddie nodded. 'I guess I'll have to be on me guard the rest of me time 'ere. I can't wait to get to Sussex.'

He sank down on his bottom bunk and thought how nice it would be not to hear so many clanking doors. Shortly after he'd be settled into life at Ford he'd be free to leave. Free to go home to Gosport and his mum and Summer. One thing he was certain of was he had no intention of accepting the pay-out from the trust fund his mother had set up so many years ago. He knew it would mature soon.

His mother needed the money more than he did. He couldn't bear the thought of her being out in all weathers at markets and car boots, selling the gold or whatever she'd picked up from the auctions. She had Gypsy now and it wasn't a life for either of them. All the same, he was proud of her for working so hard to put a roof over the family's heads and food on the table. But Eddie was determined to pay her back for the sacrifices she'd made for him.

He'd been busy during his sentence, spending most of his time reading or in the library making notes for the future.

He knew some of the cons, including Dogface, thought he was above himself because he spent his leisure time studying. He didn't care. He supposed he got his independence from his mother.

He studied and planned because he was after *big* money.

He'd spent enough time working hard with his mate Tyrone at back-breaking jobs that barely earned them money for a good night out. The snooker hall had been a birthday gift to him from Roy, so Eddie hadn't earned it for himself. But it wouldn't be long before he was able to provide for himself. Maybe even pay back Roy monies owed …

He wondered how he'd fare working for Roy with Jamie

along for the ride. Just thinking about his half-brother made his gut turn.

While he'd been inside he had been mulling an idea over and over in his mind. If it worked, he'd leave the country for a while. He'd launder the proceeds and hopefully live a good life with Summer. That's if she'd ever have him, he thought.

Africa. That's where he wanted to start a business of his own. Years ago Roy had taken the whole family on holiday to the beach near Mombasa and Eddie had fallen in love with the place and the people.

One successful job and it would enable him to become a businessman without ever resorting to crime again. And no way was he going to step on Roy's toes. Eddie's father had creamed off some of Roy's enterprises and Roy had disposed of him, the gangland way.

Eddie's dream didn't include drugs, Roy had the monopoly there; so too with prostitution and business insurance. He was happy to leave that hard graft to Roy.

But there was one scam that Roy didn't bother with. And that one scam would net Eddie a fortune. He could then take care of his mother, Gypsy, Vera and, with a bit of luck, Summer as well, for as long as they lived.

Eddie began whistling along with an old song playing on his radio.

'That's "Wheel of Fortune" by the Beverly Sisters, ain't it?' Ginge said.

Eddie nodded. 'Used to be my dad's favourite song.'

CHAPTER 3

'If 'er kid's getting 'urt, why don't she keep 'im indoors?'

Daisy handed the wet plate to Vera, who began drying it with a striped tea towel, and said, 'Daisy, what you thinkin' of, girl? You knows you can't keep an eleven-year-old boy indoors. An' his mother wants to find out where he got that bleedin' games console. He didn't get the money for it from 'er an' them things don't come cheap. He won't tell 'er nothin', says it's a secret.'

Guilt crept inside Vera's head like the unwanted guest it was. Wasn't she keeping a secret too? Usually she and Daisy were honest with each other but this time Vera couldn't bring herself to share her problem.

Vera caught sight of herself in the wall mirror. Her cheeks were sunk in and her eyes had lost their sparkle. Even the addition of her new extra-long false eyelashes didn't disguise her worry.

Daisy pulled the plug from the sink and the water gurgled down the drain. Vera saw her gazing at the swirling water as though mesmerised.

'So when did this mate of yours from Old Road tell you all this?' Daisy asked.

'This morning. She came in specially to see me in Heavenly Bodies. One of me girls was just getting stuff out for a whipping an' in Mandy walks like she owns the place. I know she turned a few tricks for me but—'

Daisy interrupted her. 'An' it's her son what's covered in bruises and cuts?'

Vera sighed and plugged in the electric kettle. 'Why don't you listen to me? It's her grandson. Mandy's my age. Sandra's Paulie's mum.'

The talk about children made Vera think about Gypsy and how before she was born Daisy was unsure whether the child might have belonged to Alec. Vera had liked the talented but depressed painter who worked in Daisychains, the club she and Daisy had once owned. The union between Alec and Daisy was a one-night stand: Daisy had needed comfort and Alec was lonely. So lonely, he'd later taken his own life.

Roy knew nothing of this and there was no reason to tell him now, Vera thought. Not when he often had some little scrubber hanging on his arm. When Daisy had realised she was pregnant she was over the moon and so was Roy. As soon as Gyp was born anyone could see the child was the spit of Roy.

Gyp called him Daddy Roy, but her birth certificate proclaimed her name as Gypsy Lane, not Kemp, as Roy had envisaged. Secrets, it was all about secrets and the keeping of them, Vera thought. Her heartbeat was loud and her mouth was dry. She couldn't tell Daisy her own secret. No. Daisy had enough worries on her plate at present.

Vera watched Daisy reach up, putting the last of the saucepans on the top shelf. The remnants of the smell from the chops Daisy had cooked for lunch was still in the air. Vera took a deep breath. She hadn't been able to eat much but she'd done her best with the pudding of vanilla cake.

'So! This woman who was on the game with you an' now

lives in Old Road 'as a daughter who 'as a son who's covered in cuts and bruises and won't talk about it an' now he's come 'ome with a games console?'

Vera smiled. So Daisy was listening to her after all.

'Yes.'

Now Daisy was spooning tea into the brown earthenware teapot. 'Why're you gettin' bleedin' involved?'

'Do you need to ask? This kid is eleven years old,' Vera said. 'Besides, Mandy 'as 'er mum living with her as well an' she's at death's door. Little Paulie loves his nan to bits, always fussin' over her.'

'I got me own boys to worry about,' Daisy said, 'though – and I know I shouldn't say this, Vera – but with Jamie under Roy's wing for a while I do feel a different person.'

'An' your heart ain't big enough to worry about another little boy as well?'

Daisy sighed. 'So you wants me to come with you?' The boiling water gurgled into the teapot.

'Yes. An' I wants you to come an' help me manage Heavenly Bodies, Dais. I don't like to think of you still out in this freezin' cold weather working the markets to make up your money. The pub's different, but you ain't full time there. Besides, I'm gettin' old. I may not last much longer.'

Daisy looked at her with mock horror. 'Old be buggered,' she said.

Vera, who had ignored her age until now, said, 'It's catching up with me, Dais.'

Daisy snorted and then the corners of her mouth crinkled to a laugh. 'The time for you to worry about bein' old is when you can't sprinkle gallons of Californian Poppy on yourself.' Vera felt uncomfortable under Daisy's laughter. 'If you was old you'd be wearing zip up booties not 'igh 'eels, an' you'd stuff yourself into bras with bones in, and them corsets with strings on. You ain't 'alf a daft cow, our Vera.'

This was one of the reasons she was scared to talk to Daisy about the changes happening to her. Daisy was apt to fly off the handle or sometimes, as now, laugh her fears away.

A splattering of rain hit the window. Daisy should have been at Fareham Market, but after the Christmas rush people didn't have the cash to spend on her jewellery. Daisy sighed and Vera knew she was thinking of the pitch fee she'd still have to cough up whether she was there or not. Anyway, Gyp was at home, where she belonged, playing with her toys in front of the guarded fire in the sitting room.

'All right for tonight, Daisy?' Vera sipped at her tea as Daisy nodded. 'Don't you get peeved when you take orders from the owners in the White Swan, especially after bein' your own boss in Daisychains?'

'No. It's honest work, ain't it? And the place might be a bit run down but the folks are just like you an' me an' I'd rather be among people who don't 'ave plums in their mouth and put on airs an' graces.'

'If you worked for me as a manageress, I'd pay you more money. Sex don't really go out of fashion, does it?'

'Maybe not. But it sticks in me craw that you insists I takes rent off you to live 'ere in Western Way. I don't want to be beholden to you or anyone, not when you worked mostly on your back for what you got. Besides, you already got a manageress. What you gonna do with her, sack her when she don't deserve it? I ain't stupid. You can't afford to take people on just because you feels sorry for them.'

Vera felt her face crumpling like a screwed-up paper bag. Daisy put her arms around her, but Vera pushed her away, saying, 'I'm only tryin' to 'elp.'

Daisy sniffed. 'I've always managed to find the money to keep this place going, 'aven't I? If it hadn't been for Eddie Lane I wouldn't even *have* a house in Alverstoke.'

She went quiet and Vera knew she was thinking of the handsome bastard who had been young Eddie's father and Daisy's one true love. Vera saw Daisy purse her lips and close her eyes. There were times, even after all these years, when Daisy missed Eddie so bad she wanted to die; Vera understood this.

'I ain't so green as I'm cabbage-looking, girly. I overheard you asking Roy to buy your little house in Greece. An' he said no, didn't he? An' I knows why.'

'You are such a nosy bugger, our Vera. Okay, tell me why?'

'Because Eddie Lane bequeathed it to you along with this place an' that piddly little MG, and that's all you got left of the man you truly loved. Even a fuckin' 'ard bastard like Roy Kemp knows what it all means to you. He also knows somewhere in that equation you got feelings for 'im. It's about time you made your mind up ...'

This time, Vera saw, Daisy couldn't help herself. A tear trickled down her face, and she turned her head away. Vera passed her a clean tea towel.

'Wipe your eyes, girl, you done good, bringin' up the boys single-'anded and keeping 'ouse an' 'ome together.'

Daisy gave a long sigh that wracked her body, then she wiped her face. 'Vera, it's such a struggle an' ... an' ... there's times I want Roy to look after me just so I won't need to keep up the effort any more. Then I realise just how well off I really am. A house, a job, kids I love, and you – the best friend anyone could wish for.'

Vera was stroking her hair. She wondered what she would do if she didn't have Daisy to look after. This was another reason why her own secret had to stay hidden.

'You only got to say the word an' Roy'll come running, Dais. Now he's free you could wed 'im.'

'I know. But he ain't my Eddie and I don't even want to think about the soddin' drug deals an' all the other shit he's involved in.'

'True, Dais, but you got memories of your Eddie an' no one can take them away from you. Some women ain't ever been truly loved in all their lives.'

Daisy breathed out slowly. 'I'm my own person; why should I marry Roy?'

'I think love comes into it.'

'If he asks, I'll give him the same answer as always. He's got to give up his way of life. Drugs comin' in from abroad to be bought by kids, and people wrecking their lives an' breaking the 'earts of the families what loves them. All that business of gang warfare an' bloodshed. You know I've seen enough poverty and unhappiness in me life, Vera, and as long as I can earn me living I will. Mind you,' she said softly, 'if he was to live in Gosport an' leave his business for someone else to take over I might just jump at the chance ... But he won't leave London and I won't leave my home in Gosport.'

'If your Eddie takes over Roy's business how will you feel about that?'

'Just because Roy's been grooming him all his life to step into his shoes don't mean to say my Eddie will.'

'But how will you feel if he does?'

'Eddie will do as he wants to do. He won't ask my permission, and for that I'm thankful. I'll back him to the hilt because I know he won't be like Roy, Eddie is his own man. But what I'd like more than anything is for my two boys to settle their differences.'

'Silly cow.' Vera pursed her lips as she applied her poppy-red lipstick. 'They'll never fall into each other's arms.' She stepped back and stared at her reflection in the small mirror. 'I reckon another thing you need to think about is telling Vinnie that you're about to ship his son off to that gangster. That detective might 'ave something to say about that.'

Daisy's face was a picture.

'I don't want to speak to 'im,' she said.

'Your own conscience won't let you not talk to him,' Vera said, thinking about the good-looking detective who had been Daisy's lover and was Jamie's father. She went to the bread bin. She lifted up the lid and took out a roll of notes with a piece of paper beneath the rubber band.

'What you got there?' Daisy was close on her heels.

'I found this earlier. I reckon Roy left it for you.'

Daisy took the money. 'I didn't ask him for no bleedin' 'andouts,' she said.

'It ain't for you,' Vera said. 'So I reckon you got to take it.'

'For Gyp' the note said.

'See,' said Vera, 'just when you think it's never gonna stop rainin' a bit of sunshine appears.' The wind blew a fresh barrage of sleet against the windows.

'You ain't 'alf a daft tart, you know that, Vera?'

Vera grinned at her.

'You still ain't said if you're goin' to come round to Old Road with me to find out about young Paulie?'

'And you're like a bleedin' drippin' tap, keepin' on.'

Vera smiled. 'I'll take that as a yes then, shall I?'

CHAPTER 4

Daisy's eyes strayed from the road towards Alver Bridge.

Vera, as though reading her mind, said, 'Used to be a poor-house there a long time ago.' Almost obscuring Daisy's view of the road, she waved towards Blake's Engineering Works. 'I bet Alver Creek over the years 'as 'ad a few unwanted babies dumped in it.'

'Jesus Christ, you ain't 'alf in a good mood this morning. Can't you think about somethin' nice?'

'Well, it ain't nice when we're goin' to visit an old mate of mine whose grandchild is getting ten bales of shit kicked out of him.'

Daisy didn't answer. Instead she glanced at the small boats moored in the mud of the creek. Most of them seemed to be in various stages of decay. The gasworks loomed over the narrow streets. Despite the drizzle, a couple of kids played marbles in the gutter. They looked skinny and streetwise. Daisy was suddenly very glad Gyp was happily playing in the crèche run by an ex-nurse in Vectis Road, only a stone's throw from Western Way. The kids paused in their playing as Daisy slowed down. Vera was peering at the house numbers.

'I 'ope my car's still in one piece when we comes out of 'er house,' said Daisy, eyeing a noisy football game in progress further up the road.

'Ask them nippers to keep an eye on it.'

Daisy said, 'You can give them a couple of bob then. I'm only 'ere because of you.'

'Pull up, this is the place.'

Daisy drew the two-seater to a halt outside the terraced house then quickly ran round to the passenger side of the car to let out Vera, who could never find the car's door handle. Vera emerged, puffing and panting and straightening her tight skirt and frilly blouse over which she wore a short jacket.

'C'mere,' Vera called to the boy and girl. 'You two bleeders want to earn a shillin' or two?' The boy looked hesitant but the girl stood up, pushed her long fringe out of her eyes and said, 'What we got to do?'

'Mind this car.'

'We can do that, missus,' said the boy.

Vera nodded then walked towards a scruffy blue-painted door. Almost immediately it was opened by an overweight woman with dark roots in her straw-blonde hair.

'Mandy,' Vera said and fell into her arms. Daisy reckoned both women to be around the same age, but Vera seemed to have defied the years.

'Come inside and meet my Sandra,' said Mandy.

Sandra was a clone of her mother, sitting sullenly on the overstuffed sofa. There was a smell of sickness in the air. 'Sandra's had the kettle on. Do you take sugar?' Both Daisy and Vera shook their heads. Sandra heaved herself up. Daisy could almost hear the sofa groan with relief but it was short-lived as Mandy sat down in Sandra's place.

After the pleasantries were over and Sandra had emerged from the kitchen with four mismatched mugs, Daisy asked, 'You thought of going to the cop shop?'

Daisy watched a long hair floating on the top of her tea and immediately put her mug on the scuffed lino at the side of the sofa.

'Don't be fuckin' stupid, Daisy,' Vera answered.

Mandy said, 'If we complain to the rozzers our little Paulie could be taken into care before we gets 'ome from the station. He was given a caution for stealing from Woolies, remember, and we 'ad a right to-do with the child welfare people. I don't want to go down that road again. Especially as I got a police record for beatin' up that bastard I married, an' a few fines for sellin' meself to punters. They'll say Paulie needs a more stable environment. Stable maybe,' said Mandy, shaking back her hair, 'but he won't get loved like he is 'ere.'

Sandra burst into tears. 'I wanna know who's 'urting my boy.'

'You reckon he might be gettin' bullied at school?'

'If anything, my Paulie can take care of 'imself in that department.' Sandra dabbed at her eyes with a none-too-clean handkerchief.

'You can be bullied just as hurtfully with words,' Daisy offered. She wanted to ask why Mandy beat up her husband but Vera got in first with that question.

'The fucker kept boozin' all the money away and knockin' me about. Even when I was up the duff I still got clouted. One day I couldn't take it any more, so I waited until he reeled 'ome from the Robin Hood and I set about him with a cricket bat. Christmas Eve it was. We got indoors and then the fuckin' tree went over, the police were called and I'd very nearly killed 'im. He was pretty messed up, blood everywhere, an' the bastard pressed charges. I kept tellin' the coppers he fell off the bleedin' pavement when he was drunk. Even now I don't know what came over me.'

'You was the worm turning, I expect,' said Vera, with a sigh that puffed out her cheeks. She took a swig of her tea.

33

'So just Paulie an' you an Sandra, an' nan lives 'ere?'

'Yes, Daisy,' Mandy said. 'Me mum's upstairs. She's bad with 'er lungs. Not likely to last until Easter."

'You must be out of your mind with worry,' said Vera. Something was not quite to her liking with the tea and she set her full cup down on the scratched coffee table.

'Course. But that's not all of it,' said Mandy. 'When I was out doin' a bit of solicitin' one night, Sandra ran off with a bleedin' soldier. Went up to Aldershot, she did. When the coppers found me it was to tell me Paulie 'ad been taken off to some place in the country because he'd got pissed out of his tiny skull on some vodka and was found lyin' in the 'igh street.'

Mandy paused and looked about her. 'I reckon it all came about by Nan just gettin' seriously ill. The sodding welfare carted me mum off to this hospice place and she was creatin' blue murder because she wanted to be 'ome in her own bed in the room she shares with Paulie.'

'That bastard soldier was already married,' sniffed Sandra.

'That 'is kiddie?' Vera pointed to Sandra's swell of a belly. Sandra nodded.

'Okay,' said Daisy. 'I think I got everything straight in me mind, but I can't really see what me an' Vera can do ...'

'Please, Daisy, please, Vera,' Mandy beseeched. Daisy saw a chord had been touched in Vera's heart and there'd be no going back now. They'd both do the best they could to find out what was going on. Daisy knew Vera would ask punters in Heavenly Bodies and she herself would interrogate customers from the pub for information. But really, Daisy thought, Paulie was just a little boy who was getting into scraps.

Vera sighed and nodded and Daisy saw relief lighten Mandy's face. One of Vera's eyelashes had come unstuck and was at an angle on her eyelid. Daisy longed to reach over and smooth it back into place but didn't want to draw attention to Vera's plight.

'We already 'ad the school round 'ere because Paulie's started playin' truant. Mr May, the bastard headmaster, sent this letter 'ome as well. He says when Paulie is in the classroom he's as dozy as shit.' She got up and waddled to the mantelpiece and took a crumpled envelope from behind the clock and passed it to Daisy. Daisy waved it away.

'It's okay,' she said, 'I believe you. What does Paulie say about that?'

'Nothin'. Even when I said he was goin' to end up beaten to death an' floating in the harbour like that other boy his age, he didn't say nothin'.'

'That was a bit strong, wasn't it?' Daisy remembered reading about that boy in the *Evening News*.

'No, Daisy, it wasn't. Who knows what happened to that poor little bleeder? I just wanted Paulie to confide in me. He's 'ardly ever indoors, an' when he is he spends most of his time up with Nan. He's gettin' money from somewhere because he's always buyin' her little treats. I can't afford to give him no money. An' fuck knows where he's gettin' dosh for a brand-new Atari console, an' there's a bleedin' BMX bike out the back. Second-hand it might be, but it's a bleedin' Mongoose an' you know them bikes ain't cheap.' Tears began to form in her eyes. Daisy put out her hand and touched the woman's fleshy arm but Mandy shook her off. 'Come on upstairs and see the room he shares with Nan,' she said.

Daisy looked at Vera, who shrugged her shoulders.

Upstairs, the smell of sickness was worse.

Mandy opened the door of a bedroom a mere slit and, turning, put her finger to her lips.

'Don't make too much noise, Nan's just had her medicine an' she's asleep. She usually sleeps about six hours at a time.' Mandy opened the door wider. 'Paulie sleeps in that bed over there in the corner. Not in the same bed as 'is nan,' she said proudly, pointing to surprisingly clean bedding with bright patchwork quilts covering both beds. Then her face fell, 'Sandra an' me is in the front. We only got two bedrooms, see?'

Daisy nodded. In one single bed pushed up against the wall was a small mound that could only have been Nan. From the rasping sounds coming from the woman's throat, Daisy reckoned she wasn't long for this world. Maybe the next one would be kinder, Daisy thought, pushing a tear away from her cheek. Certainly Paulie's bed was near enough for him to lie there and gaze into his nan's dying face.

'Couldn't he sleep on the sofa downstairs?' Daisy asked.

'Won't do it,' whispered Mandy. 'You think I ain't begged him?'

On the wall were posters and pictures cut from magazines. Poppies in a field, their red cheerfulness bright against the grubby wallpaper; waves crashing against rocks; a deer grazing in a woodland glen. Daisy stared at them all.

'Paulie cuts them from books and magazines. Nan grew up in the country an' he reckons it makes her feel more at 'ome,' said Mandy. It was then Daisy realised what was different about this room from the rest of the house. Apart from the boxed Atari standing neatly against the wall and the small chest of drawers upon which a woman's vanity set sat, this room was tidy. Unlike the downstairs rooms that looked as though a bomb had hit them. 'She won't never leave 'ere,' whispered Mandy. 'Only in 'er box.'

Daisy saw a gorgeous pink dressing gown hanging from a

nail on the back of the door. Underneath the bed was a pair of satin slippers. Both articles of clothing looked unworn.

Shiny rows of farm animals were stacked on the mantelpiece of the boarded-up fireplace. New, thought Daisy. Mandy must have seen her staring at them.

'Paulie buys 'em from the market for 'er.' Her voice grew defiant. 'He don't get the money from me.'

'Let's get out of 'ere, Dais,' said Vera. 'I've seen enough.'

Daisy wiped her eyes with the back of her hand as they trooped down the stairs and back into the living room.

'Paulie don't want to leave 'er. All the time he was in that foster 'ome and Nan was in the 'ospital, he pined for her. Anyone would think she was his bleedin' mother, not Sandra!'

'So you got no men livin' in the 'ouse?' Vera asked.

'If you means 'ave we got a bloke 'ere who bashes Paulie, the answer's no. This is an 'ouse of women, apart from Paulie. We've 'ad enough of men what fucks and leaves, thank you very much.' Then she added, 'Follow me,' and marched out, pushing her bulk into the scullery where she pulled down the kitchen cabinet door and waved her plump arm at the tins and packets lined on the top shelf. 'Look at that.'

'They don't come cheap,' Vera whispered.

'Complan, Brand's Essence, and tins of broth and chicken soup. I can't afford stuff like that. I got to buy the cheapest brands I can find. Paulie buys it. Feeds her, too. He's 'eard it all helps to build a sick person up. I'd just like to know where he's gettin' the money from.' She paused. Tears were welling in her eyes and making channels over her dumpling cheeks. 'And I want to know who's beating the shit out of 'im.'

'Where is he now?' Dais asked. She wanted to enfold the woman in her arms but didn't like to be seen to be patronising her.

'I don't know. Like I says, he won't talk to us.'

Daisy tried again. 'How long 'as this been goin' on?'

'A while. Look, what I'm really worried about is whoever's bashin' him,' she tapped her head, 'might have done 'im some serious damage. The other morning he was bleedin' from his ear'ole. He'd thrown the soaked pillowcase away but I saw the bit of white cloth stickin' out the dustbin. The blood had to 'ave come from his ear'ole as I'd have noticed if his face had blood on it.'

'You tried carting him to Haslar Hospital?'

'When they gets kids in with bruises all over their bodies they refers 'em to the authorities, in case they're bein' abused at 'ome. It's a bit like a vicious circle, Dais,' said Vera. 'Mandy don't want to run the risk of losin' Paulie an' nosy parkers comin' round ...'

Daisy nodded. 'Well, I can see Paulie's got a family what loves 'im.' Even if 'is own mother is as thick as a plank, she thought. But it was as plain as that bleedin' crooked eyelash on Vera's lid that none of these women would harm a hair on Paulie's head. 'If he won't talk to you, he ain't gonna talk to us.'

Mandy turned to Vera. 'Look, Vera, you two knows so many people you could ask. Otherwise my boy is goin' to get killed.'

Vera paused in the doorway and put her arms around the big woman. Daisy saw Vera's eyes darken and she wondered if her friend was all right. She'd been very quiet and preoccupied lately, even before hearing about Paulie.

'I'll try,' Vera said. 'So will Daisy.'

The look of relief on Mandy's face was plain to see.

'I knew I could count on you two. God bless you,' she said. For a moment Daisy wondered if Mandy was going to enfold her in a bear hug but the moment passed. Mandy stepped back and closed the door.

The two kids were standing, one at the front and one at the rear of her car. It was still drizzling with rain.

The girl said, 'Nobody ain't touched it.' Her hair was rat's tails about her thin face.

Vera stepped towards her, money already in her hand. 'Get yourselves some chips,' she said, and laughed as the girl grabbed the coins and ran.

Daisy waited, a smile on her own face. She unlocked the vehicle's door and leaned over and opened the passenger's door.

'Thanks, Daisy,' said Vera from the car's confines.

'Don't know what you're thankin' me for. All I can do is keep me ears open in the White Swan and at the car boots and market next time I go. Maybe we could ask Roy, Vinnie too, if there's any kiddie fiddling goin' on. Though a boy from Paulie's background would surely be too streetwise to get mixed up with blokes like that.' She looked to Vera, who nodded, agreeing with her.

'We could be private eyes,' said Vera. 'Find out what's really goin' on in the underbelly of Gosport!'

Daisy drove down towards the gasworks then turned into Dock Road and out onto Stoke Road. She noticed wet washing hanging forlornly on a clothes line and women walking hopelessly about the streets dressed in raincoats and headscarves, their bare white legs stuffed into scuffed white high-heeled shoes.

'Daisy, we've got to help her,' stressed Vera. 'I've never been more determined in me life.'

'Jesus, you talk a load of crap at times,' said Daisy. 'But this time I agree with you.'

Then her mouth settled into a thin hard line remembering she had a date with Vinnie to chat about his son.

Daisy pulled in to the car park of the Queen Elizabeth Country Park. She sat looking at the trees springing to life. For once the sun was shining, and she gave a long, drawn-out sigh as she spotted the Land Rover crunching across the gravel to park alongside.

The man smiled and again Daisy was reminded of how much she'd loved him all those years ago. Vinnie left the vehicle, jumping easily down like a man who keeps his body in shape. His long legs were encased in blue jeans and a tan brown leather jacket topped a blue police-issue shirt. He was still smiling as he opened the door of her MG, giving her a hand out.

'Hello, Daisy,' he said. 'What's so important that you have to talk to me face to face?'

She looked up into his gorgeous different-coloured eyes and said, 'Let's walk for a bit. Maybe later have a cup of tea.'

Without speaking he followed her to the nearby pathway that led to the top of the hill. It had rained the night before and the grass and mud clung to Daisy's flat shoes. She thought how fresh and clean the woods smelled. Though she'd been sensible enough to wear jeans and a black polo-necked jumper, topped by a thick black padded jacket, she soon felt the cold. She snuggled into the long scarf she'd twined around her neck.

Daisy spied a clump of primroses, yellow against the brown of the fallen winter leaves and couldn't help herself.

'Oh, look,' she said. 'It's a sign spring isn't so far away after all.'

'You didn't get me here to talk about the seasons. What's up?'

Vinnie was slowing his strides so that she could keep up with him. She took a deep breath and said, 'It's Jamie.'

Vinnie stopped walking and grabbed hold of her arm. He was frowning.

'Got another girl into trouble has he?'

Daisy pulled her arm away and rounded on him.

'Not as far as I know,' she said. 'And before you ask, I've not had any communication worth telling you about from that girly in Wales. I sent her a cheque three weeks ago to help with the child's upkeep. You could do the same sometime; the boy David is your grandchild too!' She paused. 'And Jamie, to the best of my knowledge, still doesn't know where she is.'

'Good.'

They started walking again. A silence had descended over them and Daisy was worried she wouldn't have the guts to tell him. At the top of the hill was a tree trunk seat. Daisy sat down. Vinnie flopped beside her, breathing heavily.

'Didn't realise I was so out of condition,' he said. 'What about Jamie? Come on, tell me. What's happening now?'

Daisy took a deep breath and turned to face him. 'I'm tired, Vinnie. I'm trying to keep a family unit together and run around after a toddler. It's not easy ...'

'I'd have liked a little girl,' he said. His eyes bored into hers.

'Yeah, well, maybe Gyp might 'ave been yours if you hadn't dumped me because I wasn't good enough for you, an' gone back to your precious Clare ...' She didn't like herself for hurling insults but seemed unable to hold back what was in her heart.

'Don't, Daisy,' he said, putting his large hand over her smaller one. She could feel the heat of him. 'Being nasty doesn't become you. C'mon, tell me why we're here? Not to look at the primroses, surely?'

She took a deep breath. 'Jamie's going to live in London with Roy.'

Her words ran from her mouth as though they were water spilling from a tap.

He sat back on the damp seat and stared at her. For a long time he didn't speak. Then he said, 'If this gets out that my boy has a gangster looking after him, and not just any gangster but London's top face, it could endanger my promotion ...'

Daisy was stunned. 'Is that all you can think about?'

He sighed. 'No, I care about my son.' Daisy knew there was a but coming. 'But I have a family, a lifestyle to consider—'

'Arse'ole,' said Daisy. 'You're a fuckin' selfish git.'

'No. I believe you've always taken it upon yourself, Daisy, to smother both your sons with affection—'

'What d'you mean, *your* sons? Jamie belongs to you! And with no fathers around I've tried to do me bleedin' best ...'

'And most of the time it's worked.'

His eyes, Daisy thought, were dark fathomless pools. And cold.

'Is Jamie happy about this?'

Daisy nodded. 'I can't tie him to my apron strings, just because he's different.'

'I never thought a son of mine would turn out to be evil.'

'He's not evil. Misunderstood, maybe.'

Vinnie got up and brushed off his trousers. Then he turned to face her. Daisy saw the pain on his face, heard the sadness in his voice.

'I do love him, Dais. He's my son. I just don't understand why he has to give everyone such a hard time.'

Daisy rose from the seat and stood in front of him. He seemed taller than ever.

'He won't find it easy to give Roy a hard time.' She tried him with a small smile.

He put his arm around her, saying, 'If you think it's for the best …' and she breathed a sigh of relief and snuggled into his leather jacket.

'Thanks, Vinnie,' she murmured. Then she remembered. 'I got somethin' else to ask you. Has anything been said down at Gosport nick about kids bein' knocked about?'

'We get parents who overshoot the mark but nothing out of the ordinary lately.' He stepped back and looked at her.

'No. Not by their parents. Given good hidings by someone else.'

Daisy could almost see his copper's mind go into overtime but then he shook his head.

'I'll look into it.'

She sighed. She wanted to do everything she could to find out why Paulie was a victim but she honestly didn't know where to begin. Perhaps Roy knew of something peculiar going on in the area; after all, he controlled much of Gosport's vice. 'I promised someone I'd find out what I could.'

There was a silence between them, each, thought Daisy, back to their own reflections.

Vinnie was a good bloke but he tended to procrastinate. She remembered how she'd always been the parent who got Jamie out of his scrapes. Suddenly she was angry, angry at Vinnie for not taking enough interest in his own son.

She blurted out, 'Are you so blind you can't see that looking into these kids who are getting beaten up might enhance your promotion chances? Besides bein' a proper copper and savin' another child from harm?'

'Another?'

'We 'ad a lad washed up off the ferry. Don't suppose you

43

did much about that, did you? Just another bit of Gosport trash to you.'

Vinnie took a step away from her.

'What do you want me to do?' He sounded resigned.

'I want you, Mr Detective, to get up off your arse and do some detecting. No woman should be worrying about her son being knocked about the head so much his ears bleed!'

His eyes were raking her face. Once upon a time he had refused her nothing. And she knew now he really would look into the problem, for he said, 'All right, I'll get on to it. But what makes you so determined . . .'

Paulie was only a name to her. A child she'd never met. But Mandy and her daughter had asked Vera for help.

'Because it matters to Vera, an' that's bloody good enough for me.'

'C'mon, let's go down and get a cup of tea and a slice of home-made cake, they got a nice warm little coffee shop here.' Then he said softly, 'Roy must love you a great deal, almost as much as I did, to take on both your boys.'

CHAPTER 5

It was nine o'clock and Eddie gathered together his towel and shower gear. He still felt it was a luxury being at Ford Open Prison in Sussex. He reckoned they must have treated the air force like bloody royalty before the place had been converted to an open prison. There was refurbishment needed in the kitchens and shower rooms that cons willingly, or unwillingly, worked at as part of their duties, but it was a hell of an improvement on his last bleedin' hotel.

He thanked God he had a room to himself. He imagined how it would have been to have shared a room with a bloke you didn't get on with. But all that aggro at Winchester with Dogface seemed like a bad dream now.

So far he'd given the other cons a wide berth. The trouble with prisons, open or not, is that they're rife with gossip. Eddie knew this and kept himself to himself. But no matter how he tried to keep his nose clean, he could sense the jealousy from the other cons. And it was because Roy Kemp, London's most feared gangster now that the Krays were banged up, was his surrogate father.

He'd been called daddy's little helper, arse wipe, brown nose, and a lot of other names, but he'd not risen to the bait. If he retaliated to the name-calling in any way the governor would review his sentence.

That he had killed a man who was about to strangle his mother didn't cut any ice with the other cons. And why should it make them fear him? Most of them were in for similar crimes.

Eddie loved Roy like the father figure he was, but he knew working for the big man wasn't enough. Eddie needed to build a reputation of his own if he was to survive in the criminal dog-eat-dog world. Like most criminals, he dreamed of the big one that would allow him to become a respectable citizen.

Eddie sighed. He didn't intend to stay in the underworld.

It was quiet in his block this evening. Tonight was a special night. A pantomime was being held in the main dining room. It was well attended by cons and their families. Ginge, who'd miraculously been moved to Ford as well, had taken a trip along to watch. There were even less screws on duty because the cons had thrown their all into a bit of different entertainment from the crap on the television, or reading. Dressing up in drag for *Cinderella* had certainly given some of the blokes something to be happy about.

Eddie liked working in the gardens and he'd been keeping on with his course in technical drawing. He smiled to himself; never knew when he might need to draw other plans and it was just as well to able to get the dimensions of a building spot-on. It was a pity he wasn't going to be there long enough to get an academic qualification.

Not that he wanted to stay until the end of the course – until the end of his sentence suited him just fine. In two days he'd be at his mother's house, and then on to London to stay at Roy's home. That Jamie was also in London was a fucking nightmare come true. At least Roy had been thoughtful enough to get hold of a flat for Jamie so they wouldn't be in the same bloody house.

He thought of Vera's cat, Kibbles, that had died peacefully in its sleep. Because Eddie had loved the old moggie, Jamie had excavated the pet from its resting place in the garden, dug out the animal's eyes and left them on Eddie's pillow.

Of course, their mother knew nothing of this and Eddie realised how upset it would make Vera if the horror came to light. It had been the last straw for Eddie and he understood that night just how much he despised his brother.

Eddie set the shower control, which took a bit of fiddling with as the plumbing was atrocious, stood back, then shucked off his clothes. The hot water gushed over him, masking the smell of disinfectant with which they liberally doused the floors and walls.

As he faced the shiny tiles, his ears were alert to every sound and his eyes scanned the glistening wall for movements. Protect yourself at all times. Especially in the shower rooms where you could be fucked over and no one would hear a bleedin' sound.

He began humming 'Wheel of Fortune' as he lathered himself. Fucking tune was going round and round in his head. He laughed to himself as he thought perhaps it was his dead father's way of telling him to watch it.

At his feet the water jets were clearing the soap away.

He smelled him before he saw him.

Two hams of hands slammed him against the tiles. Eddie wasn't quick enough to turn.

'Fuck you,' Eddie shouted, glad he was wet and slippery, making it near impossible for Dogface and his henchman Big Mick to get a grip on him. A foot landed in the small of his back, taking him down.

'This is a surprise for you, ain't it, mush? Thought I was tucked in at Winchester nick but 'cos of the overcrowding I gets a nice billet 'ere. Didn't see no welcome from you when I arrived this afternoon, though.'

Eddie slipped but managed to grab the shower controls. His heavy weight pulled them from their moorings and he heard the water pipe groan and crack away from the wall. Eddie was now holding what looked like some strange metal sunflower until it slipped from his grasp. Water gushed everywhere.

His back was being kicked and he knew some ribs had caved in.

He heard laughter, Big Mick shouting, 'You ain't Roy Kemp's little blue-eyed boy now, are you? Just another fuckin' con gettin' done over in the showers.'

Water was cascading from the wrecked pipe like a demented upside-down waterfall, but Eddie, furious with himself for being caught out, managed to reach down for the long length of severed piping and swing it.

Turning and screaming, Eddie smashed it into the face of his enemy. Before Big Mick could speak, his mouth was like red porridge, the blood dripping and mixing with the clear waterfall of water. The floor was awash with blood but in the space of a moment when Big Mick stared at him, Eddie, with his full weight behind the blow, lashed out again with the pipe. The con went down with a split in his head.

Eddie, ignoring the pain from his ribs, faced Dogface, his feet trying for purchase on the slimy floor.

Eddie cried out, 'Tell me again why you think I need a fuckin' beating?'

'Not a beatin', a fuckin' knifing.'

The knife came down from Dogface's sleeve. Eddie saw it was a razor blade in a toothbrush handle. If he allowed Dogface to carve him he would end up with more than just scars on his face. Dogface had the advantage of shoes to grip the tiles as he danced forward. The bloke was fast on his feet for a man built like a brick shithouse.

Eddie swung the pipe. Dogface moved neatly aside. Eddie felt disadvantaged not just by his slippery feet but by his nakedness. He eyed the home-made knife.

'Come on, come and get me,' he said. With his left hand he made a beckoning motion. He could see anger and something else in Dogface's eyes. Fear. He was alone now and the bastard knew it.

Once more, Eddie swung the pipe. The shower head caught Dogface full on the jaw. Eddie heard the splintering. Then Eddie went down as one foot slid beneath him, his other knee cracking on the tiles. His broken ribs jabbed at him. Eddie was struggling to breathe. With blurred vision he saw Dogface's face and his mess of a jaw. Miraculously the man was still on his feet, still coming towards him, the razor blade glinting in the pouring water. Eddie's hands probed for the pipe, finding nothing. Eddie rolled, his knee and his ribs protesting fiercely. His hand grasped the pipe just as the knife razored his arm.

'You fuckin' bastard!'

He yelled as the pain hit him.

His voice gave him the extra spurt of strength he needed. He defied his body's pain and rose to a hunched standing position and swung the lead piping once more.

More of Dogface's teeth bounced on the tiles as the shower head reached its mark. He went down. Eddie watched as he tried to raise himself up and failed.

Eddie stood surveying the carnage of the two bloodied men.

'Fuckin' 'ell, Eddie, remind me never to take a shower with you.'

Eddie turned quickly. Ginge stood there with a pair of

brightly coloured tights over one arm and a pair of ladies' clear plastic high heels in his hand.

Eddie breathed more easily. 'I 'ad a bit of trouble, Ginge,' he said. Then he put down the pipe. As he bent down his head swam and he fell.

Ginge was at his side. He hauled him up, Eddie groaning as Ginge dunked him under the spurting water.

'You're covered in blood, mate. Don't want to give no secrets away as to who bested who from this little lot, do we? Up's a daisy,' said Ginge, as Eddie buckled at the knees again. 'Bloody good job it was me as was sent back to get the forgotten props. You gotta walk, mate, a skinny chap like me can't carry a six-footer like you.'

Eddie heard him and tied the towel around his waist when it was handed to him.

'The water ...'

'Fuck the water, let it run. Let the screws make what they will of it.'

'Dogface ... his mate?'

'Dogface ain't gonna be able to talk for a long while and his mate's 'ad it.'

Ginge was back at his side, and with his arm across his shoulder, slowly Eddie made it back to his cell. He thanked God no one passed them in the corridor. He didn't want to think about what would happen when the bodies were discovered. Dogface would take a good while to be able to speak with any clarity. Even then Eddie doubted whether he'd tell anyone he, Eddie Lane, had messed him up good and proper. If he did, he'd make himself look foolish in the eyes of the other cons.

'The water has washed away the blood,' Ginge said, peering at his upper arm. 'It's a clean cut. Can you get into bed?'

Eddie nodded and pulled back the blanket. He didn't think there was a place on his body that didn't hurt.

Ginge left him to it. His knee throbbed and his chest hurt every time he breathed.

He hated himself for what he'd done tonight. Bastards they might have been but when he went to take a shower he never figured death would walk alongside him.

All because Roy Kemp gave him handouts and cared about him.

Well, come Easter, he'd stand on his own two feet. His dream would mean using a room at Western Way. Safety and secrecy was a big issue and he knew Daisy would rather he held meetings where she could keep an eye on him. He planned on convincing his mother he'd never involve her in anything shady. With Jamie out of the way and his handpicked team ready to do his bidding, it was highly unlikely the reality of his plan would be discovered. Not unless there was a traitor among his men.

There was only one way to creep out from beneath Roy's shadow. Eddie was ready to fly.

CHAPTER 6

Vera crumpled the letter from Haslar Hospital and threw it in the rubbish bin to nestle among the tea leaves. Her hands were wet with sweat and the back of her neck wouldn't stop prickling. Her heart was racing.

She had to go back for a biopsy, whatever that was, in three days' time. It seemed the doctors weren't hanging about. Didn't that mean it was serious?

'You all right out there? Lost the kettle or something?' Daisy's voice was muffled because she was probably still cuddling into her big son who'd been in the house about ten minutes.

'I reckon we needs a new kettle, this one's taking ages to boil.' Vera concentrated hard to make her voice steady. Now certainly wasn't the time to say anything about her previous visit to the doctor's surgery and her trip to Haslar Hospital for an examination a week ago where she'd sat in the waiting room with all the other women who'd received a sentence of death, or, if they were lucky, a reprieve. Oh, how she'd wished Daisy had been with her. Everything seemed to be happening so fast.

Vera thought back to that day. 'Take off your clothes, we need to X-ray you,' the nurse had said.

'I don't usually get undressed in front of women, usually it's blokes ...' As the words had left her mouth she realised how ridiculous she sounded. One of the nurses had grinned at her.

The whole X-ray process had indeed been quite painless.

'What happens now?' Vera had asked.

'The X-ray will go to the doctor who will decide what's best for you, depending on whether that little lump looks nasty or not.' The young red-haired nurse must have seen the stricken look on Vera's face.

'Leave the worrying to us. Get dressed now.'

Vera had slipped back into her frilly underwear and put on her green silk blouse. And the next thing that happened was a letter from the hospital saying she needed to talk to the specialist. Vera had memorised the letter but tore it into a million pieces so Daisy couldn't read it.

'Two shadows.' The specialist had pointed them out to her on the X-ray. 'We don't know what they are so a biopsy could tell us that. See this one?' He pointed to a small spiderlike shadow. 'I don't like the look of this but the bigger mass ...' Again he had pointed to a shadow that seemed larger than the first one. 'It's possible this is a calcium deposit.'

Now Vera raised her hand to the side of her right breast and through her frilled blouse and pointed brassiere felt the lump that seemed as big as a pea. If only the doctor had smiled as he'd examined her.

The worry settled over her like a big black shroud.

She was convinced she was going to die. How could she inflict all this added worry on Daisy? Especially with Daisy being run off her feet down the White Swan, not to mention chasing around after a three-year-old, and looking so tired as a result.

Vera turned off the steaming kettle and filled the teapot before stirring the tea and setting the lid on and the cosy on top.

'Nearly ready,' she called. She reached up into the cupboard and took down a packet of Bourbon biscuits.

This thing under her arm couldn't be much, could it? It didn't hurt ...

She thought about her mate Lanky Sue who'd died of – she didn't want to even think the word – cancer. Sue was all skin and grief when Vera visited her in the War Memorial Hospital. Breast cancer had spread. Three days after Vera's hospital visit, Sue was dead.

Vera could hear Eddie laughing. He had a big rumbling laugh just like his father had had. And earlier, when Vera had opened the front door to him, she almost thought it *was* his father standing there with that daft grin on his face. He'd swept her up and whirled her around, saying, 'You're a sight for sore eyes, Vera. Where's me mum?'

Then Daisy had flown into his arms and dragged him into the front room.

Vera took the tray then, careful not to wobble it as she was wearing her high-heeled black fluffy mules, and left it on the coffee table next to Daisy.

Eddie smiled at her. He was a lovely-looking lad. But he looked tired, fuller in the face as he'd put on weight with all that stodgy prison food.

Vera leaned forward and pushed back the fall of hair from Eddie's forehead.

'Is that the scar Daisy told me about?' she asked. 'It runs through your eyebrow. Will the hairs eventually grow over it?'

Daisy looked at the livid pink scar. Eddie fidgeted.

'No, Vera, hair don't grow on scars,' Daisy said.

'One of the hazards of bein' inside, Vera. I was caught off guard.' He shook his hair back into place. 'Nothing to worry about. You should see the other bloke. Well, Ma,' he said.

'It'd be a bonus if I could set eyes on me little sister Gypsy.'

'She's 'aving her morning nap,' Daisy answered. Vera saw her look at the clock on the mantelpiece. 'But she'll be awake soon an' then you'll wish she was asleep again!' Daisy gripped his hand. 'How long you staying, son?'

'Not as long as I'd like, but I got a favour to ask.'

'Anything,' Daisy said.

'I'd like to use one of the bedrooms you ain't using now as a sort of conference room.'

'Conference? What you got to discuss?' Then a shadow fell across her face. 'You goin' into business? It ain't the drugs business?'

Eddie smiled and shook his head. 'No, it's something quite different. Drugs is Roy's domain. I want to make him proud of me, not do 'im down.'

Vera could almost see Daisy's mind ticking over. She'd be thinking it was better for her boy to be working things out, whatever it was, under her roof than being at Roy's or somewhere else.

Vera knew Eddie would never involve his mother in anything that would harm her or her reputation, even if he wouldn't let Daisy or her into his confidence. She said, 'If he was upstairs you'd be able to take freshly cooked cakes and scones up to the blokes what's workin' with 'im in that room. Like Violet Kemp does when Roy has his oppos round. An' you'd get to see more of Eddie.' Then Vera had a brainwave. 'I'm sure whatever it is it'd be just like when Violet Kray used to let Reggie and Roy do the same. Neither Violet has come to any harm.'

'Suppose so,' said Daisy, then she rounded on her mate. 'Who's gonna cook cakes? You'd burn everythin' and I can't be bothered.'

'Don't 'ave to be cakes, Dais. Blokes like bacon sarnies and cheese an' onion sarnies. We can cope with that, surely?'

Daisy looked happier.

Eddie said, 'I don't want to put you to any trouble, I just want a quiet place where me an' a few mates can work on a few plans I'm drawing up.'

''Course you can, son,' she said. 'I ain't even going to ask you what them plans are. I suppose you wants to keep this a secret from Roy?'

'If you don't mind, Ma.'

'I trust you not to get involved in anythin' that's going to put you back in prison?'

'Course not, Ma.' But Vera saw the dark look that clouded his eyes.

'You pouring that bleedin' tea, Vera? It'll be cold in a minute.'

'Keep yer 'air on, Daisy Lane.' Vera put the mugs in position.

'You stayin' the night?'

'I'd like to,' answered Eddie. 'Would you mind if I went down to see Summer first?'

'I'd be very upset if you didn't,' said Daisy.

'I need to get to London tomorrow.' A frown crossed Daisy's face. Vera knew Daisy had hoped he'd spend a couple of days at home. 'But I'm coming back down again to Gosport very shortly. I'll warn you beforehand. I won't just turn up with a load of me mates in tow.' He picked up his tea and drank deeply. 'Ah', he said. 'Tea's like gnat's piss inside.'

'Take a biscuit an' dip it in.' Vera moved to pass him the packet and dropped them onto a mug of tea that overturned, spilling brown liquid everywhere. 'Fuck,' she said.

'Don't worry, accidents 'appen,' said Daisy. 'Most of it went my way. I'll go and get a cloth.'

Daisy was out the door with the ruined mess of biscuits in her hands.

'You all right?' Vera asked. 'No tea over you?' Eddie shook his head.

Vera realised it was taking Daisy longer than was necessary to get a cloth. She was on her feet just as Daisy came through the doorway. One look at Daisy's frown and Vera's heart sank. Decorated with tea leaves and biscuit droppings was her letter, which Daisy pushed in front of Eddie to read.

'Vera, when was you goin' to tell me about this?' Daisy was angry, her face red and blotchy.

Eddie took the letter and read it.

'What does this mean, Vera?' Worry crept over his face.

Vera shrugged. She felt sick to her boots and ready to burst into tears. She'd so wanted to confide in Daisy, but not like this, not with all this bad feeling.

'I would 'ave told you when I was ready. There just 'asn't been the right time ...'

For a single moment Daisy stood firmly planted in front of her, her green eyes searching Vera's dark ones. Vera thought Daisy was so angry she might strike her, then she leaned forward and gathered Vera into her arms.

'You couldn't keep a secret like this to yourself, you know.'

'I'm shit scared but I don't want no one's pity if the biopsy turns out bad. Don't tell anyone, please?' She looked from Daisy to Eddie.

'I promise,' said Daisy. She turned to her son. 'You don't know nothin' about this, right?'

He nodded.

'When you got to go to this biopsy thing?' She snatched back the letter from Eddie. 'What's a bleedin' biopsy anyway?'

'They put a needle in and draw off fluid. Then they can

find out the best way to treat it – or if anything needs to be treated,' said Eddie.

'You knows a lot about it, Eddie,' Daisy said. 'As for you, Lady Muck, you ain't going to no 'ospital unless I comes with you, understand?'

Vera dissolved into tears. It seemed as if all the suppressed worry needed to flow out of her.

'Will it hurt?'

Eddie shook his head. 'They must have explained it's a normal procedure and over with in five minutes. Most people worry about cancer when they find lumps and bumps but nine out of ten times the lumps are non-cancerous.'

'That's exactly what I was told.' Vera smiled shakily. 'I'm so relieved you knows about this now, Dais, but suppose I 'as to 'ave me body cut up?' She grabbed hold of Daisy's hand. 'Oh, Dais, I don't want to die.'

CHAPTER 7

'That's a nice ring, Roy.'

'Want to try it on, Jamie?'

Roy gave him a knowing smile and wriggled off his pinky ring, then watched as Jamie placed it on the small finger of his left hand. Jamie then stuck out his arm, admiring the gold and onyx band. Roy watched him preening for a few moments then went back to the problem in hand.

'So who took my fucking money?' Roy stared at Eddie, then back at Jamie, who seemed not the slightest bit interested in Roy's question. Jamie was still approving the ring, then he ran his fingers through the fall of his blond hair that never seemed to stay in place. Roy glanced over at Eddie, who looked up and met his eyes. Eddie shook his head and slid an elastic band around a bundle of notes.

Roy didn't need an answer to his question. Testing Eddie with large sums of money had already proved his trustworthiness. Jamie wriggled on the chair so that he was sitting in a more comfortable position, his long legs splayed out.

Roy sighed. 'You two might 'ave to sit at my mother's table until I finds out the fuckin' truth.'

'Where's Charles?' Eddie asked. Roy's heart thudded. In that split second it could have been Eddie's father sitting there. Years ago Eddie Lane senior had moved in on Roy's territory.

Eddie had been in love with the skinny blonde Daisy Lane, so was Roy. When it became clear Eddie was taking the piss and moving in on his manor, Roy had given him enough rope to hang himself then had him taken to one of his brothels in Forton Road. Eddie had paid with his life – the ultimate price for crossing Roy Kemp.

'Charles is on an errand,' Roy said.

Who'd have thought, twenty-odd years on, Eddie Lane's boy would be like a son to Roy Kemp? And Daisy? Roy thought he'd go on caring for the daft bitch until the end of time, even if she wouldn't live with him. Mind you if they *could* live together, he'd be the happiest bloke on earth. He and Daisy and young Gypsy needed to be a proper family.

But Daisy didn't want to come to London to live with him.

That didn't mean he had to live like a fucking monk, though, did it? He thought of Eve, empty-headed Eve. A good fuck, but because of the vast difference in their ages she had nothing of interest for him except sex. And sometimes her vigour fair wore him out. She was a youngster on the make but he knew other men envied his ability to draw the pretty girls and he liked that.

Roy asked again. 'Who took the money?'

Jamie was still admiring the ring. Eddie went on counting.

It wasn't as if it was a large amount of money to go missing. Two hundred pounds. A drop in the ocean. If either one of Daisy's boys had asked him for the money he'd have handed over twice as much, willingly.

Roy looked back at Jamie. He was six feet tall, blond, and pretty as a bleedin' picture but he had a stone for a heart. Jamie picked up the *Daily Mirror* and began leafing through the pages.

The money Eddie was counting was insurance money.

Shops, bars and clubs paid Roy money to keep trouble from their premises. Of course, if a week's money wasn't paid, then Roy brought trouble to their doors anyway. It was an old ruse that had kept the Kray twins solvent for years. Roy liked it that Reggie and Ronnie had given their blessings to him to take over most of their holdings. Violet Kray, being his mother's oldest friend, didn't want for anything. Roy made sure of that, even visited her regularly, making sure the twins had enough money stashed to ease their thirty-year sentences.

'You shouldn't leave money on the mantelpiece,' said Jamie, putting down the paper. 'Not with the amount of thieves you 'as comin' and goin' in this house.'

Again he held out his fingers, pleased with the look of the ring on his hand.

The kitchen door opened and Roy's stepfather, Charles, came in. Throwing his coat over the back of a kitchen chair, he looked at Roy with his sea-blue eyes.

'All right, Charles?' asked Roy. Charles sat down at the table and Eddie moved up to make room for him.

'What's goin' on in 'ere besides the money counting?' Charles frowned. 'You can cut the bad atmosphere with a knife.'

Roy shook his head at Charles. He'd had enough now. He didn't like being taken for a mug. He turned to Jamie.

'Listen, you little shit,' he said, his tone like ice. 'No one takes money from me. Not in me own home. I leave stuff around and I expect it to be where I left it.'

Jamie opened his mouth to protest but Roy interrupted him.

'Get over 'ere.'

Jamie pushed himself away from the table and stood up. He had a sort of swagger about him that infuriated Roy. He ambled over to the sink.

Roy passed him a clean tea towel. 'My mum's cooking us a damn good dinner, so the least we can do is show her our appreciation.' Jamie picked up a flat baking dish and began wiping it dry.

'In this 'ouse we like to show gratitude. You do something nice for me, I do something nice for you, you agree with that?' Roy kept his voice low.

'Oh, yeah.' Jamie put the baking dish on top of the cooker then picked up a mixing bowl. Roy was finishing off the cutlery.

'It's also good to think we can trust each other absolutely.'

'I agree with that,' said Jamie. The mixing bowl was set in the cupboard. Since the wiping up was now done he left the tea towel draped on the side of the sink.

Roy folded his towel and dropped it on the draining board. Then taking hold of Jamie's hand he examined it carefully.

'You know that ring looks nice on you. You got the right kind of fingers for chunky rings.'

Jamie preened, resting his hand on the draining board, and stretched out his fingers.

'It does look the dog's bollocks, Roy ...' He smiled into Roy's face.

In the blink of an eye Roy had picked up the cleaver used by his mother for cutting the pork and brought it down on Jamie's hand. Part of the small finger spun into the room.

'Fuckin' 'ell!' Jamie danced about with his hand beneath his armpit. Blood was staining his white T-shirt bright red.

'Jesus!' Eddie had jumped to his feet. Piles of money and banknotes flew everywhere.

'You bastard, you fuckin' bastard!'

Roy looked quite unperturbed. He put the blood-smeared cleaver down on the kitchen table. With both hands he quickly grabbed Jamie's shoulders and pulled him towards him. Face to face he grinned at Jamie. Roy could smell the fear on the lad's breath.

'I'm telling you now, boy, no one – got that? – no one, steals from me. Understand?'

Jamie nodded and Roy saw the tears in his eyes. He almost felt sorry for him. He'd known the lad all his life, knew everything about him, good and bad. And there wasn't much that was good about Jamie Lane.

Charles said, 'I've got his finger.' He put the digit into a piece of kitchen roll and folded it up.

'Charles, take the little bleeder to the hospital casualty department. Tell 'em he's been doin' a bit of vigorous do-it-yourself-ing.'

'Come on, lad,' said Charles as Roy thrust Jamie away from him.

Stumbling, Jamie cried, 'You took the top of me little finger right off, you bastard. It fuckin' 'urts!' Tears were running down his face now and blood was dripping onto the carpet. Jamie held his injured hand tight to his chest.

Roy said, 'Cut the bad language, Jamie. You know my mother doesn't like it.'

Jamie was staring at him as though he couldn't believe his words or his lack of sympathy.

'Where is it? Where's me finger?' Wild-eyed, he looked about him.

Charles showed him the small bloodstained package.

'I got it,' he said. 'Come on, lad, let's get out of here.'

'Bugger your finger, you little cunt,' said Roy. 'Where's my ring? Worth a lot of money that is.'

Eddie handed Roy the ring and Roy slipped it back on his pinky finger. Roy shook his head.

'Your mother should have taught you years ago that you don't shit on your own doorstep.' He straightened his hand and stretched out his fingers, looking at the ring. 'It didn't fuckin' suit you, anyway.'

CHAPTER 8

'What's the matter, little pup?'

Jamie bent down and patted the mongrel's matted hair. He wondered if he'd ever get used to seeing his left hand without the top of his pinky finger. It was almost healed now but the hospital hadn't been able to do more for him than put a stitch or two over the base of the knuckle. That bastard Roy had no right to maim him. Not for a poxy two hundred quid. If his mother knew, she'd go daft, but he didn't want her to find out. Not just yet. He didn't like upsetting his mother.

He looked at the puckered skin with disgust, then sat up on the wooden bench facing the strip of Solent water that divided Gosport from Portsmouth and peered across the harbour. He could see Nelson's flagship, HMS *Victory*, in dry dock. It had become a visitor attraction. He looked at his watch; by now there'd be queues of people waiting to walk over the hallowed ship. He remembered, when he was just a kid, his mother and Vera taking him and Eddie to clamber across the oak boards. It wasn't even very big, not like some of today's warships.

Eddie, despite being the elder brother, had been scared of the small, dark, low ceilings and Vera had comforted him and wiped his tears. Jamie had laughed at Eddie, but even then he'd known Eddie was 'the chosen one', the boy who could do no wrong.

He wondered where Eddie was now. Visiting Summer, no doubt.

And going about it all wrong. Tiptoeing round her, always scared she'd knock him back when he told her how much he cared about her. Silly bloody fool, Eddie was. If Summer belonged to him, he'd have got into her knickers long before now. He wondered if she was still a virgin. Probably, he thought. To Eddie, Summer was pure. Jamie had overheard his mother talking to Eddie one night and Eddie saying he'd wait until their wedding night if that was what Summer wanted. Silly sod, he thought, he'd have given her one and showed her who was the man.

The sea smelled of slime and mud. Its colour was a dank grey, not the bright blue you saw in brochures advertising holidays to Spain. He watched as a crowd of people disgorged from a ferry boat and began streaming up the pontoon.

The mongrel nuzzled into Jamie's hand.

'I know what you want, pal,' he said, opening the paper bag he'd put on the wooden seat beside him. He pulled out a currant bun he'd bought from The Dive café and bit into its softness, then crumbled off a chunk and gave it to the mutt. He watched the dog gobble it down. 'Hungry, aren't you, pal?' The dog wagged his scrappy tail on the concrete and looked expectantly at him.

Jamie bit into the curranty sweetness and gave another morsel to the dog. The bun reminded him of the near darkness of the underground café, sitting between Vera and Daisy with Eddie facing them. It was warm and cosy down there. He'd felt safe in that café, same as he felt safe in his bedroom at Western Way.

He was beginning to like being on his own in the London flat. Why should he worry about not being asked to live with

Roy, Roy's mum and Charles in that poky terraced house that Violet said she'd only leave in her wooden box. Of course Eddie, dear Eddie, got to live there, didn't he? *But then, Eddie was like a son to Roy, wasn't he?*

If it wasn't for the money he got off Roy, he'd bugger off abroad somewhere hot. His own father certainly wouldn't miss him. No, he was happy enough living in the country with his beloved Clare and their son Jack who was so goody-goody it made Jamie want to puke. He spat on the concrete. Fuck the lot of them.

He was just a copper's bastard, unwanted by the fuckin' copper.

Jamie wondered if Roy was buying something pretty for that scrubber, Eve, he'd taken to showing off in London. Roy hadn't broadcast the news yet that he had a fancy piece. Jamie was fairly sure his mother had guessed though. One thing Jamie would never allow and that was for any other woman to take his mother's place in Roy's heart. Roy mustn't be allowed to hurt Daisy or Gypsy.

'Not right if he's casting Mum on the scrap heap,' he said, feeding another piece of bun to the dog. 'And Gyp's his daughter. She don't need a father what fucks about.'

He stared at his hand.

He'd get even with Roy Kemp someday, he vowed. The dog's tail swept dust and fag ends from the concrete as it waited expectantly.

'Nice girly, little Gyp.' He patted the dog and smiled to himself thinking about the chubby youngster with her slate-grey eyes and constant chatter.

His sister would climb on his lap with her picture book and make him read to her and colour in pictures of princesses and fairies. And questions? She was full of them, and in the middle of a sentence when he was replying, she'd ask, 'Why?'

Everything was 'why' to her and he'd explain as patiently as he could.

He missed her and he missed his mother, but the money from Roy was useful. He sighed before delving into the bag on the seat and taking out the second and last bun.

Perhaps he'd pop in and see his mother before he drove back to London. One thing for sure, he'd go round and see if he could spy on Summer. Wasn't right that Eddie had everything, even a gorgeous little thing like her.

Just thinking about her caused him to feel his hard-on swelling against his jeans. What he wouldn't give to fuck her. Stunning little thing, with the most pert breasts he'd ever seen. He wondered what they'd look like without the confines of her clothes. Sweet meat, thought Jamie. The nearer the bone, the sweeter the meat.

He also had to look up Heinz. Heinz owed him money from the nice little earner Jamie had going in Roy's deserted brothel in Forton Road. Young boys fighting and being cheered on by a load of sad fucks who bet on them to knock ten bales of shit out of each other.

Heinz also organised dog fighting over at Browndown. Another fight-to-the-death operation that brought in a fair whack of money of which Jamie took a hefty slice.

Jamie thought he owed a visit to that little bint who liked a bit of slapping around before she begged to be fucked. It was only a short walk to the South Street flat where she lived. Maybe he'd better go to her first and give her the benefit of his hard-on.

He put a piece of bun in his mouth and chewed absently. The dog put his head on one side and stared, his tongue lolling. Jamie gave him the last morsel. The bun was gone in a second. And still the dog sat and watched him with huge sad brown eyes.

Jamie got up, crumpling the paper bag before he threw it to the ground. He looked at the dog waiting expectantly.

'Fuck off!' he said and kicked the animal so hard the dog yelped before it slunk painfully away, still whining.

Eddie turned his car into North Street, past Murphy's the ironmongers, past the Fox public house, and parked on the spare bit of ground opposite his uncle's second-hand book shop. He smiled to himself at the name of the shop, The Book Shop. Not a great deal of imagination there, he thought, but then his Uncle Bri was one of the most down-to-earth people he knew.

He looked at his watch. It was too early for the shop to be open but he wanted to see Summer so bad it hurt. They'd be eating breakfast, he guessed.

He sat for a while, thinking it had been quicker to drive down from London than he'd envisaged.

He sniffed. He wasn't happy with the way things were going. That Jamie, the fucking psycho, was in London working for Roy.

He consoled himself that if everything he was planning worked according to his arrangements, then he would get far enough away from Jamie not to have to worry about him ever again.

He couldn't blame his mother for asking Roy to keep an eye on his brother. He certainly didn't begrudge his mother a bit of time off. Time off to her meant working harder than ever and asking questions left, right and centre about the boy being knocked about.

Excitement welled up in Eddie at the thought of being close

to Summer. They'd written to each other and confessed their love, and she'd agreed that a long engagement would be a sham. Marriage was what they both wanted, and soon.

Eddie saw the notice on the bookshop's door turn to 'Open'.

His stomach churned with anticipation.

He got out of his Aston Martin Bulldog and began walking across the grass, sidestepping the dog shit.

As Eddie opened the door, recognition dawned on Bri's face and the tall red-haired man's face broke into a smile. He grabbed Eddie's arm and began pumping it.

'Good to see you, Eddie.' This was his father's brother. Once he had been a market stallholder and his strength showed in his firm handshake.

'Hello, Uncle Bri,' returned Eddie, as he was pulled into an embrace.

'I like your wheels.' Bri nodded towards the car.

'Not had her five minutes; did a deal with one of Roy's mates,' he said.

Bri's face grew serious. 'You all right?' He stepped back, staring hard at him.

'After being inside, you mean?' Eddie nodded, then grinned. 'All part of the rich bleedin' pattern of life, I guess. But not an experience I wish to repeat.'

'If you hadn't acted so fast, Daisy would be dead now. You saved your mother's life.'

'I killed a man, Bri.' Eddie's voice was low. 'I had to pay a price and now I'm ready to start over,' he said.

He looked at his uncle's comforting surroundings. Books everywhere, piled on shelves, in corners and even stacked on the floor.

'I bet you had to look out for yourself in the nick?'

Eddie nodded. He thought about Dogface. He wasn't

proud of the way he'd had to survive in prison. He'd sworn to himself he'd never hurt another living being as long as he lived.

'I don't want to talk about the past, not even think about it,' Eddie said quietly.

'Well, I'm bloody glad to see you,' Bri said. Eddie's heart warmed at his uncle's words. 'An' I know someone else who'll be more than happy you've called round.'

Bri's eyes turned towards the carpeted staircase that led to the flat above the shop.

'I hope so.' Eddie's heart had started pounding against his chest. This was the moment he'd waited for, yet the one he feared the most.

His palms were wet with perspiration. It had been a long time since he'd set eyes on Summer, refusing her a visiting order as he didn't want her to see him in prison. Letters had professed their true feelings for each other.

'Go and find out.'

Eddie, his heart in his mouth, began to climb the stairs.

She was at the sink, washing up. Her fall of strawberry-blonde hair hung low on her shoulders. A kimono of green silk was tied loosely around her body, doing a very bad job of disguising her curves. Eddie could smell the remains of a cooked breakfast. Summer turned her head.

'Eddie!' Throwing back cutlery into the soapy water, she ran into his arms.

'You nearly knocked me over!' He laughed. Her wet hands held his face and he didn't care. Her lips found his.

It was the first grown-up kiss she'd ever bestowed on him and it was worth waiting for. He breathed deeply of the peachy smell of her.

Her eyes found his scar. She ran a finger lightly across its surface. He saw her about to question him and he took her hand away and kissed her fingers.

'Don't ask,' he said.

She nodded. 'I lived for your letters. Not being able to see you was awful.'

'I didn't want you to visit me in a place like that.' He thought of Winchester Prison, of the other cons leering at her ... Then Ford flashed through his mind He'd known it would have taken just one visit from her and when she'd left he'd have walked out of the open prison to follow her.

She stepped closer. 'I love you, Eddie. I didn't know how much before.'

His eyes roved over her face, drinking in each feature.

'I've waited a long time to hear you say that. When I heard you'd taken that job as nanny to the two children in Edinburgh with the possibility of travelling abroad, I believed you'd never return to Gosport ...'

'I had to grow up, Eddie. I couldn't see love was right in front of me then. Absence makes the heart grow fonder, as Auntie Vera would say.'

Eddie's heart missed a beat. He really was the luckiest man in the whole world. He took a deep breath.

'If I was to ask you to marry me as quickly as possible, what would you say?'

A smile split her face. 'I'd answer yes, you know I would.'

She reached no higher than his chest and she fitted against his body as though that was where she was meant to be. He sighed with pleasure. 'That's all right then.'

'Yes, yes, yes.' Her eyes were as bright as stars. He wanted to kiss her some more, but with the possibility of her father climbing the stairs any moment, the flat wasn't the right place to be.

'Get dressed,' he ordered. 'I'll take you out.'

'Where?'

'Wherever you like. Shopping, if you want.' She frowned. He loved the way her nose tilted upwards and he adored the rich whisky-brown of her eyes.

'Somewhere quiet where we can be alone might be nice,' she said.

'I'd like that.' He smiled.

While she dressed in her bedroom, Eddie finished her chore of wiping up. Then he went down and waited while Bri served a customer. He began humming 'Wheel of Fortune'.

Bri said, 'Everything all right with you and Summer?'

Eddie nodded. 'You know I'll look after her, don't you?' He stepped from one foot to the other, waiting for his uncle's reply. 'I've asked her to marry me.'

Bri said, 'About bloody time. Many years ago I asked you to watch out for the wilful little madam, Eddie, and I couldn't be happier that you've finally both got it together. I suppose the next thing will be an engagement party?'

'Actually, no. We want to marry as soon as possible. We'll have a big do then.'

He thought about the job he'd planned. Time was of the essence.

Bri nodded. 'Why you humming that particular song?'

Eddie looked at Bri. 'I dunno. It's in me head all the time. Why?'

'I remember it was your dad's favourite song. Try not to whistle it when your mum's around. It'll break her heart, especially with you the spittin' image of him.'

'Okay,' said Eddie, thoughtfully. 'Thanks for the tip.'

Just then Summer came downstairs, wrapped in a fake Afghan coat that was only a few shades lighter in colour than her eyes. Around her neck trailed a long multi-coloured scarf, and white boots completed the vision. Eddie thought she was the most beautiful woman on earth and vowed one day he'd deck her out in diamonds.

'I see you can scrub up well.' He laughed. She came to him, slipping her arm through his.

'Has he told you, Dad?'

''Course he has and I couldn't be happier.'

'Has he explained we don't want to hang about?'

Bri nodded.

Eddie felt as though his heart was fit to burst. He thought of the surprise Summer would find when they reached his car. He'd already shopped in the market for enough flowers to fill the rear of the Aston Martin and in his pocket he had a small square box containing a ring that he'd taken absolutely ages to decide on from a London jeweller.

His joy was suddenly dimmed as Bri asked, 'What kind of car does that brother of yours drive?'

'It's a sunset-red Capri.'

Bri put his hand on Eddie's arm. 'Not ten minutes ago a red car was parked next to yours opposite the shop. I thought it funny that the driver never got out.'

Eddie's heart missed a beat.

'I bloody 'ope it wasn't Jamie,' he said. He pursed his lips together before he said, 'Capri's are a popular ride.'

Summer snuggled into him. He looked down at her and smiled into her eyes. But deep down, he feared trouble ahead.

CHAPTER 9

'Don't, Mum. Please?' He couldn't stand it when she was on the gear and it seemed she was on it all the time now.

'I need to, Earl, honey.'

He watched his mother trying to find a vein, any vein to inject herself. She was drunk already and so skinny her arms and legs looked like sticks. She didn't smell like his mother with the sharp stink of piss that was clinging to her, and she didn't look like his mother any more with her body full of septic needle marks.

She hoisted her leg and stared at the back of her knee. A crusty sore was still oozing pus. But she got the needle in anyway, swearing because it took so long, and then she moaned and stared at him as though she didn't know who the fuck he was or remember she was a twenty-five-year-old wreck and his mother. She fell back on the sofa.

Earl hated the smell of shit and sick mixed together. Used dirty tissues were like large filthy snowflakes covering her. His mother.

Once upon a time, when they'd first come to live in Portsmouth, his pretty mother was bossy about cleanliness and nail-sharp with her talk. He loved it that they would watch quiz programmes on the television together and she called out the answers, always right, of course, way before the contestants. Not any more. Sometimes she couldn't remember her own name or his.

The room was full of people he didn't know and the music was loud. He remembered when his mother used to sing while she tidied. She'd grasp his hands and pull him to his feet, making him dance wildly until they both fell, exhausted and laughing, to the carpet. He'd felt happy then. Now she never cleaned anything and didn't even worry that the second-hand needles were dirty.

Earl felt like crap. But he knew he wouldn't be sick because his stomach was empty. He hadn't eaten yesterday. He couldn't remember when he'd last had food.

His mother was out of it now, in never-never land on the sofa. Big Louis crawled over to where she lay, pulled her legs apart. He mouthed at Earl as he humped his mother's still form, 'Look away, you piece of shit.'

Then Louis gasped and his face screwed up like he was in pain. He rolled away and fell asleep.

Earl was hungry. His mother had said it was to be a party. Only no one had brought food.

There were empty bottles and cans strewn about. The rolled-up carpet and rubbish that his mother had thrown behind the sofa was his bed for the night.

He couldn't go into the bedroom that he and his mum usually shared. He'd seen Alice, and Tom Shaw, his mum's friend with the scars on his face, go in there. People were talking and the music was still loud but Earl thought he'd better sleep.

When he woke there were only a couple of men in the room, both fast asleep. They were both druggies and came to the flat a lot, sometimes with cans of beer for his mum. He stood up, his stomach rumbling.

He went round to the front of the sofa and looked at his

mum. She was very still and her eyes were wide open. He knew no one slept with their eyes wide open, and besides, his mum made funny gurgling noises when she was asleep.

He bent over her and touched her cheek. It was cold. And she didn't blink. Not even when he put his eyes close to hers. Her skirt was round her waist. He didn't like to see her like that so he pulled her skirt down to cover her nakedness. Still she didn't move.

He shook her shoulder, but she didn't wake and shout at him like she usually did. Earl was frightened. She looked just like Uncle Tony did when he had overdosed. His mother said Uncle Tony had died happy. He suddenly knew then that his mother was dead.

Tears began to prick his eyes. He knew he couldn't stay in the flat. They would come for him. They would take him away and put him back in that place, where the older boys would hurt him. Waiting until it was night-time and then dragging him from his bed and taking down his pyjama bottoms and putting their things in him, making him bleed. He ran away from the home but he was brought back, and because the older boys told him no one would believe him he kept quiet. So they took turns in hurting him again and again.

He used to sit with his face pressed against the window, waiting for his mum to come. Just when he thought she must have forgotten all about him, she'd turned up in a posh car with a man.

'This is your Uncle Maurie,' said his mum. She'd looked pretty, with her hair coloured blonde.

Maurie called him 'Kid' and brought them to this flat.

Earl didn't like being on his own at nights.

'I have to earn a living,' his mother told him. And she filled up the fridge with good stuff to eat. Then there were only chips, that his mother would give him the money to buy. He'd run down the road to the Moorgate Chippy and wait in the queue and the big woman with the yellow hair would give him the crackling pieces as well as extra chips.

That's when the men came to the flat and his mum would disappear into the bedroom with them. They gave her money and sometimes funny-smelling stuff that his mother would roll into long cigarettes. Then Maurie would come round and take the money off her. When she cried, Maurie hit her. When he ran to stop Maurie, he was thrown across the room.

Earl stopped going to school because the other kids laughed at him for wearing smelly clothes. He didn't have any clean ones left in his drawer. He missed his lessons. Which was a shame because he was good at arithmetic and spelling. They sent a woman round to see his mother about him not going to school but his mum was asleep on the sofa and when the knocking on the door finally made her wake up, she had a row with the woman.

Earl knew there wasn't any money in the flat but he looked anyway. Then he kissed his mum on her cold cheek and opened the door and went out into the rain.

He walked down Queen Street and stopped near Portsmouth Hard. He'd never been on a ferry boat. Then he walked over to the harbour railway station and sat on the steps, where it was a bit drier. Through the iron railings he could see gulls scooping bits of food up from the mud. The tide was out and it smelled salty but he liked it better than the smell in the flat.

'C'mon you lot, keep together.' The man who spoke was wearing a long mackintosh that went right down to his shoes. Behind him in a straggling line were children. Some were his age, some a little younger. He wondered if it was a school outing but they weren't wearing uniforms. 'Keep up,' warned the man, who had a little moustache.

It was then Earl had an idea.

He jumped up from the step and walked close to the children in the direction of the pontoon. The ticket man punching holes in the tickets said something to the man in the mackintosh. Then he pulled up his coat collar and waved all the children, including Earl, on to the ferry boat.

Once on board, Earl climbed the stairs to the top deck. He didn't care that it was raining hard, he was finally on a boat.

There were warships in Portsmouth Dockyard, all grey, but he couldn't see any sailors to wave to. It was busy on the strip of water between Gosport and Portsmouth and he thought how exciting it was to be alone on the top deck even if he was soaked through to his bones.

Now he could see the Gosport pontoon and the children below, along with the other passengers, standing up ready to get off the boat. He ran down the steps and hung about in the midst of the children. No one took any notice of him.

The ferry boat bumped against the jetty and he watched as the boatman threw the rope in figures of eight around the bollards. The man looked at him and smiled and Earl's heart started beating fast. Suppose they realised he didn't have a ticket?

Then the gate was opened to let passengers off. Earl walked slowly with everyone else until he reached the ramp that led into the town. Then he began running, just in case the boatman called him back.

At the end of the ferry walkway he could see the bus station and the taxi rank and, beyond, a pool hall called Eddie's. Next to it was a club with the name Daisy's in black paint.

A market filled the street in front of him. Stallholders were taking off plastic coverings that they'd used to protect their goods from the showers and were laughing and calling to each other. Now, as he walked through stalls selling pretty clothes, side by side with wet fish merchants and butchers, he began to feel happier. Until his stomach growled.

He stopped at a fruit stall where the owner was laughing and serving a woman who had a small child in a pushchair. He could see fallen fruit in the gutter at the back of the display. The stall was set up in front of a sort of shop. Through the shop's window he could see blue leather sofas with glass tables and flowers in vases.

Through the window he came face to face with a small dark-haired woman in a frilly red blouse and black tight skirt. She was staring at him, her eyes narrowed almost as though she could see right inside him. Earl looked down at the bruised fruit at his feet, lying near an old crisp packet and a dog-end. The shiny green apple was only bruised on one side and the orange looked perfect. There was an open ruined brown paper bag with what looked like peaches in. They were a bit squashed and some were brown but Earl wasn't fussy.

He looked at the woman on the other side of the window but she seemed to have disappeared, so he bent down and scooped up the fruit, jamming as much as he could into his trouser pockets and rolling the rest into his jumper.

The hand that suddenly gripped his arm frightened the hell out of him and he let go of his jumper, watching with horror as his dinner rolled away.

'Ouch!' He tried to twist away but found the grip was like iron.

It was the woman.

'Ouch, let me go!'

'Oh, no you don't, Sonny Jim. What are you doin' scavenging for old fruit?'

'Nothin'!' Earl was scared. Suppose the woman let the man hit him?

'You're hungry, ain't you?'

Earl stopped wriggling and stood quite still. He felt as though he might cry but instead he nodded his head.

'Thought as much,' said the woman. With her free hand she took from her skirt pocket a fifty-pence piece. 'Take this and buy yourself some chips,' she said, loosening her grip on him.

Earl grabbed at the money. Then he slid from her grasp and was away between the market shoppers like a hot knife through butter. He heard the woman laugh. He turned back to look at her and saw she had her hands on her hips, talking to the stallholder who was smiling down at her.

He'd liked her. She smelled nice, like poppies, and she had on false eyelashes.

He didn't buy chips; instead he went into the cake shop and bought a loaf of bread, eating it as he walked along the road, the market far behind him now. It had started raining again, making the bread soggy as he stuffed it into his mouth.

He thought again of his mother and how he wouldn't see her any more and this time he couldn't help himself as he cried, his tears mixing with the rain.

He kept on walking. He had to find somewhere to shelter from the rain. That's when he saw the dog. It stood in his way on the pavement. He tried to tiptoe around the dog but it barked. It danced up to him, its teeth snapping at his hand and leaving white slobber on his skin.

Earl ran. For a moment he thought he was safe but then the dog, still barking, was running alongside him.

The dog tried to jump up at him. Then Earl saw a gate that was half open set in a high brick wall.

He didn't worry that he never knew what was behind the wall, only that he must get away from the dog.

He put out his hands, pushed open the gate and slid inside, slamming it shut behind him. The dog, on the other side of the wall, was still barking but Earl breathed a sigh of relief. He was safe now.

He looked around him. He was in the front garden of a tall house. There was a big chestnut tree, similar to one he'd climbed to get conkers. 'Chestnut House' said the flaking wooden sign nailed to the front wall. The door to the house was ajar.

He bent down behind some tall dead weeds and waited for someone to come out and tell him off. After a while he got braver and climbed the steps to the front door and pushed it wide open.

There was hardly any furniture. He felt braver and discovered there were stairs going down to a long kitchen. There was a huge room, the biggest room he'd ever seen, and in the middle was a large cage.

'Hello!' There was no answer. Earl walked all around the cage. He wondered what kind of animal had lived in it. It was big enough for a lion or a tiger. He could smell damp and cat's pee, and cigarette ends were trodden into the wooden floor that had bits of carpet stuck here and there. A window looked out over a back garden that was full of brown weeds.

He climbed the stairs and found himself in what he supposed was a bedroom. He walked around and was amazed that there were five other rooms with old beds in or mattresses on the floor. There was smelly rubbish and beer cans and bottles everywhere.

He climbed to another lot of rooms. These looked similar to the ones below. Outside the rain was lashing against the small windows and coming in through the broken panes. He knew it wasn't late but the dark sky made it feel like night-time. He was sure now that he was alone in the house.

Earl went into the smallest room where there was a mattress on the floor that seemed cleaner than the rest and he smoothed it out. It wasn't all that damp although it was stained, but he'd slept on worse so he didn't care. In another room, he pulled down from the windows a pair of dirty velvet curtains. The dust made him cough. He carried them into the room where the mattress was. The curtains were lined and the lining didn't smell so much. He put one over the mattress and tucked it in. As the curtains were long he folded another one in four and laid it over his makeshift bed.

It took a long time for him to feel warm. He left the remains of his bread and two oranges right by the side of the bed where he could see them. He felt happy that he had some food to wake up to.

Outside the wind and rain were lashing against the old house and Earl couldn't stop thinking about his mum. After he had cried and thought he would never be able to stop crying, he slept.

CHAPTER 10

'I reckon it's the next exit, Rudmore roundabout.'

'Thanks, Eddie. Roy said he wanted two of us on the job in case anything goes wrong.'

'What can go wrong?'

Although it was early morning and winter-dark, Eddie could make out the silhouettes of ships in the breaker's yard across the motorway.

Eddie considered Roy's drugs empire, his prostitution rackets. If Roy needed to off a bloke it was a job that had to be done. Eddie didn't want to be like that.

'What if I don't want to take over Roy's manor?'

'Don't be silly, lad. What bloke in his right mind wouldn't want it? Been grooming you for years, ain't he?'

'I want to make it on my own. You don't know how hard it was in the nick persuading the other cons I wasn't hangin' on to Roy Kemp's shirt-tails.'

'You got a lot of your mother in you an' she's an independent bitch.'

Eddie smiled. He knew the old bugger meant it kindly.

Charles drove down a side street. Through his open window Eddie could smell burning rubber. Charles leaned forward to switch off the radio, first pausing to listen to the news headlines.

'What d'you reckon to that Dennis Nilsen, then? Bits of bleedin' bodies all over the place. He might be a civil servant but he's a bloody nutter.'

'Sixteen so far. Young blokes,' said Eddie. His stomach turned thinking about it.

He thought instead of the money he was going to come into soon.

'What you thinking about, lad?'

'My trust fund matures soon.'

'That'd be the money your mother swindled out of Roy when they first met.'

Eddie rounded on him. 'No, it ain't. It's clean money, Charles. Roy let her keep the dosh because he'd never known a woman able to best him at long-firming scams. She vowed she'd never touch the money and she put it in trust for me. Ever since, she's been trying to raise money for a similar gift to Jamie but times have been hard for our family.'

'What you plannin' on using it for?'

'I'd like to do something for Mum.'

'You're a good lad.'

'Shut up, you daft bugger.' Eddie saw the two lorries parked up ahead in front of the transport café.

'They're already here,' said Charles. He patted his breast pocket and Eddie realised he was carrying a weapon. Eddie had refused Roy's offer of a piece but he always kept his father's flick knife within easy reach.

Eddie watched as Charles got out the car and ambled over. He saw him pass two of the men slips of paper, then, after shaking hands with him, the men climbed into the cabs of the lorries. Charles returned to the Merc. The lorries began to move.

'We follow them to the industrial estate then hand the job over to someone else.'

Eddie shrugged. 'What's in the lorries?'

'Cooking oil.'

'Cooking oil?'

'Don't bleedin' ask if you don't believe it, parrot.'

Eddie realised then that these were the drugs from Kenya with the oil as a cover. No one was going to worry about a consignment of cooking oil. Good concealment for cocaine.

He shook his head. 'The big man took me to Kenya an' I met his pals. I swore one day I'd go back. It's a fucking lovely country.' Eddie grinned at Charles. 'So in ten minutes or so we're done?'

'Yes.'

'Then what?'

'We go round to your mother's for a cuppa, you're stopping for the afternoon and I'm goin' on to Southampton to where the Rosebowl Casino's having a bit of trouble with some toady croupier whose pilfering is getting on Roy's nerves.'

Eddie's heart started thumping. Charles didn't know he'd got blokes coming to his mother's place this afternoon for the first meeting about the proposed heist. Would he be able to trust them? Would they get on with each other? Petty jealousies could cause unrest unless stamped out immediately.

'We gonna mention Roy and his bit of stuff?'

Eddie's thoughts were scattered. 'I don't want me mum hurt more than necessary,' he replied.

'Then you're the best one to tell her,' said Charles.

Eddie nodded, but he felt like a traitor.

Daisy had to raise herself on tiptoe to throw her arms around Eddie's neck. 'This is a nice surprise.' Gyp was dancing about in the hallway. Her sturdy legs were encased in one correctly fitted white sock; the other sock trailed along the parquet floor like a clown's shoe. Daisy laughed as Gyp threw herself at Eddie the moment he bent down to kiss her.

'You're strangling me,' Eddie said. Daisy could see Gyp's arms were tight around his neck. He staggered further into the hall so that Charles could come in out of the biting cold and the door could be closed on the foul weather. Gyp didn't let him go until Daisy bent down to disentangle the little girl's arms.

'Eddie, Eddie, Eddie,' sang out Gyp.

'Say hello to Charles, Gyp.'

'Hello, hello,' the child repeated. Daisy couldn't help herself laughing at Gyp's antics. Every day the child was a source of wonder to her. From the moment she threw herself onto Daisy's bed in the mornings, assuming she wasn't already in it, to the moment Daisy stood over her, gazing at her perfect angelic features and watching her sleep.

'What 'ave I got in 'ere?' Charles asked, bending down to Gyp's level. Gyp giggled as she tried to prise apart his closed hand. When he let it open a fifty-pence piece lay there.

'Mine, mine,' sang Gyp, running down the hall with the coin.

Vera poked her head round the kitchen door. 'You spoil this child,' she said, then smiled. She had two curlers in the front of her hair. 'You two want a cuppa?'

'Sure do,' said Eddie, stepping away from his mother. Daisy watched his broad shoulders as he went to enfold Vera in a hug.

In the kitchen, Vera's make-up, as usual, was spread across the table. Daisy walked across the room to the ironing board and removed the plug, coiling the lead around the iron.

'It's really lovely to see you, son,' she repeated. That was one thing she knew about Eddie. She could let him go and he'd return. His dad had been like that.

Charles went over to Vera and put his arms around her. 'Violet sends her love,' he said.

Eddie took off his coat and put it over the back of a chair then sat down and stretched out his long legs. Daisy could see he had something on his mind. He looked towards Vera, who was plugging in the electric kettle, then back at Daisy.

'Do you want a glass of orange, sweetie?' Vera asked Gyp.

'Yes, please, Auntie.' Gyp climbed on Eddie's knee. 'Where's Jamie?'

There was a hush.

Eddie looked into her face. 'He's at work, lovey.'

'Where's Daddy Roy?'

Daisy noticed this time that instead of a hush, the silence was as subtle as a slap round the face.

'What's up?' she asked. 'Something's not happened to him, has it?'

'Let's go out into the garden, Mum,' Eddie said.

Daisy, her heart pounding, allowed herself to be escorted out the kitchen door. She shivered at the cold. Eddie draped his suit jacket across her shoulders as she sat on the edge of the fishpond, and sat down on the icy concrete beside her. She thought suddenly of all the times, as a little boy, he'd sat with Vera's moggie Kibbles, watching the fish in exactly the same place she sat now.

'Don't beat around the bush,' she said. 'Out with it.'

'Roy's seeing someone,' he said. He gathered one of her hands in his. Her heart froze. For a moment she was quiet, then she gave a long sigh, gathered all her strength together and gave him a weak smile.

'He's a free agent,' she said, trying hard not to let the wobble in her voice become obvious. She realised for Eddie to give her this information, this new woman was more than someone

Roy needed to show off for the night at some function or other.

'I don't think it'll last,' he said.

'Why you telling me this, then? No one says anything when he's with some little scrubber, an' they come an' go.'

'He's setting her up in a flat.'

Daisy was silent. There was no smart answer she could give to this piece of information. Roy had never before paid the rent on a place for any of his casual fucks.

'Me own fault,' she said finally. 'I can't give him what he wants, and that's to be with him all the time.' She thought of all she and Roy had meant to each other over the years.

'He wants you,' Eddie snapped.

'So it seems,' she said bitterly. She was aware of Eddie's warmth, his closeness. Yet Daisy had never felt so completely alone. 'What's she like?'

'Small and blonde and has a look of you about her but there the resemblance ends. I reckon she's a gold-digger.'

'How old?'

'Mid-twenties, I reckon,' answered Eddie.

'How long's he been seeing her?'

'Few weeks now. Jamie's really cut up about it. He barely speaks to the girl. Reckons for Roy to tolerate any woman for more than a couple of days is a real insult to you and Gyp.'

Daisy made a few quick mental sums, relieved that when she and Roy had last made love the girl couldn't possibly have been on the scene. She didn't know why, but that seemed to make her feel better.

'It won't last,' Eddie insisted.

Daisy smiled at him, 'You're the silly one now,' she said. 'Roy's entitled to be loved. Oh, I don't mean the tarts he fucks, but it is about time he had someone in his life who loves him for himself.'

'You don't mean that … You all right?'

Daisy wiped her eyes and nodded. She stared at the large piece of torn wire netting and remembered Roy saying he'd fix it.

'Let's go in before Vera eats all the Bourbons,' she said. Her voice sounded strange, even to herself.

She allowed her son to take her back into the warmth of her kitchen.

'I told Charles about that kiddie that's getting beat up,' Vera said.

Life goes on, Daisy thought. 'What d'you reckon?' She thought of the pictures cut out from magazines and stuck on his nan's bedroom wall to make the woman feel better. She and Vera had come up against a closed door where this problem was concerned but they both felt something was very, very wrong. She must telephone Vinnie to find out if there was any progress.

'Want me to mention this to Roy?'

'I think I do, Charles.' Daisy knew Roy hated kids being exploited in any way.

When Charles had gone and Eddie had disappeared upstairs to his meeting room, Vera put her arms around Daisy.

'You knows you only got to click your fingers an' Roy'll come running back, tail between his legs, Dais.'

'Not sure I want 'im,' said Daisy airily.

'Who's talkin' about wanting him? You an' 'im is so en-twined, one little scrubber ain't about to prise you apart. You need each other.' Vera unrolled her curler and took a brush to her hair.

'Need *him*? I always thought I was so bleedin' self-contained I never needed no one.'

But as the words fell from her lips, she knew it wasn't true.

Vera said, 'We all needs someone, Dais.'

Tyrone was the first to arrive.

'You gonna tell us what all this is about, Eddie?'

'When everyone's arrived.' His mate frowned at him. 'Upstairs, first on the right.' Eddie nodded towards the stairs as another knock sounded on the front door.

Jet and Big Col had arrived together.

From the hall Eddie could hear the men chatting upstairs. His mum and Vera were clattering about in the kitchen with the radio playing softly.

Clive arrived. 'Jesus, it took me ages to find this place.'

'You're here and that's what matters.'

Eddie went upstairs with Clive following. The men were sitting around the large table, and already the meeting room was full of cigarette smoke. From a locked cupboard Eddie took a folder, threw it on the table and sat down facing the door.

'Now do we get to find out what this is about?' Ty stared at Eddie, who nodded.

'You might not know each other now, but by the time this is over we'll be fuckin' sick of each other.' Col laughed.

'What's the job?' Jet sat back on his chair.

Eddie took maps from the folder and he distributed them to his waiting mates.

'I picked the lot of you because I'm familiar with each and everyone's work. I think I can trust you, but I have to *know* I can trust you. You'll not be aware of the actual venue until nearer the time of the job.' He paused.

'What'll we get out of this?' Tyrone asked.

'More money than you could envisage.'

Tyrone whistled. Clive said, 'This map. Is this it?'

Eddie nodded. His heart was beating fast. So far the effort of appearing in control seemed to be working, outwardly at least.

Jet asked, 'This anything to do with Roy Kemp? Drugs?'

'No. I promise you no one should get hurt. It's a robbery. Planned to perfection.' He pointed to the map each of them held. 'Timing is of the essence. Waiting around is essential. Secrecy vital. And fucking dangerous – which is why I picked you top blokes to do it. We'll go in this way.' He fingered the paper. 'We'll get a van in for the pickings, and sort the money off premises.'

'But where the fuck *is* this place?' Jet was turning his piece of paper round and round.

Eddie smiled. The map contained arrows showing the routes inside the building. Rooms were clearly marked as were safes, exits and cameras. But no telltale outside street names and no local buildings were specified. He looked at his watch. His mum was bound to knock on the door soon with tea and sandwiches.

'You don't need to know where, what or when for the moment. But I'd like to go over this map with you then answer a few questions before I collect them up again. Then if any of you wants out, no harm done.'

A voice boomed from the end of the table, 'Got it all worked out, ain't you, Eddie?'

'Without a doubt, Ty. Without a fuckin' doubt.'

CHAPTER 11

'Pint of Brickwoods, please, Daisy.'

'Coming up,' she said, with a smile she didn't think she had in her. Straight from the pump the beer foamed over the rim of the glass and she set it on the bar top in front of Old Ned. She took his money, exact small change as usual, and he carried his precious pint over to the table in the corner.

Cigarette smoke hung in the bar and the music came from a radio, playing softly so the customers wouldn't complain.

The clock said nine and there was a peculiar sense of gloom like a shroud covering everything. The atmosphere fitted Daisy's own mood.

She couldn't stop worrying about Vera. In Vera's presence she had to put on a brave face but when she was alone in her room she gave full rein to her fears.

Tomorrow morning they had another appointment at Haslar Hospital. Vera was due to be told the results of further tests they'd done on her.

If the worst came to the worst, whatever would she do without Vera?

She mustn't think of that. It was easier to think about Roy and the new love in his life. Daisy tried not to let anyone see how upset she was about his affair with Eve, but inside she felt dead. She honestly never thought Roy would get serious about anyone else. She and him knew each other so well, shared so much history.

'Gin please, Daisy.' Daisy snapped herself out of her morbid thoughts and turned to the optics.

'How's your arthritis, Sal?'

'Bearing up, Dais, bearing up.'

That was the thing about a pub that hadn't yet been modernised into a theme bar, Daisy thought. Customers liked to know there was somewhere familiar they could enjoy a gossip and a drink and a little moan about their ailments. They didn't want the young yobbos coming in, starting fights, nor did they want poncy cocktails or bar meals with fancy names.

'But my feet 'urt,' said Sal.

'You're on 'em all day, ain't yer, Sal, in that greengrocer's? No wonder your feet are playin' up,' said Daisy, pushing a lock of blonde hair back behind her ear. She passed Sal her drink.

'Cheers, love.' Sal drank half quickly, almost as if she thought Daisy might snatch the gin back.

'So 'ave you heard about little Derek Hartington?' Sal asked.

'That eleven-year-old from the wooden houses up the road?' A blond-haired kiddie came to Daisy's mind. 'Cheeky little devil?'

'That's him,' said Sal. 'Or was him.'

'Whatever do you mean?'

Sal looked about her then leaned across the bar. Daisy moved forward so they wouldn't be overheard.

'His mother found him 'anging in the shed.'

Daisy went cold. It took her a while to gather herself together to ask, 'What happened?'

'The kiddie 'ad come 'ome with a nearly new bike, one of them expensive Diamond Back BMXs. His mum couldn't afford to buy him one, see?'

'Where did he get it from?'

'Wouldn't say. Any more than he'd tell her where he was getting the bruises and cuts that was appearing on 'im.'

Daisy gasped. Immediately she thought of Paulie. Was there some connection between the two boys?

'The bruises and cuts to his body were so bad that the school informed the welfare, who went to see Derek's mum. Of course she was terrified they'd take Derek off her, even though she'd never laid a finger on 'im.'

'Bloody hell,' said Daisy. 'Must have been bad. Didn't his mother see what a state he was in?'

'No. He kept himself covered up at home and his mother left the house before him in the mornings to clean that block of new flats down Mumby Road. Most nights she was out cleaning again an' trusted 'im to get 'imself off to bed. Derek told her things would get better now he had his bike. All she could get out of him was it was over, he'd got what he wanted, which was the bloody bike.'

Sal was glassy-eyed now but Daisy knew she could hold her gin and only had to walk three doors along to her home.

'Put another in there, Dais.' Sal smiled, showing brown teeth. 'I shouldn't really, but ...'

Daisy put another measure of clear liquid in front of the old woman.

Sal took a good sip and smacked her lips.

'After Derek said it was all over, he stayed indoors a lot, only venturing outside riding on his beloved bike and to polish the damn thing. His bruises began to heal.'

'So everything was fine?'

'No, Dais. Two days ago his bike got stolen. He was inconsolable. All he kept repeating to 'er was "I worked 'ard for that bike, Mum."'

'How d'you know all this, Sal?'

'I lives only a couple of doors away from the poor cow, don't I? She's wrung out like a wet rag.'

Daisy saw a sudden glint in Sal's eyes. ''Ere, Dais, you reckon I could organise a whip-round for her?'

'You don't think it's rubbin' 'er nose in 'er grief? Money ain't gonna bring 'er boy back.'

'No, I bleedin' don't. She ain't left the house, so there'll be no money comin' in until she pulls herself together. If she does.'

'I think that's a brilliant idea then, Sal. Can I come round with you when you gives it to her?'

Sal's face lit up. 'I was 'oping you'd take it to her, Dais.'

Daisy reached up to the top shelf and took down a large empty decorative cigar box. She opened the till and took out two five-pound notes. She'd pay back the White Swan's till later when her wages came through. Tucking the money into the tin, she turned back to Sal.

'This is a start,' she said, and pushed the tin into Sal's work-worn hands. Then another gin went into Sal's empty glass and Daisy said, 'A bit of Dutch courage before you goes around on your poorly feet, asking people for donations.'

'So that's that, Daisy. That biopsy thing shows I definitely got breast cancer.'

Since leaving the hospital Vera hadn't spoken, but now they were in the open air and walking across the grass towards the car park she gave voice to the test results.

Daisy slipped her hand through her friend's arm.

'Haslar Hospital is the best hospital in the south of England. They'll sort it.'

'And you were there when the specialist said an operation

might be successful, and if I don't have an op the disease will take its course, which means I'll die.' The truth had a life of its own and Vera was numb with shock.

'Daisy, I don't want to leave you.' Vera burst into tears. She put her face in Daisy's neck and sobbed, allowing Daisy to make soothing sounds and pat her back as though she was a child.

'It's karma, ain't it, Dais? All my life I've showed off me figure and now it's all come full circle and me life's bein' taken from me for me vanity.'

Daisy glared at her. 'If you think I'm going to keep on agreein' with you while you starts bein' maudlin, you got another think coming ...'

When they reached the car park, Daisy opened the car door for her and Vera slid inside.

'We'll get through this, Vera, you and me, you'll see.'

Daisy handed her a piece of kitchen roll and Vera blew her nose. She stared out the window.

'Bloody 'ell!' Was she seeing things? 'Look who's over there, Daisy.' She waved towards a Mercedes car.

'Vera, behave yourself,' snapped Daisy.

Inside the back of the car sat a thin man wearing horn-rimmed glasses. His hair was swept back from his forehead and cut in a short military style. He was staring straight ahead.

Vera felt a wave of excitement rush through her.

'That's Major Carter!' Vera couldn't believe her eyes. Never in her life before had she ever seen the major in any other place in Gosport except for his own big house in The Crescent at Alverstoke or in his car when he'd collected her.

She thought of the time when she was living down Bert's caff, before she ever owned the massage parlour in the High Street, how the major would come in his car to pick her up.

Most times he employed a driver with a peaked cap. He'd be sitting all dressed up in the back seat and she would climb inside wearing her skimpy maid's outfit.

'I used to wear me crotchless knickers an' a long coat an' we used to go back to 'is place where he took off his clothes and put on a butler's outfit and bossed me around, and then it was my turn to make him do things like lick me shoes. Then we 'ad sex—'

'You can stop right there, Vera,' said Daisy. 'I don't think I want to know any more.' Daisy screwed up her eyes.

'Okay, Dais. But I bet he still remembers me an' my feather duster.'

That's when the idea came to her. If she was going to lose bits of herself, she was going to do it in style.

''Ang about,' she said to Daisy. 'Come an' get me out of this bleedin box.' Daisy got out of the MG and opened the door for her. As soon as Vera was free she ran, stumbling on her high heels, across the tarmac. Reaching the big car she banged on the window, surprising the man inside. He was alone in the rear of the vehicle.

The major turned at the noise. Vera saw he had a rug across his knees.

'Cooee, Major? Remember me?'

For a few seconds he looked at her blankly then a smile broke his face in two.

'You still livin' in the same place?' She had to yell for he seemed not to realise it would be better to wind the window down than to cup his ear with his hand.

His forehead creased as though the effort of listening to her was rather more than he could cope with. But then he nodded.

The MG's horn sounded. Gyp was at the crèche in Vectis

Road and Vera knew Daisy didn't want to be late picking her up.

Vera turned and waved at Daisy. Then leaned her face close to the car's window and mouthed once more to the major.

'See you tonight,' she said.

'Whatever was all that about?' Daisy asked when Vera returned.

'Once upon a time he used to cancel all his appointments when I said I'd see him. We used to 'ave such good sex together. Daisy Lane,' Vera said, 'I'm goin' out tonight an' I'm not charging him a penny!'

Daisy was ironing when Vera got home.

'You're early,' she said. 'I thought you might stay the night with your major.'

After tossing her pink feather duster on to the draining board, Vera took off her long black coat. She was wearing a very short black dress with a plunging neckline, black fishnets, a white starched apron and high-heeled red peep-toed shoes.

'Bloody karma, Dais. Everything 'appens for a reason. All I wanted to do was prove to meself I still had a bit of sex appeal.'

'Come on, tell me about it. You don't look very 'appy.'

A big sigh escaped from Vera. 'Well,' she said. 'I gets out of the taxi in The Crescent and goes up the big flight of steps to the major's house. I undoes the buttons on me coat so he can get a good look at what's on offer and grips me feather duster before I rings the doorbell.

'As soon as I 'ears footsteps an' reckons the door's goin' to open I whips off me coat an' stands so he can see me open-crotch knickers an' me flesh above me stockin' tops an' I says, "Hello, big boy," an' waves me feather duster and ...'

'And?' asked Daisy.

'Some dragon of a nurse with hairs on 'er chin is standin' there, all dressed in blue an' white. She got a look on 'er face like a bowl of sour cream, "If you've come to see the major, he's just had his enema. His Alzheimer's has been bad today, but he *is* awake," she said. 'I was bleedin' flabbergasted. It didn't dawn on me that the old duck 'ad gone a bit funny like. So I looks at her 'orrible mug an' says, "Tell the major I'm sorry but I got another dustin' job to go to."'

CHAPTER 12

Earl didn't want to go out but he was hungry. He'd woken up not feeling well but knew this was one time he wasn't going to be able to go back to sleep again. His head hurt and he was cold. He'd been all through the big house looking for stuff to use as blankets but although he'd found more smelly curtains and an old coat, he'd shivered and shivered until he'd slept. A gust of wind bringing with it a spattering of sleety rain hit the broken window.

He yawned and stumbled unsteadily to his feet.

He thought about his mother but he refused to cry again. Carefully holding on to the banister rail, he moved one step at a time down the endless stairs. No one had come into the house all the days he'd been there but it didn't really feel deserted. He looked at the cage in the big room off the kitchen. It was such a strange object to have inside a house. Perhaps the previous owners had had pets; cats, maybe, or a dog, for he could smell the pong animals made.

At the sink he drank water straight from the tap then went out of the front door into the rain. There was no point in trying to close the door and make the house safe because he'd discovered the back door didn't lock properly.

He pulled his thin jacket around him and walked in the

direction of the town. In minutes he was wet through and his teeth were chattering.

He hoped the market would be there. He might find some fruit on the pavement again.

Earl wondered if he'd see the pretty woman who'd given him the fifty pence. The money was just a memory now. His stomach growled. There was a wind blowing off the Solent and it seemed as if it was taking him a long time to reach the High Street and, when he did, his heart sank. There wasn't a stall in sight.

Why didn't he think about it before he left the house?

The rain. No one comes out in the cold rain. So the stall-holders hadn't turned up.

Earl walked the length of the High Street, passing unhappy shoppers who seemed just as fed up as he was. He could smell coffee, and tea, warmth, and the lovely aroma of sticky buns coming from The Dive café on the corner near the bus terminal.

Tears filled his eyes. He looked down into the heat of the underground caff and sighed. Not much point in going down if he had no money.

He walked across the road. Then he saw her again, his dark-haired angel from the funny shop with the blue sofas.

He stood outside Heavenly Bodies and watched her. She looked very tired. Her sparkle seemed to have gone. She bustled about on her high heels, with her tight skirt giving her just enough room to walk. Her green frilled blouse was made of some shiny material that glistened as she moved. She was talking to a pretty girl with blonde hair who was wearing a white overall.

And then, as though sensing someone was watching her, she looked across at him. He knew he had a silly smile on his face but she grinned back at him. Oh, she was lovely, he thought.

He knew she hadn't forgotten him. He saw her go to the till drawer and take out a coin then walk towards the door.

And then he panicked. He began to run. He heard the ting of the doorbell and the clack clack of her heels on the freezing wet pavement and then he slipped and fell.

The woman bent down to him. She smelled nice. Her perfume reminded him of fields full of poppies.

'Gotcha,' she said.

He looked up at her. Surprised she wasn't as young as he first thought she was.

'What's your name, boy?' She pulled him to his feet.

'Earl,' he said. He was too exhausted to lie.

'And am I right in thinking you got no place to go ...?' Her long nails were digging into his arm.

'How do you know that?'

'You're wearing the same smelly clothes you were in last time I saw you looking in my window.'

'I'm sorry ...'

'Sorry you're wearing smelly clothes or sorry you looked in my window?'

'Both,' he said, looking down at the wet pavement.

The woman held out fifty pence. Earl snatched at it.

'Your're bleedin' 'ungry as well, ain't you?'

'What of it?' He was feeling braver now he had money for food.

'Well, my name's Vera and there ain't no need for you to starve ...'

Earl didn't want a grown-up telling him what to do, he'd had too much of that in the past. He took a deep breath before he scooted towards the ferry and away from his nosy friend.

'Cup of tea please and a bun with butter in it,' said Earl, when he reached the caff.

He could see the man with the moustache looking him up and down so he put the fifty pence on the table. 'I got money, I can pay.'

The man grinned at him and passed over the tea.

Earl pocketed the change and took the tea and bun through and sat at a table. He put his hands around the hot mug, warming them, then he put the tea down and started on the bun, which disappeared within a few seconds. He felt better already. He knew he was getting thinner because his clothes hung on him now. He wished he had some others to put on, nice clean ones. He could remember when his mother made him change his clothes all the time, even when they weren't very dirty, but that was far back in his past.

Almost as long ago as when he had asked her about his father.

Earl knew he had a dad because his mother had had a letter from him before they moved to the flat in Portsmouth. She read the letter then tore it up. He never knew the contents.

Earl sat in the warm café, watching the customers come and go, long after his tea had gone. He liked the look and smell of the bacon sandwiches the bus conductors and drivers ate with their thick brown tea but he knew he didn't have enough money to buy one.

'You can't stay in 'ere all day without buying, laddie. I got a business to run.' Earl looked up into the proprietor's face. In his hands he had another cup of tea and two buns. 'Get this inside you and be on your way, son.'

Earl felt like he was going to cry.

'Thank you,' he said. Ten minutes later he was outside and walking down Mumby Road. The rain had stopped but the wind was still bitterly cold. Earl jingled the coins in his pocket and reckoned he had enough to buy some chips later. He didn't want to think about the rest of the day. He didn't want to go back to the old house but it was too cold to tramp around the streets and, besides, he'd come over all tired.

He reached Chestnut House and pushed open the door. He thought he heard a rustling noise but knew old houses creaked a lot. His heart started beating fast as he climbed the stairs to his makeshift bed.

In the room stood a boy about his own age. He saw the surprise on the boy's face and then the boy began to walk towards him.

'You come to take Derek's place?' The skinny lad had on a coloured paisley shirt and covering it was a brown quilted jacket that was elasticated at the waist. He was also wearing jeans and trainers.

Earl shook his head. 'Who's Derek?'

'The lad what killed himself.' The boy looked at him as though he should know all about it. Then he rubbed his ear and blinked hard. Earl saw he had bruises on the side of his face.

The boy didn't seem surprised to see Earl there. 'I don't know nothin' about a boy what killed himself,' Earl said.

The boy blinked hard again. Earl thought he had a nervous twitch. He'd seen druggies with all kinds of spasms and tremblings. Surely this boy didn't take drugs?

'Why did this Derek kill 'imself?'

'I reckon Heinz was at the bottom of it. Derek had been fighting for a good while. He wanted a BMX bike an' his mum couldn't afford one, so he kept on fighting an' suckin' dick. You know what that is, don't you?'

Earl knew all about this. His mother had sometimes done it to blokes to get packets of stuff. He nodded.

'But why did he kill himself?'

'Derek finally got his bike off Heinz, he's the man what runs the fights, but he told him that he didn't want to do it any more. He'd got what he wanted, see? Mind you, he'd taken a lot of punishment, Derek had.'

'So?'

'His bike got stolen. We reckon, me an' some of the other boys, that Heinz didn't want him to leave so he taught Derek a lesson. He stole his bike. Next day Derek's mum found him strung up in their shed.' He looked at Earl then asked, 'Anyway, why are you sleeping in 'ere?'

'I ain't.'

'I ain't come up the Solent in a bleedin' bucket. I can see you are.' He pointed to the pile of smelly rags on the floor. 'You're a runaway, ain't you? What's your name?' The boy shook his head as though trying to dislodge something in his skull.

'Earl.' He was taller than the other boy so decided he wasn't a threat. Anyway it was nice to talk to someone, especially someone his own age. 'What's yours?'

'Paulie.' The boy walked round him as if assessing him in some way, then said, 'Got any money?'

Earl shook his head. He didn't think Paulie would take his few coins off him but felt it was better to say he had nothing.

'What you doin' in 'ere anyway?' Earl asked.

'I come to set the place up for tonight. A few chairs for the front row seats an' all that. Heinz gives me a bit extra to make sure the place is ready so the fights can go ahead. I spends most of my money on me nan, see, she's ill, an I don't want her to die.' Earl saw a shadow pass over the boy's face then he blinked a lot as though he had something in his eyes. 'Wouldn't do for Heinz to come into Chestnut House an' find the rozzers here, would it?'

Earl had no idea what Paulie meant. 'Why would the police care about a bit of fighting?'

'Ain't allowed, is it?' Paulie said. 'Kids fighting and their parents urging them on.'

Earl wasn't sure he heard right. 'Why would their mums an' dads want them to get hurt?'

'It's a way to get money for drugs or beer. If their sprog wins.'

'What d'you mean?'

'We gets a fighting partner an' we gets locked in that cage downstairs. The only way to get out is to go on beatin' ten bales of shit out of the boy we're knockin' about until he's unconscious or can't stand up. There's a lot of money bet on us. Specially me now I been doing it a while,' he said proudly. He grinned at Earl. 'I gets the crowd so riled up they cheers and cheers.'

'People watch this?'

'Sure they do. We fights naked and anything goes. Punching, stamping, anything. There ain't no rules. You should hear the mums an' dads cheering. This place gets packed out with people. Heinz calls us his bits of rough trade.'

'That's horrible,' said Earl. He didn't understand why anyone would want to willingly get hurt or grown-ups encourage kids to hurt each other. He'd known blokes give drugs to kids so they'd get hooked on it and he'd seen other kids smoking weed. He wouldn't do it for he'd seen what it did to his mum. Again he watched as Paulie shook his head and rubbed at his eyes.

'What's the matter with your head and eyes?'

'I've taken a few knocks,' said Paulie. 'It feels like water is rushing around in me head an' me eyes is blurred.'

'Have you been to the doctor?'

'No, 'cos I'd have to explain, wouldn't I, silly sod. Besides, if the authorities found out they'd take me away from me mum and nan. Heinz is always threatening to tell them if I don't do what he wants. Anyway, as the blood's stopped comin' out me ears it shows it's gettin' better of its own accord.'

'Does your mum know about your fighting?'

'Don't be bloody stupid! She be right down the bleedin' cop shop. I keep makin' excuses to 'er about the bruises, but most of the time it's easier to say nothin'. Anyway, how come you're sleepin' in 'ere?'

'I ran away. Not that anybody'll come looking for me.'

Then Earl told Paulie about his mum. At one point he began to cry but he gathered himself together again and asked, 'Why you fightin' if you're livin at 'ome and there ain't no rucks at your 'ouse nor no drugs?'

'Like I told you, I want to buy me nan stuff, make her feel better. She ain't me nan really, she's me gran's mum, but she was always there for me. She used to take me for walks to see the swans an' cuddle me and ruffle me 'air. Me nan always listened to me. Then she got sick.' He shrugged. 'My mum can't afford to buy me nothin' an my dad pissed off years ago, but I got an Atari and a Mongoose bike an' my nan don't want for nothing.' His voice was harder now. He looked Earl straight in the eyes and said, 'I'm a good fighter, I makes a fair screw. I got a fiver last fight.' Earl heard the pride in his voice.

'A whole fiver?' Earl knew a fiver would keep him in chips for ages. He was quiet, thinking, then he asked, 'How often do you fight?'

'Heinz got to get matches together so he can 'ave enough

people to make a profit. He's not the boss of it all, someone else is, Jamie Lane. Jamie Lane found us this place to use.' He waved an arm around the room. 'Heinz sorts it all out. You thinkin' you could do it?'

Earl stepped from one foot to the other. He shrugged his shoulders.

'You got to remember it's no use you being a cry-baby and wanting to be let out of the cage. The people will boo you. Though if you look like you being beaten to death and there's no hope of you bein' able to stand up, Heinz will stop the fight and declare your partner the winner. You might get a couple of quid if you lose but you don't expect to get paid if you don't come up with the goods, do you?'

Earl listened. Paulie seemed so wise and he was wearing warm clothes, clothes that Earl wished he had. He thought about the Atari Paulie had and the Mongoose bike. He'd always wanted a decent bike. Most of all, he needed money for food. He couldn't depend on fallen fruit from traders' stalls. 'I'm a good fighter. How old was Derek?'

'What are you? About the same age as me? Eleven?'

Earl nodded. 'Eleven,' he answered. He wasn't eleven for another eight months but he guessed it was best to say he was the same age as Paulie.

'If you're thinkin' you might take Derek's place, it's Heinz who has the say-so an' he won't be here for another half-hour or so. Course, if you do fight, I expect he'll let you stay in this house as well.'

'Would he really?'

'Dunno. 'Ang on, what about school?'

'I ain't been to school for ages an' they got to find me first.'

Paulie nodded, then Earl watched as the boy's head shook of its own accord and when his eyes focused on Earl again he

said, 'Okay, we'll talk about what you got to do as I'm sortin'
out the chairs an' stuff. One thing you must promise never to
do.'

'What's that?' Earl asked.

'You mustn't let anyone know what's goin' on ...'

'Oh, I won't,' broke in Earl. Paulie took a Mars Bar out of
his pocket and passed it to Earl. Earl grabbed at it.

'I knew you could be trusted,' said Paulie.

'Do you like doing what you do?' Earl stared at the bruises
on his new friend's face.

'Not really. It was a lark at first, but now Heinz 'as got me
where he wants me 'cos he knows I need the money.'

Earl twisted his hands together and his skinny wrists showed
beneath his dirty jumper.

'So do I.'

CHAPTER 13

'I've set Eve up in her own flat,' said Roy.

His mother was basting a leg of lamb. The potatoes sitting around the meat were golden and making his mouth water. Violet's face was stony, her lips pressed into two thin lines. Roy waited for an answer and didn't get one.

'Jesus Christ,' said Roy. 'I know you don't like it, but am I never to be free of Daisy Lane? Ain't it enough I got one of her sons under me roof and another round the bleedin' corner?'

His mother faced him, her eyes hard. Even the tea towel she held in her hand looked like a dangerous weapon, thought Roy.

'Don't you swear at me. Have you forgot Daisy's got your kiddie?'

'Sorry, Ma. And no, I haven't forgotten about my Gyp but Eve makes me laugh,' he said.

'Ken Dodd makes me laugh but I don't want to shack up with him,' said his mother. 'An' you wouldn't be employing Daisy's boys if you didn't care for them and her.'

'I *do* care, but our relationship comes with too many hang-ups. You know she won't leave Gosport, says it's her home.'

'Well, it is, so what?'

'What am I supposed to do? Visit every weekend like a lovesick puppy?'

'If I remember rightly, that's exactly what you used to do. She'd come to London one weekend and you'd go down there. Then you had an affair an' it all went wrong.'

Roy took a deep breath. He rued the day he'd ever hurt Daisy. 'That was a bad mistake, Ma.'

'So get over it.'

Roy sat down at the kitchen table and his mother slammed a mug of tea in front of him. 'I do care about her,' he said.

'I think you really love her.'

'I do love 'er, the silly bitch.' There wasn't much point in disagreeing with his mother.

'You're swearing again and I don't like it. Not in my kitchen, and that brings us back to the beginning of our conversation. Why have you set Eve up in a flat?'

'Because it's what she wanted.'

Violet Kemp raised her eyes heavenwards.

'Little gold-digger.'

'You just don't like her, do you?'

'No.' Violet began cutting a thin wedge of lemon cake. 'Eat this, but it's all you're getting. Don't want to spoil dinner, do we?'

Roy took a bite and rolled his eyes. 'This is a lovely bit of cake, Ma. Listen,' he said as he brushed crumbs from his shirt, 'Eve's a kid, she got no problems to bring to this relationship.'

'Now we're getting somewhere.'

Violet picked up his empty plate and put it in the sink that was filled with hot soapy water.

'I need a woman on me arm for functions and special do's. Daisy won't come up to London more than is absolutely necessary.'

''Course not. She got little Gyp to consider. Can't go leaving her every five minutes—'

116

'Ma,' Roy broke in. 'There's just no pleasing you at times. I'm a grown man an' I can do whatever I want ...' He stared at her blue-rinsed curly permed hair that made her round rosy face look younger. Her eyes were like pieces of flint as she said, 'That's where you're wrong, son. Just don't bring that girl round here.'

'Have you finished them sandwiches yet?'

'Nearly, Dais,' answered Vera. She was at the kitchen table topping slices of brown bread with cheese and onion. Daisy watched as she cut the stacked sandwiches in two then arranged them on a plate. The smell of pickled onions and chutney tickled her senses. 'I've already made the tea an' it's just setting. The corned beef sarnies are ready for the tray.' Vera nodded towards a tea towel covering food. 'You want me to take the tray up or you goin' to do it?' The radio was on and Stevie Wonder was singing his heart out.

'I want to take up the sandwiches,' said Daisy. 'My Eddie's sat at a big table with his mates all around him. God knows what them plans are, usually he got them papers locked away in that room. I wish I knew what he was up to ...'

'An' that's precisely why he's got them locked away. So you can't 'ave a nose. He feels the drawings are safer here.'

'He can't leave them at Roy's place, can he? Violet would soon find out, you can't hide anything away from her hawk eyes. Though I wonder what job requires all them plans.'

'Ask Tyrone then.'

'No, I don't like to. An' if I did, I knows he won't say a dicky bird. Neither would I ask any of the other blokes he's got up there.' Daisy was counting the cups and saucers on the tray.

'Stop drivin' yourself daft with all this bleedin' wonderin',

Dais. You know as well as I do that whatever scam young Eddie's got tucked up his sleeve, no one will get hurt. It might well be against the bleedin' law, but then, I runs a massage parlour an' that ain't exactly on the level, is it? But I wouldn't hurt a hair of anyone's head and neither would your Eddie. An' it won't be anything that Roy dabbles in, no drugs or prostitution or murders. That reminds me ...' Vera frowned. 'The child what hanged himself. Did you mention it to Roy?'

Daisy stared at Vera. 'I don't think either of us is in the mood for cosy chats. I don't want to talk to Roy until he wants to talk to me, but I did have a long phone call with Violet and she'll have told him. The thing is, Vera, Roy's in London and the kids is down 'ere. I think me and you 'ave got to be more vigilant.' Daisy thought for a moment then asked, 'You seen that little boy again what picked up the fruit from Arnie's stall?'

'No, but if he's sleeping rough around 'ere I'll not be long in finding out.'

Daisy put the sugar bowl on the tray.

'I wonder why Eddie don't want Jamie to know what he's doing?'

'Do you really 'ave to ask that, Daisy? Jamie's a bloody unexploded bomb.'

Jamie watched her walking ahead of him down Gosport High Street. Red wool coat nipped in at the waist, black high heels and a shoulder bag swinging against her hip. Summer's hair was loose, a golden sheet of gloss pouring down her back and moving gently in the breeze.

She paused to look in the window of Bishop's shoe shop. He stepped back into the doorway of Boots but she was busy studying the shoes, not looking along the High Street.

It was nice feeling the warmth of the sun on his face. The change in the weather probably gave Summer her jaunty steps. Though she wouldn't be so happy if she knew how often he parked on the spare bit of ground further up from The Book Shop, hoping for a glimpse of her at the windows of the flat or the long waits he endured yearning for her to emerge into the street.

Jamie knew there was no point in him casually calling on his uncle and Summer, he wasn't wanted there. Uncle Bri despised him and Summer only had eyes for Eddie.

But Jamie didn't care. He'd have her one day, whether she wanted him or not ...

She was walking again, small neat steps and every so often she shook her hair back from off her face so that it tumbled enticingly across her shoulders. Oh, how he longed to bury his face in that sweet-smelling hair.

At the pet shop Summer went straight in. He was hidden but near enough to hear the chime of the shop's doorbell.

Peering among the assorted advertisements stuck on the window he saw her talking to the assistant. After a while she was taken through into the back room. What on earth was she up to?

Jamie crossed the busy high street and stood behind the flower stall. He still had a good view of the pet shop.

After a while Summer opened the door, waved to the assistant and stepped out into the market crowd. She walked quickly back the way she had come.

From stall to stall he watched her.

At North Street she turned down to The Book Shop.

He saw her re-enter the shop and speak to her father, who grinned at her then kissed her tenderly on her forehead. She then disappeared up the stairs to the flat.

He stood for a long while in the doorway of the photographers, just in case she came out again. Eventually he walked to his car, got inside and sat there waiting. His brother was marrying Summer at Easter.

He had never wanted anything or anyone as much as he wanted her.

One day Summer would discover that.

He turned the key in the engine. He'd go back to Western Way and see what his dear brother Eddie was up to.

CHAPTER 14

Staring at the men sitting around the table, Eddie hoped he really could trust them. These were all criminals skilled in their lines of work. These were men who wouldn't talk if the police became involved, men who wouldn't run risks to get caught. Men who could be richer than they'd ever dreamed possible by this coming Easter.

Eddie took off the jacket to his dark blue suit and sat down at the head of the large table, making himself comfortable before unrolling his large drawing. All that he'd learned while he'd been inside was now coming to fruition.

'I've done a lot of research on other robberies and the mistakes that led to the capture of men. After the Great Train Robbery, the coppers found fingerprints and palm prints. That's not going to happen to us.' He looked across the table before he continued. 'For months now, this has been in the planning stages.' He tapped the plan in front of him. 'I started this while I was inside and completed it on my release. I repeat, we ain't going to leave nothing behind to incriminate us, not a fag end nor an apple core.' He stared at the expectant faces. 'And there will be no violence.'

Mumbling and fidgeting filled the room. 'Again, I repeat: no sawn-offs, no guns, no knives.'

'We got to have *something* to frighten the numptys. Who's

going to obey us an' do what we wants if we go in unarmed?' This was Jet speaking, so called because of his jet-black hair that Eddie knew was enhanced via a bottle nowadays. Jet was running a legitimate scaffolding business in Islington, with his young wife doing all the office work. But he hankered after the old days when he spent his youth ducking and diving. One more job, he'd confided to Eddie, the *big* one, would enable him to take his Sally to Spain, where they could invest in some property. He was the best driver Eddie had ever known.

'We can always ask nicely and say please!' Big Col laughed at his own joke.

A red-haired, roly-poly bloke but surprisingly light on his feet, Col kept the men in fits of laughter with a never-ending flood of stories concerning his latest female conquests. That he was and had been married to the same woman for thirty years meant she either suspected nothing or was a bleedin' saint.

Eddie opened a drawer at his end of the table. 'These are what we'll use.' He took out an odd-shaped gun.

'What the fuck's that?' Col demanded.

'This gives off an electric shock from a distance, Col. The shock disrupts control of the muscles.' Voices became raised. 'Anyone who disagrees with having one of these instead of the more formal weapons had better get out now.' At his ultimatum, the murmurings stopped.

'You gonna tell us what that bleedin' thing is?' asked Tyrone. He had been Eddie's mate for as long as he could remember; Eddie would trust Tyrone with his life.

'It's a taser. Gives off a volt of electricity. Enough to quieten down someone but not enough to kill 'em, unless that someone's got a dicky heart an' I'm sure where we're going everyone's got to be pretty fit to work there.' He slid the gun along the table. 'Anyone not come across these little beauties before?'

It was then his ears picked up a sound outside in the hallway. He flew across the room and threw the door open. He caught sight of Jamie's jacket sleeve as his brother's bedroom door closed.

Eddie sighed. The fucking little turd had been eavesdropping. He took a deep breath before going back inside the room. Wouldn't do to let the men see he'd been shaken up. It might destroy their confidence in him. But what would Jamie do with any conversations he'd overheard? Grass him to the coppers? All eyes were upon him as he gave a fair imitation of a smile and said, 'Can't be too careful. One day I'll swing for that black cat from next door.'

It was good to see the relief on their faces.

'Now, where was I? Oh, yes, anyone not seen these little beauties before?'

Tyrone shook his head and picked the taser up as though it was going to explode in his hand.

'Don't worry, Ty, it's powerless at present,' Eddie said.

Tyrone looked relieved. 'How does it work?'

'Cartridges are fitted.'

'Is this what they call a stun gun?'

'Sure is, Clive,' said Eddie with a smile. Clive, when he was in Parkhurst doing time for armed robbery, had found out his wife was shagging everything in trousers. Upon his release he divorced her, and was now running a car breakers yard in Putney and living with a little blonde who had a kiddie by him. He fancied a nice house in a Hampshire village within walking distance of the local pub and a pony for his little girl. Eddie said, 'I don't intend anyone, them or us, should get hurt. Any questions?'

The gun was being examined and passed along. There were no questions.

'Okay,' Eddie said, smoothing down the corners of the large drawing. 'This raid's going to be a highly professional job, an astonishing gamble which, if all of you play your allotted parts, will make each of you richer than you ever dreamed possible. So,' Eddie said, 'let's get this show on the road.'

Jamie sprawled over the wooden garden seat beneath the oak tree. He didn't bother to look up when Eddie thumped himself down beside him.

'How much did you hear?'

Jamie shrugged. 'Enough.'

'What are you going to do about it?'

'Nothing.'

The smirk on his brother's face told Eddie that Jamie was lying. Jamie held his hands out in front of him as though admiring his nails. He frowned as his eyes lit upon the missing top of his pinky finger.

A cheeky sparrow attacked some seed his mother had left on the bird table.

'Remember when you went shooting at the birds you'd enticed to that table? Squirrels, too, a right fuckin' bloodbath. I gave you a hiding, didn't I, Jamie?'

Jamie moved his legs so they were straight out in front of him, his heels sunk in the damp earth of the lawn.

'I remember.'

'If you so much as breathe a dicky bird to anyone, I'll kill you. Understand?'

Jamie turned his head.

'Oh, I won't breathe a word. Not to Roy nor to the coppers, and I'd only need to ring me dad for that, wouldn't I? No, I'll

124

keep quiet about your nice little earner. Should be a decent screw in Safety Services.'

This was too easy, thought Eddie. Jamie wouldn't let a secret like this go without getting in on it somehow.

'So you heard everything?'

'All I needed.' Jamie ran his fingers through his blond hair and gave Eddie a big smile. 'I'm very good at listening at doors, you know I am. By the way, I hope you'll be happy with Summer. I haven't bought you a wedding present but I *will* get an invite to the wedding, won't I?'

Eddie was angry. He leaned forward and grabbed Jamie's lapels.

'Don't ever mention her name, cocksucker!'

'Ooh, touchy!'

Jamie brushed his hands away and sat back. 'I said I wouldn't tell anyone about the robbery. Good idea, by the way, and well thought out. But there is a price for my silence.'

Eddie rose from the seat and stood over him. 'What do you want? And how do I know you'll keep your promise?'

'If I open my mouth, I won't get the half of your share I'm expecting.'

Eddie let the words sink in. He stared down at his younger brother and the hate boiled away inside him until it overflowed. He hauled Jamie to his feet and gave him a single blow to the side of his face, causing him to stagger backwards against the bench and slide down. Eddie's shoes slid on the damp grass and he fell on top of Jamie. Too late, he saw the lump of wood that Jamie had lifted from the ground coming towards him.

'Fucker!' Jamie shouted as the log caught Eddie on the shoulder. Eddie staggered as the pain ran through his arm. Jamie threw himself at him and they rolled towards the fish-pond.

'Met your match, me darlin' brother.' Jamie's voice was breathless. 'I ain't no kid for you to boss around.'

Eddie managed to twist his head away as Jamie's hand grabbed at his face. A few whacks on the stone surround and the bastard would have him. Jamie was right, he was strong and lithe and easily a match for Eddie. They rolled until Eddie hauled himself to his knees, taking Jamie with him, and hit out with a kidney punch that made his brother gasp. Eddie had one more punch left but it was enough for Jamie to twist and fall forward, toppling on to the broken wire of the pond.

Eddie, his breath coming in gasps, managed a strangled laugh.

Jamie, sitting in the water with his knees up to his chest, was surrounded by green lily fronds. Eddie was still trying to laugh when the back door flew open and his mother came out.

'Stop that fightin'!' Daisy screamed. Her body paused in mid-run as she stared at Jamie. 'You'll catch your bleedin' death in there.'

Daisy put out her hand to help Jamie up and as he rose from the muck his jacket caught on the wire netting and a long ripping sound filled the air.

'Did you do this?' She glared at Eddie and he nodded. 'Ought to be bleedin' ashamed of yourselves, fighting at your age.'

Eddie saw Jamie's teeth were chattering, but that didn't stop him grinning and saying, 'Half, remember. Half, bruv.'

Eve looked around the flat Roy had found for her. Gas fires, square rooms, and scope for improvement when she started using the credit card Roy had given her last night.

'Don't be afraid to use it, pet,' he'd said.

And she wouldn't be. By Christ, she wouldn't be. She

switched the radio on and The Police were singing 'Every Little Thing She Does Is Magic'. Eve smiled to herself. That song just about summed up her sex life with Roy Kemp when she had him begging her to take it easy before she gave him a bleedin' heart attack.

She smiled to herself as she ran her fingers along the back of the moquette sofa. Christ, but she was glad to get out of the council flat where she'd been living with her parents and four brothers. Fucking wasters, the lot of them. Her brothers only cared about drugs and fanny and her father was forever trying to feel her up. She'd have left long ago if she'd had somewhere to go and if there'd been someone to look after her mother before she passed away from TB.

It had been a chance meeting with Roy that had brought her to this happy state.

She'd been a hostess at The Blue Moon, one of Roy's clubs. One night he'd come in in a hell of a temper because the woman he was keen on, Daisy Lane, had said she wouldn't go with him to an opening of an old mate's new club at Bethnal Green with a theatre visit to follow.

He had been standing by the bar, slowly drinking himself silly and staring at the tickets when she rubbed up against him, apologising profusely of course, and after chatting for a while, he'd asked, 'Wanna come?' He'd run his fingers through his gypsy curls.

'I'm working,' she said.

'I'm the boss so I'll give you time off. Not only that but I won't dock your wages.'

And that was the start of it and she thanked her lucky stars. Not because she liked his fumblings but because he spent money on her. And now she had a place of her own and a credit card so she could buy anything she fancied.

And all she had to do was smile and open her legs, which wasn't a hardship when she thought of all it brought her.

He was a man who could command a killing at the flick of his fingers. Did he frighten her? Of course he bloody did. But was she afraid? No, because she knew that all the time she had the balance of power in the bedroom, he wouldn't harm her.

Eve sauntered into the bedroom. She'd visit Debenhams and order a new bed today. This one with the cast iron frame was positively ancient. She might even have a walk through their clothing department. Oh yes, she had plans for this flat. Two floors up in the heart of London's West End, even the bleedin' address was glamorous. Roy Kemp was a name, a face. He belonged to her now. Only the Krays had been more notorious than Roy, and they were banged up in prison.

That first night Roy had fucked her he'd said, 'Good to know you aren't going to get out of this bed and go home.' The big man was lonely, that was a certainty.

She would leave the flat soon, after making a note of all she'd buy, and have it delivered. She needed a gown, something svelte and sexy, Roy said. In black, he'd told her. And high heels, also black. Roy was taking her to some fancy do after Michael Heseltine had been appointed Defence Secretary. She wasn't sure who Michael Heseltine was but she loved parties.

'Don't drink,' Roy had warned her. She knew she got giggly after a couple of wets but wasn't that what drink was for, to make you feel good and ready for a laugh?

Eve wasn't sure about the mould he was trying to cast her in, but if it kept him coming with the handouts she didn't care. When she went to that party, she promised herself, she'd just have a couple of glasses of bubbly.

She looked at her new watch. It was early yet. She had plenty of time to shop for the dress and get her hair done. She even had time to go and see *Sophie's Choice* at the cinema. She quite liked Meryl Streep.

Now, she thought, if it was Eddie Lane setting her up in a flat her life would be complete. She thought of his long dark eyelashes framing those green eyes. And what about those broad shoulders? She wondered about the size of his cock and how she wouldn't mind waking up in bed next to him. She daydreamed for a moment then came back to earth.

She opened a wardrobe door and stared at herself in a mirror. Short blonde hair, blue eyes, and although she was reed slim, her breasts were decent handfuls.

Perhaps one day she might get it together with Eddie Lane. If she did, she'd be the first in a long line of bints he usually ignored.

He wasn't queer but he never bothered with the women. It was said he'd had his fill of tarts and was only interested in one woman. A Gosport girl.

Eve reckoned she must be some looker for him to turn down the offers that came his way. And Jamie Lane?

He was a kid. Actually, he wasn't. He was only a year younger than her, tall and cute-looking. A little like an angelic young Billy Idol. Not that he smiled much. He looked as though he had a lot on his mind. But he had a good body on him and spent a lot of time staring at her as though he was weighing her up.

Eve reckoned the closer she got to Roy, the closer she'd get to Eddie – and who knows?

Fancy her being in bed with both the brothers? Now that would be really something.

CHAPTER 15

'Why didn't he ask my mother to accompany him to this do?' Jamie asked. Already he was fed up with hanging about in the corner, watching Roy Kemp's back.

'Roy did, ages ago, but she turned him down. Said she couldn't take time off from working in the pub.' Charles shrugged his shoulders. His iron-grey hair and his broad shoulders hinted at the big bloke he'd been in his youth.

'I admire me mum's principles but sometimes she's stupid. I wouldn't work in a poxy pub when I'd been given the opportunity to come up to London for the opening of a new club.'

'Trouble with your mother is she don't like to let people down,' Charles said. Jamie saw he had his eye on a couple of young girls who'd come in dressed in mini skirts but they waltzed up to Bert Cameron and threw their arms around him.

'They work in Cameron's club,' said Jamie. He saw Charles relax. 'I really love me mum but why she'd work for a measly couple of quid when Roy could put her on easy street for the rest of her life is beyond me.'

The air was thick with cigarette smoke mixed with perfume. Out on the packed dance floor, Roy was cheek to cheek with Eve. Jamie noted her long slinky black dress and high heels. From the back, she could have been mistaken for his mother.

Jamie looked down at his own dark suit, new and expensive. He couldn't quite afford Savile Row yet but his involvement in the fight club back in Gosport was proving lucrative and, with the money Roy paid him, he was getting there. Of course, when Eddie paid him his share of the robbery proceeds for keeping his mouth shut, he'd be in clover.

Charles too was in a suit and he looked much younger than his actual age, thought Jamie. If crime bought a person clean-cut looks and good clobber, he was all for it.

Jamie handed Charles a glass of champagne and took one for himself from the tray that was practically shoved in his face. The pert redhead with an overdone mascara job grinned at him. He looked across at Roy who had Eve draped all over him like a bleedin' chair cover.

Charles returned his still full glass to the tray.

'Best not,' he said. 'Roy doesn't like us drinking on the job.'

Jamie shrugged and downed the liquid in one mouthful. He called back the girl and took another glass of champagne.

'Do you always do what he says, Charles? You can give him twenty years easy. And you're married to his mother, for fuck's sake.'

'It's called respect, Jamie. Something you don't seem to know much about.'

Jamie turned away. The miserable fucker might look the gangster part in his silk tie and shiny shoes, but he was nothing but a bleedin' flunky for Roy Kemp.

Jamie set his glass down and stared at his hand. His knuckle had healed nicely. But he'd not forget in a hurry what that bastard Roy Kemp had done to him. The fucker didn't mar his body without getting paid back somehow.

Jamie stared about him. Red velvet, chandeliers and polished bar tops gave the clip joints authenticity. A backhander to the coppers on the manor and the place was seldom raided. He looked across the crowded room to the table where Roy was now sitting with his blonde bint. She sat one side of him, her head on his shoulder, and dear brother Eddie sat on the other side of the big man.

Eve had been picking at her food, frightened of spoiling her figure no doubt. Boy, did she have a pair of knockers on her. Every time she bent forward, they almost slipped out of that low-cut dress.

She'd given him the once-over and he knew she'd be gagging for it if he made a move on her. The little tart was more of an age for him, not Roy bleedin' Kemp. Still, he had to give it to the old guy. The women flocked around him. Like flies on shit. Perhaps it was his name. Roy Kemp, like Reg or Ronnie Kray. Names touched with glamour.

And there was his brother, soaking it all up like a bit of fried bread and a runny egg. Silk shirt, a nice suit, a carbon copy of Mr Big himself.

Soft bloody Eddie. Always giving his mother handouts she refused, then found left in the kitchen in the breadbin or the bleedin' fridge.

Not that he minded his mother getting the money, because she needed it. But Eddie earned more than he did so Jamie's smaller gifts looked mean.

'Go and check the doormen, Jamie, make sure there's no problems,' Charles said.

Jamie nodded. Thank Christ he wasn't staying glued to the old fart.

He walked jauntily round the edge of the dance floor, watching the noisy crowd, the men especially, for signs of aggression.

That's what he was tonight, he thought, a bleedin' minder. Making sure to defuse any trouble before it really started.

He passed a mirrored wall and caught sight of his reflection. He looked good. He stared at his shortened pinky finger then ran his hand through his long blond hair. The lack of his fingertip had taken some getting used at first but now it had become a talking point for women he picked up. Not that he told them the truth, that he'd had it sliced off for stealing.

His version was he had been lying aboard a dhow sailing the coastline of Mombasa in Africa, trailing his fingers in the sea when something in the water had bitten him. Women fell for it every time.

Jamie knew now that if he ever intended crossing Roy again, he'd better make sure he'd never get caught.

Of course, his mother believed losing part of his finger had been a pure accident. He thought it better not to worry her.

He saw the red-haired waitress about to enter the Ladies.

'Wait up,' he said.

She stopped and smiled at him.

'I reckon you could do with a bit of company.'

'Sure of yourself, aren't you?' she said, opening the lavatory door.

'Not really,' Jamie said. 'In this world you 'ave to take what you want and be grateful.'

'An' what is it you want?' she asked. He'd followed her in, paused, then held open a cubicle door for her.

'Same thing you do,' he replied. She stepped ahead of him and he followed, pulling up her black skirt with one hand and opening his fly with the other 'Bend over,' he said. The flowery scent of her perfume mixed with her musk rose to greet him.

It was like slipping a warm knife through butter, he thought afterwards as he sidled up to Charles in the ballroom.

'Everything okay?' Charles asked.

'Sure is,' said Jamie.

CHAPTER 16

Daisy wiped the bar top, mopping up the spilled beer. Next, she pushed up the wooden flap and went out into the public bar so she could clean tables and empty ashtrays into a metal bin.

'You all right, Doris?'

The old woman was always the first in the bar and the last to leave.

Poor old bat, thought Daisy, she's eighty if she's a day and can just about make it across Forton Road from Albert Street on them swollen legs of hers. But Doris was never without her make-up skilfully applied and her hair in its usual wartime bleached pageboy style.

'Better today, Dais, thanks for asking.'

That's what Daisy liked about the White Swan: its customers. The salt of the earth people, always ready for a laugh no matter what their lives were like at home.

'I've heard whispers that this pub might close down if there ain't no one to run it properly.' Doris tipped her the wink.

'You saying my best ain't good enough, Doris?'

Daisy knew the old girl was only confirming the news she herself had heard on the grapevine.

'What I am sayin', Daisy, love, is that you'd be the perfect landlady.'

The White Swan was a round-fronted, white-painted building on the corner of Ferrol Road. On the roof a huge white stone swan presided over the entrance. It wasn't a big place but it was busy – mainly due to the past efforts of Annie and Jim Ward and the fact they paid good wages.

'So what happened to that whip-round for Nora Hartington? The mother of that kiddie what 'anged himself?' Doris asked suddenly.

'Sal started it and I finished it. We collected nearly seventy pounds in that bottle.' Daisy pointed to a large whisky bottle. 'We started with a cigar box and the donations soon filled that. I'm going round to the old fishermen's cottages later when we're closed up here. Me mate Vera's coming as well.'

'You got a heart of gold, Daisy, you 'ave,' said Doris.

Daisy rang the bell to signal the bar would be closing after ten minutes drinking-up time.

'I think I'll be off then, Dais. See you tomorrow.'

'You take care, Doris.'

Vera was now behind the bar, dunking glasses in the washing up machine as though her life depended on it.

'C'mon, you lot, ain't you got no 'omes to go to?'

The stragglers drifted out and Daisy began collecting stray glasses.

'Was Gyp asleep when you left?'

Vera said, 'Stop worrying. That girl from across the road is sitting in your living room watching your telly an' eatin' a plate of shop-bought cakes. She'll phone if anything's wrong.'

Daisy nodded. 'Can you finish the sweeping and cleaning while I cash up?'

'Yeah. You know, Dais, this reminds me of when we 'ad the caff down the town and we used to clean up together and mop those bleedin' stairs. Do you remember?'

Daisy looked up from the open till. 'You an' me got a lot to remember, Vera, good times and bad.'

She forced herself back to the job of counting out money and putting it in little bags for the bank.

With the place safely locked up for the night and clutching a wad of notes in a paper bag, Daisy put her arm through Vera's as they walked along Ferrol Road towards the small wooden houses known locally as fishermen's cottages.

'You don't think she'll be upset about us bringing the money around at this time of night?'

'Na, Dais. I reckon she'll be sitting in the kitchen crying and will be glad we've called. Grief's a terrible thing.'

The wooden houses faced Ferrol Road with their front doors opening on to the pavement.

'Here it is,' whispered Vera. She knocked softly on the door. The noise echoed in the still of the night. 'See,' said Vera. 'There's a light on and someone's coming.'

At first the door opened just a crack. Daisy said, 'Mrs Hartington? I'm Daisy Lane. We're from the White Swan. I hope you don't think it's an imposition but the regulars 'ave clubbed together ...'

The door opened wider to show a thin woman with tears running unheeded down her cheeks.

'Everyone's being so kind.' She sniffed. 'Do come in.'

Daisy stuffed the roll of notes into the woman's hand, wishing she'd written on a card to go with it.

'I ... I can't possibly ...'

''Course you can,' said Vera.

Nora Hartington led them through as though in a dream. The cottage was immaculately clean but poorly furnished, like the woman didn't have much but what she had she treasured.

'I'm sorry it's so late ...' Vera said.

'I don't sleep,' said the woman. 'Would you like a cup of tea?'

Daisy didn't really want tea but she sensed Nora needed to be busy.

'That'd be nice,' she said. Vera nodded.

Nora looked at the money in her hand. 'I can't take all this,' she said.

'Yes, you can,' said Vera. 'Daisy's customers knew your lad. It's the least we could do.'

The woman pulled out a chair from beneath the table and collapsed onto it. Vera took her cue and filled the kettle and switched it on.

'He was all I 'ad, see? My old man walked out when Derek was born.'

'I guess money has been tight,' said Vera.

'Three cleaning jobs, I've got. And scrubbin' other people's dirty floors don't bring in the money.'

Daisy got up from her chair and put her arms around the distraught woman. This made her sob. Alarmed, Daisy looked towards Vera who mouthed the words, *let her cry*.

The kettle was whistling. Vera found the cups and tea bags and made three cups of tea, then asked, 'Was it the loss of the bike made him do it?'

The woman disentangled herself from Daisy and said, 'I think it was. He hadn't been well for ages. I thought he was being bullied at school. He was covered in welts and bruises, but when I asked him about the state of his body he didn't want to talk.' She sipped at her tea.

Daisy looked at Vera. The knowing look she received in return was enough to tell Daisy that this child and young Paulie were somehow connected.

'I couldn't get him to open up about it,' she went on. 'After he came home with the bike, he wouldn't tell me how he managed to pay for it or where it had come from. Well, for a couple of weeks Derek hardly left this house except to go out on that bike. He was almost back to his own sunny self, then the bike got stolen.' She pointed through the kitchen window down towards the shed. 'My lad breathed his last in that place an' I got to live here. I wish I could pull the bloody shed apart with me own hands.'

Nora finished drinking her tea. 'I got no money to move,' she said, her voice bitter. 'You must think I'm awful going on like this.'

Vera shook her head. 'It's natural. I'd like to ask you a question, if you don't mind.' Mrs Hartington nodded.

'Did your boy ever mention a lad named Paulie? He'd be the same age as 'e was.'

'No. I never heard of that name. Why are you asking?' She looked confused.

'I can't explain now,' Daisy replied, 'but Vera and I are going to try to get to the bottom of why your son died. That's if you don't mind?'

'Mind? Why should I mind? The police down in South Street are not that bothered. A detective called round. Nice bloke with odd-coloured eyes. But as yet nothing's come of that, an' I need to know what's behind this.' She blew her nose into a surprisingly white handkerchief.

'Right, no promises, but we'll visit you again if we may?' Daisy looked to Vera for confirmation. Vera nodded.

'I'd be glad of it,' she said. 'And I'd like you to thank your customers for me, Daisy, for this money.'

Daisy and Vera kissed her goodnight and walked out into the chill air of Ferrol Road.

When they got to the spare bit of ground where Daisy's

car was parked, Vera said, 'I reckon you should have another word with DCI Vinnie Endersby.'

'So do I.'

'No good me asking you to talk to Roy Kemp, is it? You and your bleedin' pride.'

'I don't have any bleedin' pride when kiddies are getting hurt, even if Roy is chasing that bit of tail. I'll phone him as soon as we get in.'

'Well, Daisy, now we got two young boys what's been badly knocked about and possibly connected to them is the dead boy. Paulie mustn't be allowed to end up the same way as Derek.'

CHAPTER 17

The stars looked like diamonds sitting in black velvet, thought Eddie. He squeezed Summer's hand.

'You're not cold, are you?' He looked at her sitting on the bench beside him in the Ferry Gardens. The last ferry boat had just come in and people were trailing up the pontoon.

'How can I be cold, cuddled into you?' she said. His eyes met hers and he smiled. 'This just seems a funny place for you to suggest we sit after that gorgeous meal we just ate in Roy's club.' Summer kissed him lightly on the lips and ran her fingers over his scar. Her touch was electric.

He withdrew the box and pressed it into her hand, using his thumbnail to snap back the lid.

In the dullness of the ferry's lamplight, the diamonds winked and glinted as though they had a life of their own.

Summer gasped. She took the ring from its nest and handed it to Eddie. 'It's beautiful,' she whispered as he slipped it on her engagement finger.

Eddie decided he'd made a good choice. 'Does it fit okay?'

'It does, and it's the most beautiful thing I've ever owned.' She lifted her face for a kiss.

'I've had that ring since before I asked you to be my wife. The day I put flowers in my car for you was when I intended to offer it. But though you said you'd marry me I still thought you'd need time to think about it.'

'Silly,' she said. 'All these years I've waited for you and now you finally belong to me.'

She kissed him again.

'I just love it when you kiss me, Summer,' he said. He crushed her to his chest.

'Ouch!' Summer pulled away. 'What have you got in your pocket?'

'Are you all right?'

Summer put her hand inside his jacket pocket and pulled out his wallet, a couple of receipts, a comb – and a flick knife.

'Aha!' she said, turning the knife around in her fingers. 'Your father's favourite weapon. I forgot you hardly ever go out without this.'

'I'd use it too, if I needed to protect you.' He took it from her along with the wallet and papers and slipped them into his trouser pocket. 'Sorry.' He pulled her towards him again.

He'd never looked at another woman since he'd been home, and now he knew he wouldn't ever again. Summer was all he'd ever wanted. He'd waited his whole life for her to love him.

All the plans he had started making when he was inside to ensure Summer would want for nothing in the future could now be brought to fruition. Within weeks he'd have as much money as he'd always dreamed of. He dismissed Jamie's threats, but all the same he'd have to watch his brother carefully. As long as Jamie thought he was in for a cut of the proceeds, he'd keep his mouth shut. Eddie intended never to scrimp and save like his mother had done. No, he wanted to look after his family, be the man they all came to when help and advice was needed.

Summer was looking intently at the ring.

'The ring is legit,' he said. Hoping she wasn't wondering if it was part of one of Roy's deals. 'There is something else I have to say, though.' He took a deep breath. 'I am what I am, Summer. The son of a Gosport gangster. I work for a London face. But with a bit of luck, soon I'll be leaving all that behind.'

She nodded. 'I know you'll never hurt me and whatever happens in the future, we'll be sharing a life together.'

'I love you, Summer. What more can I say?'

'Fair enough, then,' she said. 'I'm glad we're getting married as soon as possible.'

'Yes!' The word burst from his lips like it had been trapped in his mouth.

She started to laugh. 'Did you really think I might want a long engagement? You've just given me a ring. Easter. We shouldn't wait a moment longer than Easter. Your mother treats me like a daughter, always has. And my dad's so happy to be transferring me over to your safekeeping, he'll be dancing on the tables.'

Eddie started to laugh. His arms were tight around Summer's body. It was a dizzying awareness, this knowledge that she loved him. She sat up and smiled at him. He'd never made a move to touch her beyond kissing. He didn't want to upset the natural balance of things even though his passion and desire for her seeped from his skin. Now, here in the lamplight, he was lost in her smell as his hands slid slowly around her waist. He was overcome with the desire to kiss every single part of her.

But he had to tell her.

'Vera's ill. It's cancer.' As in most families, secrets didn't really stay secret for long, he thought. 'Suppose the operation shows the cancer has spread? Suppose she doesn't have that long to live? I want Vera to be as happy as she can be *now*.

And she will be happy for us. I want to see her laugh and dance at our wedding.'

Summer was silent for a while, digesting the information. 'I already knew she was ill – my dad told me. I'm sorry, Eddie. I know how much she means to you. The sooner we get married then, the sooner she can dance.'

Eddie pulled Summer to her feet and swung her around. Her brilliant golden hair flew around her face.

'Families and secrets, eh?' He didn't wait for an answer. 'Shall we go abroad for our honeymoon?'

'Have you been thinking about this for a long time?'

'I have,' Eddie said. He was urging their two bodies together. Then he smiled and closed his eyes. 'Africa,' he said. 'I want to show you wild animals. I want to show you space, space to dream by a warm sea as blue as the sky.

She smiled and melted into him.

'I'll go anywhere with you,' she said.

For a moment he allowed the night to envelop them. 'I told you I want out of Roy Kemp's clutches. But the day before we marry, I have business to attend to. Call it my stag party.'

'I'm not even going to ask what it is.'

Eddie looked at her mouth with its softly pouting lower lip and leaned forward to kiss her.

He paused, seeing a movement in the bushes alongside the boat builders' wall. Dread filled his heart.

His eyes searched the darkness but he saw nothing.

'What's the matter?' Now he could sense Summer's unease.

Her eyes met his. He could feel her shivering. He took off his jacket and put it around her. 'Nothing can hurt you,' he said. 'You belong to me now.'

But he was sure someone had been watching them.

CHAPTER 18

Earl was aware that whatever trials he'd had to overcome in the past weeks, it was going to get tougher tonight. He sat, Paulie at his side, on the stairs of Chestnut House waiting for Heinz to call him down.

He had been nervous about asking Heinz if he could fight so was surprised when the blond-haired man with the pale blue eyes had thrown back his head and laughed.

'Ain't often I gets kids asking,' he had said. 'Mostly I 'ave to force 'em. Where do you live, squirt?'

Paulie had nudged him. 'Go on, tell 'im.' Earl noted Paulie hadn't got rid of his head twitch.

'I don't live anywhere. I been sleeping upstairs.'

'Have you?' Heinz was very pale. Earl didn't think he'd ever seen such a white-skinned man in all his life. The blue veins of blood pulsed at his temple. A sickly perfume came from him. 'I might 'ave to charge you rent. Where's your mother? Father?'

'Me mother's dead and I don't have no dad, neither.'

The man sucked on his teeth and then said, 'As it 'appens, because young Derek's no longer with us but has already been billed to fight Sammie Doe, you can take 'is place.'

Paulie whistled and Earl saw fear pass over his face.

Heinz must have noticed as well for he glared at Paulie,

whose hands seemed to have a shaking life of their own, then he said, 'Got to start somewhere, kid. And so what if it's with one of the sneakiest fighters? The crowd'll love it. You know what to expect?'

Earl thought of the money. The fact that he was starving made him all the more determined to fight.

'I know,' said Earl. Heinz grinned at him. Earl had never seen teeth that white; they reminded him of the wolf in Little Red Riding Hood.

'Good boy,' said Heinz. 'But I'll remind you of the rules in case our Paulie here's forgotten to tell you. The cage door's locked with the pair of you inside. There's no rounds so it's a fight to the finish. I have the say-so for when the cage can be unlocked. You understand?'

Earl nodded. His head was reeling. But the man was speaking again.

'Ever fought before?' Earl shook his head. He didn't want to tell this man that he'd had many brawls with kids, some older and bigger than himself when they'd called his mum a 'fucking smack 'ead whore'.

'Okay,' said Heinz. 'We'll see what you're made of. I'll announce to the crowd you're fighting in young Derek's place. Might even up the takings ...' Earl could see his mind was more on the money than explaining about the fight rules, so he coughed politely and Heinz, brought back to earth, looked straight into his eyes and said, 'It's no holds barred. And you fight unclothed so we can be sure to see every punch, every kick. Understand?' Earl nodded. 'There's another thing. You're a new boy an' I'm takin' you on face value, so don't let me down.' He put his hand on Earl's shoulder. Earl saw his fingers were short and glistening with dampness. 'This fighting business is illegal,' he whispered, 'so the crowd will be looking for blood. I repeat, no holds barred is exactly that, get it?'

Earl looked at Paulie, who nodded at him.

'Yes,' said Earl.

'I provide all the boys and this ain't a regular event. Tonight I'm thinking the dozy punters will bet heavily on you to win, being fresh sweet meat, see? Word soon gets about. And another thing.' The man tightened his grip on Earl's shoulder. 'Whatever happens in this house don't go outside these four walls, okay?'

Earl nodded then. If he won tonight, he could buy fish and chips.

'We'll be starting soon.' Heinz stared at him. 'You and Sammie Doe are first up.'

Heinz started to walk away, then turned back to Earl and grabbed hold of him 'You ain't a plant set here to find out what's going on in this house, are you?'

Earl shook himself free. 'No, I'm not.'

'If I get raided by the coppers, it'll be *you* I'll come looking for.' He stared into Earl's eyes until the boy began to shake.

Then he grinned, winked at Earl and brushed past him.

Earl's heart was still pounding. Whatever had he got himself into? Looking around the room, he saw it was fast filling up. Money was changing hands at the door, the huge wad of notes growing ever bigger in the hand of the big beefy bloke.

The chill in the air was fading with the stench of warm, unwashed flesh.

'You sure you want to do this?' Paulie asked.

Earl nodded. He saw there were women, some carrying babies in their arms, and they had parked themselves on the few chairs in the front row opposite the cage.

'Are any of these women mothers of the boys about to fight?'

'Sure,' said Paulie. 'It's a good night out for them. See that red-haired woman in the front?'

Earl's eyes skimmed the people to a woman heavily made up. She had her hand on the knee of the swarthy-looking bloke next to her. 'That's Sammie's mum.'

'Don't she mind her boy is going to get hurt?'

'She makes money on Sammie. It pays for beer. She's an alky and Sammie does his best to keep her in drink so that she'll love him. The more he fights, the more money he takes home and the more she coos over him.' Paulie stared hard at Earl. 'You're going to get a battering tonight. Heinz knows it.'

Earl felt the lump rise in his throat.

Paulie's nose was running and he wiped the red-tinged snot away on his sleeve.

'Is that Sammie's dad?'

Paulie looked over to the front row.

'Na.' He shook his head. 'That's some john she's picked up in The Queens.'

Earl felt the more he knew, the sicker he felt. In a way, it was like living in the Portsmouth flat with all the sick shit going on. But at least making friends with Paulie gave him confidence – if he didn't take any notice of Paulie telling him he'd get battered by Sammie.

'So what is this house? Don't it belong to anyone?'

''Course it does. It's owned by a London gangster named Roy Kemp. He's been going to do it up for ages but 'e ain't got around to it yet. It used to be a brothel.'

'Oh,' said Earl. He knew what a brothel was. He felt sick, but wasn't sure whether it was from apprehension or hunger. He stood up.

The red-haired kid sauntered up from the kitchen area and immediately a cheer rose. Earl was surprised to see he was wearing a sort of black cape that covered his body. He walked around the small area in front of the cage, grinning and showing a space where one of his front teeth used to be. He stood tall, well built, and Earl knew he mustn't show his fear, even though he was nearly crapping himself.

'Watch for Sammie to go inside the cage then you follow him,' said Heinz.

Another cheer went up. Heinz walked to the cage and stood in front of the open door. Earl started to shake.

'Ladies and gentlemen, I give you ...'

'Get on with it, ya big poof,' came a cry from the audience. Heinz didn't turn a hair but shouted clearly, 'Sammie Doe.' The crowd went mad and Earl could hear the stamp of feet on the rotten carpet.

A smartly dressed bloke in a suit and overcoat now stood at the rear of the room near the door. He'd caught Earl's attention because most of the blokes and women were dressed in scruffy parka jackets. His eyes went back to his opponent.

Sammie walked confidently to the cage, took off his cape and threw it towards his mother, who caught it and then blew her son a kiss.

'Go down now, dozy.'

Earl jumped at Paulie's voice and threw his last stinking sock on the stairs.

He shuffled down the rest of the stairs, his hands in front of his penis. He'd never taken all his clothes off in public before and felt shy.

'A newcomer tonight, folks.' He heard clapping and a solitary whistle. 'This is Earl.' Another couple of claps followed.

Earl walked over to the cage. He was very conscious of his naked state. He stepped inside the cage and felt a sharp jab on his nose.

Even before the cage door had been locked, Sammie Doe had drawn first blood.

Earl was confident his nose wasn't broken. He wiped the blood away on his arm, and jumped back as the red-haired lad let go a right-hand punch that missed but then his left fist hit Earl on his cheek just below his eye and Earl's head scrambled. The crowd were roaring now.

'C'mon, Sammie!'

Earl could tell Sammie was no mug. He was used to winning. Earl shook his head, and blood flew from his nose and he threw a body punch at the lad then a left into his jaw. Sammie seemed surprised as the thrust took him backwards.

'You little fucker,' he snarled and went at Earl with five or six fast blows to his stomach then he raised a hand with his fingers set in claws and raked the side of Earl's face. Earl felt the pain and it made his eyes water. Sammie turned to the audience for applause. Earl took the chance to thump Sammie in the guts. Earl saw the wind go out of Sammie but he could also see the boy's beady brown eyes staring back at him with hate. Earl grabbed him by the shoulders and headbutted him. Then, while the boy was shaking his head, trying to work out what happened, Earl headbutted him again.

The crowd was going mad. Earl heard the throaty voice of Sammie's mother cheering her boy on, and he felt sad for Sammie that his mother would want her child to get battered. But not so sad that he couldn't grab Sammie by the arms and then chuck him back so he slammed against the cage bars. Sammie slid down.

Earl unloaded kick after kick. Sammie couldn't get up. A sliver of blood appeared at the corner of his mouth and sweat was running down his face, mixing with big fat tears. He tried to double up to avoid Earl but Earl kept kicking while Sammie lay on the floor, covering his head with his arms.

And the noise the crowd made was terrifying.

Earl was still kicking when he felt an arm on his shoulder. He turned to punch out but Heinz caught his fist and said, 'It's over, lad. You've won.' Heinz signalled to the beefy bloke and he entered the cage to remove Sammie.

'I got a feelin' you could make me a lot of money.' Heinz was grinning broadly, teeth big and shiny.

Earl's head felt as though it wasn't connected to him as he stood side by side with Heinz. Earl wanted to throw up. Heinz pushed his arm up in the air. 'I give you the *winner*!'

Earl looked across at the bleeding broken lump of a boy being lifted and carried out and said, 'Is he goin' to be all right?'

Heinz shrugged.

He pulled away from Heinz, mumbling about throwing up, and pushing himself through the mass of people, he raced up the stairs. When he'd finished vomiting down the bathroom's blocked up and stinking lavatory, he climbed further up the stairs to what he considered his room and fell, still naked, sweating and covered in Sammie's blood, onto his makeshift bed.

He'd never felt more alone. He started to cry. He hadn't liked hitting Sammie. He went on crying until he fell asleep.

When Earl woke in the morning he was still alone.

His body was stiff and covered in bruises. He examined his face in the sliver of mirror he'd found and saw it was puffy. One eye was almost shut, and the place on his cheek where Sammie had raked his nails was raised and red. He knew he had to wash himself and, even more importantly, eat.

He looked at his smelly trainers on the floor beside him. Stuffed inside one was a five-pound note.

CHAPTER 19

'You don't like her, do you, Charles?'

'None of your business.'

Jamie moved from one foot to the other. Standing in draughty doorways to avert trouble from local gangs seemed to be what he did most these days and he was pissed off with it.

Charles never seemed to mind that he didn't get invited to sit at the top table where Roy and Eddie entertained business associates and drank champagne. All he and Charles got was the offer of a meal *after* the event.

The event tonight was Roy's opening of a Revue Bar in Soho. Roy was doing a bit of entertaining in The Glass Slipper, his new club.

'I'll take that as a no, you don't like her,' said Jamie.

He glanced at the dancers with their near-nude outfits and outrageous feathered hats, and heels that were twice the height of Vera's.

Jamie had on a new suit with a waistcoat to match. He quite fancied himself in it. It was charcoal grey and he had a yellow slim tie over his light grey shirt.

But time and again his eyes were drawn to Eve. What a slut, he thought. Already she was waving her fork around and loudly gesturing for her glass to be refilled. His brother was sitting, as usual, next to Roy but his face was expressionless. Like the woman didn't fucking exist. If Jamie had his way, she wouldn't exist for much longer.

'Did you see see 'er givin' Eddie the old go ahead?' Jamie asked.

'Bloody good job Eddie ignores her,' Charles said.

'Yeah, well, he's a bloody saint, is our Eddie.'

But then, why should Eddie respond to that slut when he had Summer, the girl Jamie thought was closest to an angel? Jamie looked at Charles and saw he was watching Eve.

'Comes from the gutter and she'll stay in the gutter,' said Jamie. Charles didn't answer. Jamie brushed a stray bit of cotton off his immaculate suit.

The big man, Roy, was throwing money at the cunt like there was no tomorrow. To the best of his knowledge, Roy still hadn't gone down to Gosport to see Daisy. Sensible woman that Daisy was she'd said Roy was doing what he felt a man had to do. But he knew his mother had had her heart broken by the slob.

Perhaps, just like most blokes, Roy felt he didn't need to justify his actions to anyone.

Jamie hated that he felt such anger towards Roy.

He'd always thought of Roy as being the one constant man in his mother's life. Hadn't he been there for both him and Eddie when they were growing up? And wasn't he still a sort of father figure?

Jamie's own father, the great detective Vinnie Endersby, was a twat Jamie wouldn't piss on if he was on fire. He'd treated his mother like shit, discarding her to go back to his wife. When he was younger, he'd listened at his mother's bedroom door and heard her crying at nights and knew nothing he could say or do would take away her pain. When he was a kid he'd thought how fucking grown-ups make rules for kids to live by. But grown-ups seldom lived by those rules.

Roy knew nothing about Vera's illness, and Jamie had decided it wasn't up to him to open his mouth about it. He'd also heard a few rumours that his mother was trying to find out why that crazy kid from Ferrol Road had topped himself. And all because that kid Paulie was Vera's mate's boy. Perhaps it was time he shut down the operation, nice little earner though it was, before his mother found out about his involvement.

Jamie had given his mother no end of grief but she always loved him and she showed it. He'd let her think it was her decision for him to leave Western Way for his own flat in London. But it was what he'd wanted all the time, independence, more money, and the chance for him to show how much he loved her and little Gyp.

Roy owed his daughter a visit as well, the bastard. Gyp needed her father just as he'd needed his father, Vinnie, all those years ago.

He watched the dancers, mostly old men, sweating and puffing their guts out to keep up with their slag partners, always much younger than themselves. But interspersed among them there were young blokes, poofs or wannabes hoping to catch the eye of the men who wielded the power behind London's underworld.

He saw the bloke, ill-fitting suit on his lanky frame, weave his way around the outside of the small dance floor. Eddie touched Roy's arm but the big man seemed content to sit and watch the man's progress.

Jamie started forward, pushing through the cheap-scented, cigar-smoking crush. When the bloke reached the table where Roy sat, he held on to it for support.

'Fuckin' whore, you left me for this?'

As he shouted, he made a lunge at Eve who scrambled to her feet in alarm. Despite being shot away with drink, she was amazingly light on her feet, thought Jamie. Dancers near the table had stopped to watch the entertainment.

Eddie had stood up.

'Slag,' the man's voice carried above the music.

Roy, slippery as an eel, had slid from the table and now stood close to the man, shielding Eve from him. Eddie's hand went to his breast pocket and out came his father's flick knife. With a magician's touch the knife was now in Roy's hand and he lunged low and upwards. Before the man had time to sag at the knees, Roy supported him and repeated the attack.

'Fucker! Cause me grief while I'm having an evening out?' His face was impassive as he pulled the knife free and casually wiped it clean of blood on the man's suit lapels.

The man's eyeballs had rolled back into his head as Jamie threw himself forward to catch him before he crashed to the floor.

'Show's over,' Roy said. 'Keep dancing!' The crowd dispersed. Jamie marvelled that all the action had taken place in almost the blink of an eye.

'Get the fucker out, he's bleeding on the parquet.' Roy passed the knife back to Eddie. Jamie noted that the big man hadn't even creased his suit.

'Get Mac and Billy to sort him.' Eddie's green eyes flashed. 'The Thames, tell 'em. Want a hand with 'im?' The man was making gurgling noises way back in his throat.

Jamie shook his head. He didn't like it that his brother was dishing out the orders.

The bloke was skinny enough for Jamie to walk him, making it look as though it was merely a bout of drunkenness. But before he moved, he looked to Roy for reassurance. Roy said, 'When you've got him on his way, come back.'

Jamie headed to the exit, careful not to get blood on his suit, with Charles giving him a hand.

Mac said in his dour Glaswegian accent, 'Pretty nimble for an old bloke, ain't he?'

'I don't see any reason to talk about it,' Charles interrupted. 'If you value your own breath, you'll do what the boss wants.'

Mac took the dying man from Jamie. 'Get the car, Bill. Matey 'ere's goin' for a swim.'

Jamie watched the night mist swallow the men. Charles shut the door and bolted it. He touched Jamie lightly on the arm.

'Roy ain't got where he is today by letting blokes make a fool of him. He's as soft as a marshmallow to those he loves, but he rules by fear. Never forget he's taken over London's business from the Krays because he's the only one who could.'

Back on the dance floor, it was business as usual.

Eve was pouring herself another drink. Despite the heavy make-up, Jamie saw her skin was slum-white. Jamie marvelled yet again that Roy had ditched his mother for this cunt. He had never before worried about Roy's bits on the side. They came and went. But Roy seemed besotted by this slut. It wasn't as though the bitch cared anything for him. All she cared about was money and the booze she could neck.

Jamie laughed softly to himself.

'What's the matter with you?' Charles and Jamie stood at their post by the door.

'Nothing, old timer,' he answered. Diana Ross was asking, 'Why Do Fools Fall In Love?' Yeah, why indeed, he asked himself, watching Roy's table and its occupants.

Eve downed a drink in one go. As she returned her glass

to the table her hand knocked against a single red rose in a silver vase. The water spread across the tablecloth and fell into her lap. She rose from the table, pointing to the stain on her dress and laughing loudly that it looked like she'd pissed herself. The dress was ruined. Jamie watched as Roy set the vase straight and slipped the flower back. Roy raised his eyes to Charles.

Without a word to Jamie, Charles moved like a stealthy old alley cat towards the top table where he whispered something in the girl's ear.

A few seconds later, she was allowing Charles to help her out of her seat and walked unsteadily away from the table, blowing theatrical kisses as she went. Roy's face was impassive. Upon reaching Jamie, Charles whispered in his ear, 'We'll get her home before she makes a complete twat of herself and Roy. He ain't very happy about this. Nor about the appearance of this slag's old boyfriend.'

Jamie walked over to the cloakroom where the girl took one look at Eve and, with a sneer, handed Jamie a fur that was more like a bear than a coat.

Charles wrapped it around Eve, who was practically asleep on her feet.

'Tip the girl,' said Charles. Jamie pressed a note into the cloakroom girl's hand. Then Charles fumbled around in his pocket and came out with a set of car keys.

Jamie walked out into the fresh air of the car park, found the new Mercedes and drove to the front of the club beneath the garish neon sign of a glass slipper.

Eve's voice came from the depths of the fur. 'I don't want to leave the party, I want 'nother drink,' and then vomited on the kerb. Charles stepped back just in time.

Jamie felt sickened by the girl.

With the engine running, Jamie waited until she'd finished heaving then Charles bundled her inside the back of the car, slammed the door and got in the front with Jamie.

The smell of vomit on her made his stomach heave.

'Jesus fuckin' 'ell, what a poor excuse for a woman.'

'Drive the bitch home,' said Charles. He said it with such bitterness Jamie knew he'd been right that the old timer, who loved Roy like a son, was ashamed. The gangster had been shown up.

Ten minutes through the wind, drizzle and London traffic, he pulled up outside a block of flats. Roy had done well for her, thought Jamie. The large uniform building was set back from the road with a circular driveway and neatly trimmed privet hedges.

Charles jumped out first and opened the door. He pulled the girl out.

'I thought we'd have trouble with her,' he said, but Eve was like a rag doll.

'I ain't never seen my mum really drunk,' said Jamie. 'Seen her at Christmas with Vera over a bottle of sherry and the both of them all giggly, but I ain't never seen her make a fool of herself. Not like this one.'

'Let's get her upstairs,' said Charles. 'It's the second floor. Boss gave me the key.'

Holding her upright between them, Jamie and Charles walked her towards the main door and opened it. Suddenly Eve spoke.

'I've lost me bag,' she said. She tried to turn back towards the car.

'No, you don't,' said Jamie.

'I'm goin' to be sick.'

'Get her away from the fuckin' car, I don't want to be cleaning her shit off it!' yelled Charles.

Jamie pushed her head down towards the grass and she threw up. He held her so she wouldn't fall forward and when it seemed she was finished, he pulled her upright again. Charles was waiting by the open front door.

'I've left me bag behind,' she said again.

'C'mon, let's get you upstairs and into bed,' said Jamie. Charles walked on ahead, moaning about the steepness of the stairs and his knees.

'I want me bag,' she said once more. Jamie was fed up hearing about her fucking bag.

Outside her flat, he propped her up against the wall and watched Charles unlock the door. Charles slipped the keys back in his pocket.

It was in that instant the idea came to Jamie.

'Where's the bedroom?' asked Charles. Still holding the girl, Jamie looked about the flat with its new furniture and furnishings. The predominant colour was pale grey.

Charles was opening door after door.

'Stop fuckin' looking about like a bleedin' estate agent, an' find the bleedin' bedroom,' said Jamie.

'Get her over here,' said Charles, holding a door open so Jamie could walk her through into a room that was all pink frills. 'We goin' to undress her?'

'That's the last thing I want to do,' replied Jamie. 'But if you get a washcloth I'll get the worst of the crap off her face and hair. Roy won't be happy with us if we tip her into the kip like this.' He sat Eve down on the bed and looked about him. Dolls with glass eyes sat atop the wardrobe, Jamie hated the way they seemed to be staring at him. Fancy all those eyes watching you in the night while you slept.

Charles was back with a flannel. Eve was snoring and was so far out of it, Jamie doubted she was aware he was cleaning her up. He got her bear of a coat off and tossed it onto a chair. She'd managed to vomit on it and the fur was stuck together and stinking.

Charles was pulling back the pink candlewick bedspread.

Jamie pushed her flat on the bed and took off her shoes, then rolled her into the candy-striped sheets and Charles covered her up. Both men stood up and looked at each other.

'Thank Christ for that,' said Jamie.

Charles said, 'Right, little scrubber, sleep tight.' He walked out of the room, then out to the front door.

Jamie followed, drawing the door to but not closing it.

'Where to, back to Soho?' Jamie asked, catching him up.

The party was winding down when they got back to The Glass Slipper.

Roy was looking worriedly at the door, but Jamie gave him a wink that meant mission accomplished and took up his stance near the door, dismissing the tall fair-haired bloke and Anton the Greek who'd been given the job in their absence. Charles wound his way through the people and whispered in Roy's ear.

After a while, he returned. 'We're to go home if we want. Roy's going on to another party and he doesn't need us.'

'I could sure do with an early night,' said Jamie. 'You gonna give me a lift?'

'Can do,' said Charles.

Jamie watched Roy rise from his chair and Eddie get up with him. Roy put his arm across Eddie's shoulder and then Roy laughed at something Eddie said. Jamie turned away.

'You ready, Jamie?'

'Yeah,' said Jamie, 'I'm ready.'

CHAPTER 20

With a half-bottle of vodka tucked into the inside pocket of his leather jacket, Jamie, leaving his light on in the bedroom, locked his front door and left his flat. It had started raining again and, though the wind had eased, he was glad to go down the steps into the underground station, out of the inclement weather. He boarded a train, leaving it after two stops.

He'd had to stand as there were no seats available. London never sleeps, he thought. The theatre crowds were the next surge to descend like locusts on the stations. If he was lucky, he could do the job while the crowds were still in evidence.

He walked briskly down the road to Willow Court and pushed open the front door then half ran, half walked up the stairs.

At Eve's front door he listened carefully and, deeming it safe to enter, he pushed open the unlocked door and went inside.

She was lying on the bed in exactly the same position he'd left her in.

He sat on the edge and held her hand. 'C'mon, Sleeping Beauty,' he said. 'Wake up.'

He shook her shoulder and when she didn't respond, he shook her again. Successful this time, he whispered as he took out the bottle, 'Look what I've got.'

She opened her eyes. 'You've brought a party,' she said. She was still very drunk.

'And I brought me,' he said.

'You're nice,' she slurred. Her once immaculate make-up was so smudged her face looked like a clown's.

He opened the bottle and tipped it to her lips and automatically she drank greedily. Vodka ran down her lips and chin.

'Move over,' he said.

Jamie wriggled until he was by her side on the bed then he raised the bottle to her lips again. Another couple of gulps of the white stuff should do it, he reckoned.

Jamie's utter disgust for her rose.

'Steady,' he said, as she opened her eyes.

'I've lost my handbag,' she murmured before closing her eyes again.

'Steady,' he repeated as she cuddled into him.

'You want to play games?' she slurred.

'Maybe,' he said.

He knew she fancied him and she obviously thought he wanted sex. But for Jamie it was nothing to do with sex.

It was the power. The power he held over her at this moment.

When he'd left the flat's door unlatched earlier Charles had not noticed his deception. And as Charles had held the keys to this flat until he'd handed them back to Roy, who would ever know Jamie had returned?

So, too, he had power over Roy Kemp. He could take something that belonged to Kemp without ever being discovered.

Eve opened her eyes and her hand fumbled against his clothes searching for his cock. He hated himself for responding to her touch.

'Later,' he said, gruffly. 'Drink this first.'

It was as easy as giving candy to a baby, he thought. The vodka slipped down her throat and again she slept. He stashed the empty bottle in the inside pocket of his jacket. Then he slipped his jacket off, draped it on the chair by the side of the bed and turned once more to Eve.

'Wake up, bitch,' he said. He pulled her towards him, twisted her pliant body around until she was lying face down with her feet on the carpet. Reaching beneath her he ripped off her soiled knickers. The stupid bitch had pissed herself. Somehow, it added to his excitement. Then he unzipped himself and, standing over her, whispered, 'Open for Jamie, bitch.' And then he pushed into her.

'Ah, lovely,' he murmured. 'What an arse you've got, you little bitch, what a lovely tight arse.' Jamie went deeper with each thrust. Eve was making sounds like a mewling kitten but he knew she was loving it. And then Jamie began to lose it, began to go wild, shoving himself in and drawing out, harder, deeper, faster. He could feel the sweat making his shirt stick to his skin and his breath was fast and ragged. He drove deeper, further still into her, and smelled that musty female stink. He felt like some kind of giant between her thighs. And then he was almost there, gasping, throbbing and suddenly in another world, and then he shuddered, collapsed and said, 'You fuckin' bitch.'

He pulled himself off her, tucking himself in and zipping himself up. Looking down at her inert figure, he laughed as he pulled his leather jacket on.

'Stupid fucker,' he said. He heaved her to her feet, hoping she wasn't going to throw up over him. He walked her round the bed, seeing her automatically put one foot in front of the other. 'Now I know what Roy Kemp gets, I reckon you ain't worth it,' Jamie said.

'Don't want to get up,' she mumbled.

'We're going to get your handbag,' Jamie said. He managed to slip her fur coat around her and slip her arms into the wide sleeves. Those were the magic words.

'Shoes,' she muttered. 'Need shoes.'

He pushed her into a sitting position on the bed and slipped her high heels on. With difficulty he walked her to her front door and closed it tightly behind them.

He found she was quite manageable because she was not a big woman. She leaned her head against him and allowed herself to be led downstairs and out onto the driveway. He hoped he'd not meet any of her neighbours and luck was with him.

'You've caused my mother grief,' he said, as they walked arm in arm up the dark street, barely lit by lamps.

At the end of the road they mingled with the crowds of chattering people exiting from theatres and cinemas. Patrons from *No Sex Please, We're British* were pouring into the underground. He was surprised at how easy it was for him and Eve to be inconspicuous in the heavy crowds.

He bought tickets while she nestled into him, her eyes closed. He didn't attempt the turnstiles, simply showed his tickets to the duty porter and moved on down in to the bowels of London's underground.

He held her pliant body tightly. Her head lolled on his shoulder but he knew she could barely be recognisable in the depths of her fur. They were simply an anonymous couple. And if anyone gave them a second look, they'd reckon the girl was drunk.

Standing on the platform waiting for the train, he allowed himself to be pushed nearer and nearer the edge of the platform. For a split second he watched the adverts on the opposite wall. Mingling with the voices from the crowd was the scent of perfume and the smell of dirty oil from the tracks. Somewhere he could make out the plaintive sounds of a flute being played by a busker.

At last he felt the rush of warm air signalling the oncoming train. He breathed a sigh of relief. Soon it would all be over.

The train was already in sight … No time to think … He thrust Eve's warm body forward and let go of her.

He watched mesmerised as she put out her hands to break her fall before she slid over the edge of the platform and on to the tracks. It happened as easily as a black cat slinks from a low wall. He didn't wait around.

He heard the screams, the noise, the screech of brakes. Melting through the mass of people scrambling for a better look, he thought he'd never forget that last moment before the train had hit her, when she'd turned her head and he saw the accusation in her eyes.

CHAPTER 21

It was nice being out in the open air, Vera thought, clutching her takings from Heavenly Bodies. She marched through the rows of stalls and the noisy fly pitchers trying to sell stuff illegally from their suitcases. She loved the different smells that emanated from the variety of goods on display, fragrant candles and incense mingling with aromas of fresh fruit from all parts of the world.

'Hello, Fred,' she called to the fishmonger. She remembered regularly buying haddock or cod for her Kibbles off that stall and Fred always put in a bit extra.

'Wotcher, Vera,' shouted Ali, the baby clothes man. Tiny pretty clothes were hung about, gently swaying in the breeze.

She waved at him and he blew her a kiss.

Vera shivered. It was cold, and the little red suit with the fluted peplum wasn't very warm. Her toes were cold in her red high-heeled shoes and she had to watch carefully for the patches of ice still clinging to the cobbles.

'Nearly bleedin' Easter,' she moaned to Maxine, the flower girl, 'and no sign of warmth yet. There's bleedin' daffs in Daisy's garden coming up with their overcoats on.' Maxine laughed.

Vera left behind the heady scent of the hothouse blooms, thinking how lucky she was to live in an area she loved with people around her she felt comfortable with.

Then she thought about the letter she'd opened this morning, and the truth of it was she was scared. Scared of leaving these people she loved.

She shook off her morbid thoughts and went towards the bank to join the queue for the cashier.

That's when she saw him.

The young ragamuffin she'd given the money to. The lad who'd been picking wasted fruit from the gutter. He was buying chocolate. Only that wasn't what caught her attention; it was the livid scratches down his face and the state of his left eye. It was very nearly closed it was so swollen. Vera moved stealthily around so she was directly behind him. She had to know how he'd got so bruised and cut. Surely it couldn't be anything to do with Paulie's cuts and bruises and Derek's suicide . . . or could it . . .?

She let him pay for the bars of chocolate, noting that he wasn't short of money, then she clamped her arms around him.

'Jesus, you stink,' she said. His hair was lank and greasy and his clothes were so filthy and creased, she was sure he was sleeping in them. 'I want to know how you've got them marks on you,' she said, pulling him away from the stall where onlookers were beginning to gather and gawp and the stallholder was looking uneasy.

'Mind yer own bleedin' business, an' you're hurting me,' the boy yelled, 'My ribs 'urt.' He kicked her on the shins.

'Ouch, you little bleeder,' said Vera. 'Who's been knocking you about?'

He was wriggling like a fish on a hook and was twice as slippery, but Vera's grip around his body was like constricting steel rods. His bars of chocolate had fallen to the cobbles.

'Let me go, you ol' bat!' Vera twisted him round so he was facing her.

'Not until you tell me if you know a boy called Paulie.'

The lad went rigid at her words. Recognition spread across his face. Then came the blustering lie.

'Never 'eard of 'im.' And he kicked her again. This time Vera's knee took the brunt of it and she momentarily let go of him. But it was enough for him to slither out of her grasp and then he was off, hopping through the market like a flea on a dog's back.

'Little bastard,' moaned Vera, rubbing her knee.

'You all right, dear?' asked an old lady who could barely walk and held herself up with a stick. 'Little buggers, the kids are today.'

'Yes, I'm fine, thanks,' said Vera, gathering up the chocolate bars. She tottered through the market and down Hobbs Alley that came out on the quay. She'd seen the lad run straight ahead. She was taking a chance he was heading for Forton Road.

The tide was in. The creek smelled of rotten fish and seaweed. Two yachts were moored near the slipway of the boatyard. She was keeping a sharp eye out for the lad. Something made her feel that he'd run this way. Then she rounded the corner by St George's Barracks.

'Gotcha!' she said to herself. She stepped back to hide among the broken tree boughs hanging low across the pavement.

Oblivious, the lad was walking along Mumby Road.

Vera chanced he wouldn't look behind him and ran across the road to the railway line that was parallel to Forton Road. Three streets later, walking along the overgrown path, she still had him in her sights. She walked quickly down Albert Street taking care to hide as best she could by the Five Alls pub. She gazed up and down Forton Road.

'Jesus Christ,' she said to herself. 'I've lost the little toad.'

Scanning the Georgian properties, Vera noted Roy's derelict

brothel, Chestnut House, still waiting for its conversion to flats. Vera was shocked to see through the broken gate that the front door was wide open.

And even more surprised to see sitting on the stone steps, chatting away to Paulie, her little hungry friend from the market who had a kick like a mule.

Back at the house in Western Way, Daisy was hanging out washing when Vera came hobbling into the garden. A sheet flapped angrily at her.

'Whatever's the matter with you? Did you know you've got a hole in your stockings?'

'Bugger me stockings and bugger your washing. Where's Gyp?'

'Over at the crèche. I got her out the way so I could have a go at the filth in this house. I'm gonna mow the lawn when I've got this lot out.'

Daisy put a few pegs in her mouth and moved the basket of washing further down the line. Vera was gabbling away nineteen to the dozen and seemed very agitated. Daisy went on pegging out and when the last peg had left her mouth she grabbed hold of Vera's arm.

'Slow down. What's the matter?'

'Them kids!' Vera collapsed on the side of the pond and Daisy sat down beside her. She took hold of Vera's hands.

'What kids?'

'Paulie and this little lad what I been seeing around the market.'

'Paulie?'

'They're together in Roy's old brothel in Forton Road. You got to come down with me an' find out what's goin' on. This other lad 'as got bruises an' all, now.'

'Why didn't you confront them?'

'If I thought it was only them two inside the house, I would 'ave.'

Daisy pursed her lips. 'No sense in taking chances then. When was this?'

''Bout half an hour ago.'

'Okay, you open the garage door so's I can get the car out an' I'll find me coat.'

Vera disappeared in a flurry of poppies.

'Bugger me, our Vera, you must care a lot about them kiddies if you ain't stopping to change your nylons!' Daisy bundled Vera into the passenger seat and backed out on to Western Way.

She drove down Jellicoe Avenue and past the old waterworks. Waiting at the traffic lights then driving down Whitworth Road, at the Criterion cinema she turned left up Forton Road towards the White Swan.

'I'm parking on the spare bit of ground round the back. We can walk round the front.' She unbuckled Vera and helped her out of the confines of the sports car.

Daisy opened the gate to the path of Chestnut House that led up to the front door that was pulled close. Then she put her shoulder against it and it creaked open. The smell of un-washed bodies and mould swung over her.

'Fuckin' 'ell!' Vera was close behind her and gasped as the stench washed around her.

'Shhh! We want to catch whoever's in here, not give 'em a warning we're on our way. We both know this house like the backs of our hands. You take upstairs and I'll go down to the cellar room.'

'What a dump,' muttered Vera, making for the stairs as Daisy walked across the room and looked out of the back window. Tangles of blackberry bushes and an open gate met her eyes. The lock to the back door was also broken.

Daisy ran her hand along the bars of the metal cage.

'What d'you think this is for?' Her voice was hardly more than a whisper as she looked at Vera for an explanation.

'Fuck knows! And I shudder to think. Is that dried blood on the carpet inside?'

'How can you spot dried blood from where you're standing?'

'When you've seen as much of it as I 'ave you can soon tell.' Vera began to climb the carpetless stairs.

Daisy wound her way downstairs to the kitchen. The sink was full of rancid water and dishes that looked like they'd been in it for years. She spied a half bag of sugar tightly rolled and a peg clamping it together to keep out creepy crawlies. A box of Co-op tea bags sat next to the sugar. The box looked clean.

Further down in the cellar room, junk was piled high. Some of Roy's prostitutes had once used the room for business. Now it was just a stinking mass of unwanted furniture and boxes of mouldy rubbish. Everywhere there was the stench of decay.

Curiously, Daisy felt no fear. The house *was* empty, she was sure of it. But who then was making tea?

Upstairs again, she followed Vera to the bedrooms.

'Anything there?'

Vera stood in a doorway surveying a pile of curtains and old rugs.

'Not now there ain't.' She inclined her head towards the passage and wrinkled her nose. 'Jesus, don't that overflowing toilet reek?'

'The boy may have been sleepin' rough here.' Daisy pointed to the makeshift bed.

'I wouldn't mind bettin' that's where he kips.' Vera's voice was croaky.

Daisy looked at her friend and saw she had tears in her eyes. Vera had taken to the boy, thought Daisy.

'I don't want no harm to come to him,' Vera said.

'Then we'd better get a certain detective off his arse to give this little lot the once-over.'

CHAPTER 22

'Why would she do this?' Roy put his head in his hands and his elbows on the kitchen table. 'Eve had everything to live for.'

'Shift up,' his mother said. He moved along so that she could sit down next to him. Roy looked across at Eddie standing by the sink. On the ledge was his mother's favourite photograph of himself and her with Violet Kray and the twins, taken years ago at Blackpool. He saw the smile on his chubby face. He had no idea then he'd be feeling so much pain in the future.

'Charles reckoned she was going on and on about her lost handbag. It's possible she took it into her head to get back to Soho to see if she could find it,' Roy said.

Violet patted his back like he was a little boy. 'Charles also said she was sparked out on the bed when him and Jamie left her in her flat.'

'She was out of her mind with booze,' he continued. 'I suppose she could have slept for a while then woke up and decided she'd go looking for this.' He motioned to the small clutch bag on the table. 'She'd got herself to the right underground station to get back to The Glass Slipper.' He fingered the silver purse. 'I brought it home with me from the club.'

Roy pushed the bag towards Violet. She opened it, and said, 'There's nothing in here except a lipstick, key to her flat, compact and tissues. Why on earth was she making such a fuss about it?'

'That's what happens when you've 'ad a few too many to drink.' Roy sniffed. 'Something not worth worrying about when we're sober magnifies itself to monumental importance.' He wiped his eyes. 'She was such a pretty little thing, reminded me of Daisy when she was younger.'

'She was nothing like Daisy!' His mother's voice was sharp. 'That's all in your head.'

Eddie butted in before an argument could escalate. Roy knew he would, he was like his mother. Daisy often backed down to save the peace. 'Who's paying for the funeral?'

It was like an arrow in his heart. 'I don't even get to do that,' Roy said. 'Her brothers claimed what was left of the body and they're taking her home to be buried near her mother. I spoke to them on the phone only this morning and the eldest was emphatic that I wasn't wanted there.'

'He can't do that ...' said Violet.

'Mum, he can. And I have to respect family wishes, even though Eve said she wanted nothing more to do with them. Anyway, the newspapers'll make a meal out of it if I appear at the graveside. Talking of funerals, has that bloke's body been dredged up yet?'

'Ain't seen nothin' in the papers yet nor heard anything on the grapevine,' Eddie said, scratching his ear, then picking up a spoon and drumming it on the table.

'I just don't know what to do.' Roy was distraught.

'What you should do is come home with me. I'm going down to Gosport to see me mum and Summer.' Eddie ran his fingers through his dark curls. 'It's about time you cleared the air between yourself and Mum, and I need to talk to 'em about weddings and stuff.' Eddie put down the spoon after he caught Violet glaring at him.

'I don't think I could, son.' Roy wasn't sure if he'd have the guts to see Daisy. Gyp? She was different. He'd spoken to her on the phone and he'd sent her presents. Then there was the problem of the boys with welts and bruises that Vera had been bombarding him with questions about.

'Tomorrow, we'll go tomorrow. I'll drive.' Eddie was speaking as though he hadn't heard a word Roy had said. 'It's about time you sorted things. She reckons all this is her fault, you know ...'

'But why?' Eddie's words seemed to shake Roy out of himself.

Eddie said, 'If she'd come up to London a bit more, this tragedy would never have happened. That's what she's thinking ...'

'But that's not true ...'

'Well, it's her you should be talking to, not me.'

Roy looked to Violet and she nodded her approval. She got up from Roy's side and tightened the thin belt of her wraparound pinny. 'I think it's a good idea,' she said.

'I'm not bleedin' happy with the way things are goin',' said Vera. She had her hair in plastic curlers and was smothering her face and neck with pan stick. The mirror was propped against a milk bottle on the kitchen table. Gyp was sitting at the other end of the table colouring in a farm animal book, wax crayons spread all over the place.

'Shouldn't think you would be. You've put too much pan stick on the left side, you look like a ceiling what's been done with Artex,' said Daisy.

Vera peered in the mirror.

'Do I?' She began to rub furiously with a piece of kitchen roll and the tan colour became patchy.

Daisy was laughing, 'Stop it! There's nothing wrong with it. You're ever so easy to wind up. So, what ain't you happy about?'

'That ragamuffin boy from the market and Paulie messing about in Roy's old place. Paulie's mother is at her wits end.'

'Have you told her you saw him when he should have been at school?'

Vera shook her head. 'Not yet, I haven't.' She didn't want to heap more pain on his mother. The sick boy seemed well enough to have made a friend with that little scruff.

'I got to be careful, Daisy. He'll get taken off her by the authorities, taken away from that old lady what he loves. I'm beginning to think there's something goin' on with them dear boys an' it *is* all connected with the three of them, Paulie, that little scruff an' that poor hanged Derek. Maybe even that other dead boy. I also want to know why Paulie and Scruff were sitting on the steps of Roy's old brothel. I still think that lad is livin' there.'

'We 'ave to find out what's going on, Vera. You and me, we made a promise. An' God knows I've spoken to Roy enough times.' Daisy didn't want to even think about Roy. She folded the tea towel neatly over the cooker rail. Vera had got to her eyelash stage now and three attempts had resulted in crooked lashes and a lot of swearing.

'Stop right there, Vera. If I 'ave to sort out your lashes later, I might just as well save meself the trouble and do it now.'

'When I die, will you make sure me eyelashes is on right when I'm in me coffin?'

Daisy took the eyelash from Vera and squeezed a small amount of glue along its rim and snapped, 'Don't talk so bloody daft and close your eye.' Daisy repeated the exercise with the other lash and stepped back to survey her handiwork.

'You didn't answer me question, Dais.'

'No, and I ain't going to. You got the date when Haslar's going to admit you and operate. We got a weddin' to go to before that …'

'Supposing I'm riddled with it. The cancer?'

Daisy sighed.

'Perhaps it's time to let the family know,' Vera said.

'I think you'll find word's already got spread about a bit.'

'Oh, dear. D'you really think so?' Vera peered at her neck and smoothed the wrinkles. A loud knocking at the door interrupted Vera's words.

'Jesus Christ,' she said. 'That'll wake Gyp up and she's only just gone off to sleep again.' Daisy was already halfway down the hall.

Vera hadn't put on her lipstick so she set about rectifying that. She heard muffled voices and then Vinnie's bulk seemed to fill the kitchen. She thought how smart he looked in his light blue shirt, dark suit and mac that didn't disguise the breadth of his shoulders. His curly brown hair glistened with wet droplets. 'Hello, stranger,' she said. 'I see it's started raining again.'

'It's always bloody raining, Vera.' Vinnie didn't wait to be asked but sat himself down on the bench and stretched his long legs out in front of him. Then, as though he'd forgotten something, he got up and took off his mac, folded it and put it on the seat beside him.

'Nice and warm in here,' he said.

'You look like you've lost a tenner and found a penny, DCI Vinnie Endersby,' Vera said. She was liberally applying perfume over her neck. Vinnie started coughing. 'You'd better get something for that cough, Vinnie,' she said. 'Don't want it to turn to bronchitis.'

'Want a cuppa?' Daisy asked.

Vinnie nodded. 'You heard the bad news?'

Vera asked, 'What bad news? It's all bad news here in Gosport.'

Vinnie took a deep breath. 'Hampshire Constabulary have called me down here. A twelve-year-old boy was found dead off the shore in Walpole Park.'

Daisy gasped. Vera put her hand to her mouth and shook her head before she said, 'Not another boy.'

'He was only found this morning. Poor little bleeder. He'd been sexually assaulted and badly knocked about before his short life was ended.'

Vera looked at Daisy and knew the horrors going through her mind. After a long silence, Daisy was the first to speak.

'You don't usually come round to my 'ouse to discuss your cases with me.'

'Remember when you asked me to keep my eyes and ears open for anything strange going on where kids were getting bashed about? Well, this little boy looked like he'd gone ten rounds with a steamroller. Of course, it's probable he's not from around here,' Vinnie said.

'Surely kids go missing all the time?' But in her heart Vera knew it was no coincidence these boys were being hurt.

Vinnie nodded. 'I got one lad missing from Portsmouth. But he doesn't answer the description. Name's Earl Ashby. His mother was found dead with an overdose and he hasn't been seen since. His father's been notified and wants the boy returned to him.'

'Why wasn't the father in constant touch with the boy?'

Too late, Vera realised she'd hit on a raw nerve. Vinnie let it slide.

'The mother took the boy away and melted into city life. That much the father does know.'

'You got to find that lad,' said Vera. She was thinking about the boy picking up fruit in the market. No self-respecting parent would have allowed a child to go about as unwashed and as hungry as that. She could see him in her mind's eye, sitting with young Paulie on the steps of Chestnut House and chatting like they were great friends. It was on the tip of her tongue to say something to Vinnie but maybe she ought to have another word first with Roy. After all, Chestnut House was his property. And he wouldn't take too kindly to the police crawling all over the place, even if it was almost derelict.

Daisy gave her a look that would freeze a snowman. Vera knew then that Daisy felt as she did. Roy had to be informed of this latest happening before Vinnie visited Chestnut House. After all, what if Roy had something stored there? Drugs, maybe? Vera turned her back on the pair of them and started making a pot of tea.

Vera knew Roy Kemp and Vinnie Endersby had an uneasy truce. But already she saw Vinnie had picked up on the look between her and Daisy.

'Where's that tea?' Vinnie asked. 'I reckon me, you an' Daisy ought to have a little chat.'

'Vera's doin' it,' snapped Daisy. 'Can't you see her? You lost the right to 'ave me waiting on you hand and foot when you left me and went back to your wife.'

'How's Jamie?' he asked, ignoring Daisy's barb.

'Your son is doin' really well with Roy. And Eddie's getting set to wed our Summer real soon.'

'That's not a surprise, Dais. It was always on the cards. I'm happy for him.'

'How are you and Clare?' Daisy didn't care how Clare was, she simply wondered if they were happy together.

Clare and Vinnie had been separated when Daisy had come along. Daisy had no doubt whatsoever that Vinnie had loved her. At the time, Roy had had a one-night stand with a young blonde so Daisy had turned to Vinnie on the rebound. She hadn't planned on caring so much about him. It just happened.

'We're fine.' She saw the cagey look cross his face.

'What I actually meant was, are you happy?'

Vinnie moved closer, his beautiful different-coloured eyes stared straight into hers.

'What you and I had all those years ago was exciting. You know as well as I do it was never meant to be permanent.'

Daisy looked at the lines on his face that had deepened with the years but she remembered how much she'd loved him. Remembered how the skin on his back had smelled and tasted of salt as she'd nuzzled into him when he'd driven his motorbike over the hills of Kos in Greece. So too she remembered their joy at making love in the long grasses near Kefalos. Every time she visited her beloved small white house in Greece, given to her by Eddie's father, she had a million wonderful memories to take out, examine and treasure.

'It seemed permanent at the time.'

'I loved you, Daisy, but there was always Eddie's ghost between us. And you may not have realised it at the time but Roy came a close second to Eddie. You were never really mine.'

'And I wasn't the right woman, was I?'

Vinnie shook his head.

'As of now, Vinnie Endersby, I'm setting you free from my thoughts. But I hope you'll be there if Jamie needs you.'

Vinnie leaned down and kissed her on the forehead.

'He's my son,' he whispered. Then he left.

CHAPTER 23

'Will you be all right on your own, Lol?'

Lol pushed back her long blonde hair and thrust out her newly acquired bosom, courtesy of a trip to Sri Lanka.

Vera knew Lol would be fine. She was Vera's manageress, well used to dealing with stroppy clients and making sure that business ran smoothly at Heavenly Bodies. A throaty giggle came from one of the cubicles. Vera and Lol smiled at each other. The radio was playing soft romantic music.

Lol jiggled her bust.

'Yes, Lol, they look gorgeous.'

Lol preened. 'I'm well on the way for saving for the *big* operation that'll turn my body completely to a woman's.'

'Just wait 'til you come back after the summer, Lol, and start wearing really tight clothes and pants without having to worry about that bulge you tries so hard to tuck away.'

Daisy and she had taken Lol in after she'd been raped by a group of thugs near Gosport ferry. Lol was only a youngster then but she'd found her forte working in the massage parlour and had acquired a cluster of customers of her own. Vera was very proud of the small slim woman who constantly dressed in floaty clothes that emphasised her femininity.

Vera took a deep breath of the incense burning in the stand on the side shelf, lotus blossom, her favourite.

Newly decorated, the business cubicles at the back were well furnished with luxurious drapes and comfortable beds. Linens were changed after every customer.

Years ago, when she'd been working the streets or on her usual pitch near the taxi rank, Vera had dreamed of a place like this, with regular clients; a place so clean and fresh men would queue up to enter and find deliciously clean girls waiting for them. With a little bit of help from her own clients on the council and from the town hall, her dream had become a reality. Vera was now a respected citizen of Gosport. She'd worked hard all her life, she thought. If the bloody cancer wanted to take her dreams away, it would have a fight on its hands!

'If I'm not back, lock up,' Vera said to Lol.

Lol lived in the flat above Heavenly Bodies where once Vera had lived before moving in permanently with Daisy. She was happy being part of Daisy's family.

'See ya,' shouted Lol, smiling brightly.

Vera walked out into the cold misty air. Her high heels clicked as she crossed the road and trotted down Hobbs Alley.

It wasn't long before she was walking past Clarence Square, the smell of the creek almost overpowering. There were very few people about but as she passed the Railway Tavern, the door opened, letting out the smell of fags and beer – and a customer. A tall man tipped his hat to her.

'Evening, Vera.' She returned his smile and carried on into Forton Road, glad the man was walking in the direction of Spring Garden Lane and not her way. The last thing she needed tonight was company.

A provincial bus passed on its way to Fareham as she pushed open the gate to Chestnut House. The garden was dark; she took a deep breath and trod the cobbles to the front door.

It had been the cage contraption that had brought her back to Chestnut House.

Was it simply a pet cage left by a previous tenant? The bars were too wide apart to keep a domestic animal from escaping. Was it a large birdcage that had been stripped of its netting? She didn't think so.

The main door was closed but not fastened. Vera listened carefully but could hear only the normal outside sounds: a car in the distance, laughter from people walking down the road.

She was puzzled by the fact that she wasn't at all frightened as she pushed open the door and slipped inside.

Again, the smell was as bad as she remembered.

She hadn't thought to bring a torch so was grateful for the streetlamps on the road shining into the blackness. Not that it mattered; she knew exactly where she was heading.

As quietly as she could, she climbed the stairs, keeping a sharp eye out for rubbish that littered them, until she found herself outside the room where she'd seen the makeshift bed.

Listening hard but hearing no sound, she pushed open the door. Vera's eyes adjusted themselves to the gloom.

Beneath the pile of curtains, a body lay gently snoring. A pair of trainers stood side by side on the torn lino.

Vera knelt down and touched the lad's cheek.

'What—'

The suddenness of his movements startled her. He had launched himself to his feet and was towering above her. Vera tried to jump up but her tight clothes held her back and instead she fell over.

'Don't!' she cried. What if he had a knife or a blunt instrument and was about to lunge at her? Vera felt utterly helpless sitting at his feet. Her heart was beating so fast she was sure he would hear it.

'You?' Recognition spread across his face.

'Help me up!' Sleep falling away from him, he held out his hand and she grabbed it. Her other hand found purchase on a small package on the floor and she heaved herself up. When she was standing, she began brushing herself down. The boy took the package and looked at it.

'You've ruined me breakfast!' Vera saw she'd completely flattened a giant Mars Bar.

Now that her heart had stopped its frantic tattoo, Vera was glad they were almost the same height. Her courage had returned and she knew if he started any funny business, she was well able to retaliate.

'Why you following me?'

She could only tell him the truth.

'I've been worrying about you.'

He looked at her as though she'd spoken in a foreign language.

'You don't know me.'

'I don't 'ave to. You're a boy an' you're sleepin' in a shit'ole.'

'Mind your own fuckin' business.'

'That's not a nice thing to say, is it? Where d'you come from?'

'Ports ... Nowhere!'

Vera laughed. 'So, you come from Portsmouth and you're nine years old.'

He looked ashamed that the word Portsmouth had slipped out but indignant that she thought he was only nine.

'No, I ain't, I'm nearly eleven!'

Vera smiled. It was getting easier all the time.

'Where's your mum?' This time, there was no hesitation.

'She's dead.'

Vera moved towards him and put her arms around him.

Tentatively at first and then when she found no resistance, she pulled him into her warmth. After a while he wriggled away.

'Where's your dad?'

'I ain't got one.'

'I don't think that's quite true. Everyone has a dad even if they don't know where or who he is. Will you tell me your name?'

He glared at her, his eyes searching her face as though he was weighing up whether he could trust her.

'Earl.'

'That's a great name.' Vera reckoned she had enough information. Shouldn't be too difficult to find out more. How many kids of his age, named Earl, were missing from the Portsmouth area?

'Look, Earl, I don't like to think of you sleeping here. Surely you'd like a proper bed.' She sniffed. 'And a nice hot bath?'

He stepped quickly away from her.

'I ain't goin' with you. I've heard all about women what pretends to be nice to kids then does all sorts of stuff to 'em.'

Vera knew when she was beaten but she tried again.

'Where did you get all them bruises from an' that shiner?'

'I ... I can't say.'

'Why not?'

'I'll get into trouble.' Now there were tears in his eyes.

'Okay, okay.' A sweet wrapper clung to her skirt and she brushed it away. 'I'm not forcing you. You can stay here if you want.' She bent down and picked her handbag off the floor. Opening it, she took a five-pound note from her purse. 'I'm giving you this to get some decent food inside you.'

His face was a mask of disbelief.

'I want a promise from you to come to my place – you

know where it is, don't you? – if anything happens to you that you can't control. Come there. Promise me?'

He nodded.

'I'm sorry about your Mars Bar.' He took the money from her.

Out on the street again, she walked past Parham Road before she realised she was crying and that she hadn't asked him if he knew what that funny cage was for.

She hailed a taxi and when she opened the front door at Western Way, she went straight to the telephone and dialled a number.

'Vera?' the sleepy male voice asked. 'It's not Jamie again, is it?'

'No! It's not bleedin' Jamie. There's a kid dossing in Roy's old whorehouse what's in danger. He's got bruises all over him. I think you ought to sort it.'

'Wait ... I need a pencil ...' So the bugger was interested now, was he?

She replaced the handset, then picked it up and dialled again.

'Roy, there's a kid staying at Chestnut House. I hope you're gettin' your finger out about this because I don't want him to end up dead.'

The phone was down before she realised she hadn't given Roy a chance to get a word in. But Vera trusted Roy. He'd investigate. He didn't like kids getting hurt.

And then she was aware of Daisy standing beside her in her old cream dressing gown.

'I'll put the kettle on.'

After the stench in the house in Forton Road, Daisy and the warm scent of the kitchen smelled like heaven to Vera.

CHAPTER 24

'Well, that was a waste of time,' said Daisy. She turned the corner from Mayfield Road into Dock Road, narrowly missing a small child on a tricycle who had no business riding on the busy street.

'Not really,' said Vera. 'Paulie didn't look too bad, did he?'

'How can you say that when he's a bundle of nerves and there's something seriously wrong with the way he stutters and twitches? No wonder he's in no fit state for school.'

'But there weren't any fresh bruises, were there, Dais? Not visible ones.'

'No.' Daisy drew in a deep breath and let it out slowly before she said, 'His mum seemed more at ease, even if the old girl upstairs is about to pop her clogs at any time now.'

'That's when Paulie'll go to pieces,' said Vera. She leaned forward in the MG and started fiddling with the heater. Daisy slapped her hand away.

'You're completely ignorant where my car's concerned, so get your fingers off,' she ordered. 'Paulie said he didn't know nothin' of the report in the *Evening News* about that lad bein' found off Walpole Park's shoreline, didn't he? An' he still maintains he wasn't with no boy sittin' on the steps of Chestnut House.'

Daisy thought it was a good job she was used to Vera's

lavish application of Californian Poppy perfume otherwise she might become gassed by the sickly smell in the small confines of her car.

'I reckon the lad's lying. I don't like it. Well, I *know* he's lying.'

'You don't like a lot of things,' said Daisy. 'You especially didn't like that important-looking letter that came this morning for Eddie. You'd 'ave steamed it open if I hadn't taken it off you.' Vera's face was a picture.

'I could have stuck it down again; he'd never have known,' Vera said.

'If he wants us to know what the bloody thing is, he'll tell us. Anyway I already got my own thoughts on the subject.'

'Thought anything about that boy in Roy's old place?'

'Roy'll sort that, don't you worry.'

Daisy was now driving up South Street towards the ferry and Vera's massage parlour. The morning was cold, though a few rays of sunshine were trying to get through the cloud.

'It's his money come through, ain't it?'

Daisy took her eyes from the road briefly to turn and nod to Vera. Many years ago she'd set up a trust fund for Eddie. It had at last matured. She'd worked her fingers to the bone to do the same for Jamie but to no avail. It worried her that this money would make the rift even wider between her sons.

'How long you going to be attending to things in the massage parlour?' asked Daisy. They were driving past the police station now. A few stragglers waiting to be admitted to court were hanging about outside.

'Why?'

'I got to pick Gyp up at four from that birthday party. I bet her friend's mother'll be glad to get rid of her so I mustn't be late. In the meantime I'll walk round the market and you can join me on the Ferry Gardens so I can give you a lift back home.'

'Right,' said Vera.

Daisy pulled up at the end of Bemisters Lane and let Vera out.

'I wish you could open the door of my car without me 'aving to get out an' run round,' she grumbled. She watched the retreating figure of her friend walk down the cobbles of Bemisters Lane.

Daisy restarted the MG and moved down to Beach Street where she parked on the verge near the boatyard. She got and out locked the car, then walked past the boat skeletons, smelling the sawdust and the tar. The noise of saws and hammers and men at work was somehow comforting. She decided against wandering through the market, but instead crossed the road, past the bus terminal and taxi rank, and entered the Ferry Gardens. She picked an empty seat near the pontoon. There weren't that many people about. The cold had kept them indoors, she reckoned.

A ferry boat was leaving Gosport for the short trip to Portsmouth and it seemed to cut through the water like it owned that piece of the Solent. White V-shaped waves followed the boat. Daisy took a deep breath of the freezing air mixed with the brine. She loved Gosport and the abundance of excitement that seemed to hover over the town. She'd never leave there, only for holidays, and that suited her just fine.

Her mind slid to Roy and the girl, Eve, he'd cared about and the way she'd died. People did all sorts of stupid things when they were drunk. Poor Roy. He was a rogue, a gangster and at times a cruel man. But he loved the people he cared about and was generous to a fault with them. And if the girl had made him happy ...

Daisy looked towards the market and waved to a stallholder selling suitcases and handbags who'd pitched up outside Eddie's pool hall.

The pool hall was doing well enough. Tyrone was a good manager. But Eddie had his head screwed on properly. Working in London for Roy was more profitable than spending his time sorting out Gosport's drunken yobbos, some of whom seemed to think the pool cues were excellent tools for inflicting harm on each other. When Eddie relayed gossip about the fights there, Daisy closed her ears.

Across the road was Fleure's, the dress shop. She smiled to herself. She remembered buying a dress in there to wear to a London party hosted by the Krays. Vinnie had waited patiently while she'd tried on the black dress, then he'd asked her to twirl for him. It was a long time ago.

Daisy's eyes fell to the gold bangle Eddie's father had bought her. She remembered her first trip in what was to become her MG. Eddie had taken her to the New Forest. It was a special break away from working hard in Bert's Cafe. She'd loved her eldest son's father so much. What a great pity he'd never lived to see his boy get married to a woman who loved him to bits.

She thought about her life so far. She reckoned all the downs made the ups more worthwhile and she adored her boys. That all her children had different fathers made not a bit of difference to the ferocious way she loved them. If only her boys could have some kind of friendship. Come to an understanding about their differences. She looked at her watch. Not time yet to collect her beloved daughter Gypsy. Vera should be along in a short while. Daisy was so lucky to have such a good friend. She would miss her so much if … if … Daisy pushed the thoughts away.

Then she felt the tears roll unbidden down her cheeks and could do nothing about them.

A hand thrust a clean white handkerchief towards her and a voice said, 'Is it really that bad, Dais?'

She raised her eyes to see her benefactor.

'Roy! How did you know where I was?'

'I've just come from Vera's place. You weren't at the house so I figured you'd be with her. She said you'd taken a wander and I spotted you from across the road. You know how blondes in black always catch my eye.'

She gave a half-hearted smile and handed him back the hanky which he put in his pocket. He looked tired in spite of the expensive suit he was wearing. His dark overcoat was open and a yellow scarf was slung casually around his neck.

'What's up, Dais? It's not like you to give way to your feelings.'

'I dunno, Roy. It's everything.' She moved along the seat so he could sit next to her.

'I know the feeling,' he said.

'Of course you do.' She felt selfish and guilty at her casually spoken words. 'I got to collect Gyp from a birthday party. And yet I'm sitting here snivelling like a bleedin' ten-year-old.' He took her hand and smiled. She saw the tiny chip in his white front tooth and decided he looked more like David Essex the older he got. She began, 'I'm so sorry about—'

He cut her off. 'Your boy Eddie thought it a good idea for me to come down here and make my peace with you.'

'There's no bad feelings,' said Daisy. 'I just wondered why you stayed away so long. We've been through so much together ...'

She knew Roy wouldn't be drawn into baring his soul.

Instead, he said, 'Eddie's gone off to meet his mates. Did you mind me arriving unannounced?'

'Don't be silly,' she said. She was clutching at his wrist, fearful of him removing his hand. She wanted, suddenly, to be held by him. To have Roy say, 'there, there'. She looked into his slate-grey eyes and said, 'I'd have been really angry if you hadn't come to see me.'

'Honest?'

She nodded. 'Honest.'

'Come on,' he said. 'Let's go back to Western Way, collect Gyp and you can fill me in on all the current news. There's a few things I need to get off me chest with you.'

Daisy rose from the seat. 'I'm supposed to be picking Vera up to take her home.'

'She's going home by taxi. And as your Eddie's borrowed my wheels, I'll have to squeeze into your MG,' he said. To know Eddie was in Gosport brought a smile to her lips. 'Eddie'll get back to Western Way when he's finished with his mates,' Roy confirmed. 'Then maybe he and I'll take a look down at Chestnut House. I been speaking to your detective.'

'He ain't my detective!' She saw he was teasing her. 'I suppose Vera's filled you in on them battered boys as well as tellin' Vinnie?'

He nodded. 'And about the kiddie who hanged himself.'

''Ave you got something hidden at the house?'

Frown lines creased his forehead. 'No, I haven't. Whatever made you think that?'

Daisy shrugged. 'We just thought ...'

'Sometimes, Daisy love, you think too much. I simply want to know why a house I left locked up like Fort Knox has kiddies sitting in its open doorway.'

She had believed all along that whatever was going on with

the lads was nothing to do with him. His words confirmed it. She stretched up and kissed him on his cheek.

'Thank you for doing such a good job looking after my boys,' she said.

'That's another thing that's been on my mind. I knifed a bloke not so long ago and I don't want to have anything like it happen to me again. I want to hand over the manor to Eddie.'

Daisy knew she should be surprised by his words but she wasn't.

'It's always been on the cards. Though I can't imagine you doing nothing for the rest of your life, Roy.'

He shrugged.

'Is Jamie behaving himself?' she asked.

'Seems to be. I got Charles on standby in the Smoke so Jamie can have a few days off an' all.'

As though tuning into her thoughts, he said gently, 'You don't need to tell me about Vera.'

'But how—?'

'Let's just say bad news travels quickly in a family. Charles can't keep secrets.' He smiled. 'About my business, he's tighter than a clam, but give the old bugger a bit of gossip ... I wanted to send a card, or flowers, but I reckoned if Vera had wanted it made public, she'd have told me herself.'

Roy squeezed Daisy to his big frame. And with that small gesture it seemed as though everything could be made right between them.

As they walked together down Beach Street, Daisy thought how nice it was to be with a bloke who knew you so well it didn't matter if you weren't looking your best. She didn't always have to be on show with people she cared about. And then another thought struck her.

'Bugger it,' she said. 'I have to be at work at six.'

'Not tonight, Dais. Your new friend, Nora, Derek's mum, is only too happy to fill in for you. She said she could cope.'

'I beg your pardon?' Daisy thought of Roy making decisions for her behind her back.

'I shouldn't be saying anything but I know Eddie wants to talk to you.'

Daisy let his words sink in. That was different. Roy had done her a favour in asking Derek's mother to stand in. She'd forgive him, just this once.

She and Roy would always be held together with some invisible cord. But what was happening in her family that she was becoming the last person to know about things?

CHAPTER 25

Jamie rounded the corner into Beryton Road. He stopped outside the maisonettes just beyond the Ford Anglia on bricks. He got out, locked his car and wrinkled his nose at the state of the garden, covered in dogs' shit, then pushed open the broken gate. Not quite able to reach him was a skinny Alsatian on a rope lead. Blackberry bushes had taken over the path.

He walked through the main door that was propped open by a brick and entered the shared hallway. The stink of piss hit him and he stared momentarily at a syringe lying under the stairwell. His eyes were drawn to the graffiti on the stone walls. He knocked at number three.

No one answered.

He banged louder, and when still no one answered he applied his knee to the door and almost fell inside as it opened. The stench of stale marijuana and unwashed bodies made him want to puke.

On the stained sofa was a girl asleep, naked from the waist down. Her mouth was open and she was snoring. The room was in a state of chaos. Fish-and-chip papers, burger cartons and empty cheap cider bottles littered the floor. On the sofa beside her lay a syringe and a belt.

Upstairs in the bedroom, asleep on a mattress on the floor, was a very young boy, perhaps six or seven, also naked. Jamie felt the well of disgust rise to bursting point. He shook the man who was lying asleep with one leg across the lad.

'Get up you cunt, we got business.'

'What the fuck!' The blond man sat up, trying to gather his wits together.

'You really ought to make sure you lock this filthy hole up, Heinz. Any fucker can get in.' Downstairs, the dog was barking.

'What d'you want?' Heinz groped for the cigarettes on the floor beside the overflowing ashtray. He lit one, drew on it deeply, and the lad woke up, rubbing his eyes. 'Get downstairs to your mother,' he said. With eyes wide as a frightened rabbit, the skinny boy ran still unclothed downstairs.

'You dirty bastard,' Jamie said. 'Is that his mother down there?'

Heinz nodded and flicked ash on the bed. He rubbed it in, making a round grey mark that was still cleaner than the sheet.

'I suppose you keep her in gear and she lets you fuck her boy?'

Heinz laughed and ran a hand over his crew-cut blond hair. 'What are you? The fuckin' morality police?'

Jamie bent down and wrenched the man's shoulder, making sure his nails dug far into the flesh.

'Listen, you fucker, that dead boy found in Walpole Creek was one of yours, wasn't he?' He put even more pressure on Heinz's skin. 'The death made the papers and the cops are involved now. I ain't going down because of your incompetence. I found you a place to hold the fights and for that I take a percentage. That's all I do. I expect you to look after the little bleeders what fights.'

'Ouch, let go. I'll tell you what happened.'

Jamie released his hold. Heinz rubbed his shoulder and neck

and consoled himself with another lungful of smoke.

'He told me he wasn't feeling well. He was spinning some line about not being able to breathe properly. He was all right when I gave him one up the arse so I sent him in the cage. Hang about.'

Heinz took a plastic packet from nearby and started busily chopping and cutting lines of coke on a Monopoly board.

'So what happened to the boy?' Jamie asked.

'The kid went in to fight and was rubbish. The crowd started jeering and the next moment the kid was lying on the cage's floor all glassy-eyed. I got him out of there quick and set another lad to fight. No one was more surprised than me to find the boy was a goner. Must have had a dicky heart or something. We got rid of him.'

He looked at Jamie and Jamie could see he didn't give a fuck about any of it. Heinz showed him the lines and said, 'Help yourself. Plenty more where that came from.'

'I don't want any.'

'You come all the way to see me for nothin'?'

'I only want to know if everything is ready for next Saturday?'

'Thought you was pulling out,' said Heinz, rolling a note and chasing a line.

Jamie thought quickly, 'I reckon we can use the premises this one more time. Should rake in a fair few quid the Saturday before Easter. Then we'll move out.'

Heinz breathed deeply then made the other line of coke disappear.

'Don't worry so much,' Heinz said. He looked at the other two fat lines of coke and Jamie knew he'd see them off in a moment. 'Everything's in hand. Saturday's fights are with older boys. Anyway, they don't fight properly until they're eleven or twelve and hungry for something in their lives. '

'I'll never know how you conceived this idea,' Jamie said. He'd had enough of the stale air and wanted to be gone.

'Blame the parents. The fuckin' mothers are the worst where money's concerned. They make me sick the way they yell and scream for the blood to start flowing.'

'You ain't never short of boys wanting to fight. That's another thing I don't understand.'

'Word of mouth. But nothing reaches the ears of the authorities because the kids'll lose their chance to make money. By the time I've paid 'em and made them be nice to me, they're scared stiff I'll tell someone what they've been up to. I got 'em over a barrel. They'll do anything I say.'

Jamie thought about the first time he'd met Heinz down in The Dive café. Heinz was looking for a place to hold the fights and he'd made it his business to know Jamie would go along for some easy money as long as he didn't have to get too involved. Only now the whole thing was coming apart at the seams, thought Jamie.

He hadn't bargained on the dead boy. Or his father being asked to investigate the case or Daisy asking Roy for his help because a friend of Vera's had a damaged boy.

It wouldn't be long before it was discovered that Roy's old whorehouse was the venue. Then it was only a matter of time before Heinz dropped him in the shit. Unless ...

The plan grew in Jamie's head.

There was no love lost between him and Heinz. If Heinz went down he'd take Jamie with him. For sure the bastard would.

Outside Jamie got into his car and sat with the windows down, glad of the fresh air. He needed to think. He looked to where his missing pinky finger tip had been and knew Roy wouldn't hesitate to maim or painfully exact his revenge for using his premises. The fact that Jamie was Vinnie's boy would only add fuel to the fire. Vinnie and Roy had an understanding that was more of a truce between them.

And if it ever came out he'd pushed Eve onto the tracks, he'd be a goner. That stupid fucker Roy Kemp wouldn't see she had to go so Roy and his mother could get back in their old routine. And didn't little Gypsy need her daddy?

He had a lot of thinking to do. Switching on the engine, he decided to pass away a couple of hours on the slot machines at Lee on the Solent's arcade. Maybe later he'd call in on his mother. Not yet. Roy would be consoling her about Vera.

It was all about family wasn't it? His mother, Roy, Vera, himself and little Gypsy. There wasn't room for anyone else, not even Eddie.

So he would always have to make sure his mother and Gypsy were all right, wouldn't he?

CHAPTER 26

Vinnie stirred his tea, then stared across the brown-ringed Formica table at his son.

'Why d'you want to see me in a dump like this?' he asked. The Safari Café at Lee on the Solent needed a damn good clean, or pulling down. Vinnie decided pulling it down might be the better answer. Safari? The walls were painted in zebra stripes and there was a picture pinned up above the door of two bored-looking lions. The place reeked of bacon and sausage but the smells certainly didn't make Vinnie hanker for a sandwich.

'I heard about that kiddie found near Walpole Creek,' Jamie said.

'So?'

'I want to make a deal with you.' Vinnie began to laugh but stopped when he noticed that his son was deadly serious.

'I reckoned no one would see us together out here.' Jamie was idly stirring his tea and the constant scrape was getting on Vinnie's nerves.

'It's a dead cert no one I know'll come in a dump like this,' Vinnie said. 'So what's this deal you think I'm interested in?'

Jamie leaned across the table and Vinnie was once more amazed that such a good-looking young bloke had come from his loins. Perfectly in proportion, that was Jamie. Good bones, good body, neither fat nor thin and already an inch or two taller than himself.

'I know how the kiddie died.'

Vinnie whistled through his teeth.

'D'you know what you're saying, son? That little boy looked as though he'd been rough trade for some sadistic bastard.'

'Yes.'

'Come on, don't bloody stop there ...'

'You haven't said whether we've got a deal or not?' Jamie leaned away from the table and tipped his chair back on two legs.

'You haven't given me any information that's worth any-thing, yet.'

Jamie took his time in answering. 'Unknowingly, I've got mixed up in something that's escalated beyond my control.' Jamie was very concise with his words, as if he'd thought care-fully about them.

Vinnie saw Jamie lower his head as though not wanting to take this conversation further. Then his shoulders slumped and a sigh escaped his body. Vinnie's heart started beating fast. Jamie was a tearaway, a handful, a law unto himself. His son wasn't a nice person but he *was* his son.

'You can't freeze me out there,' Vinnie said. He took the spoon from Jamie's fingers and set it down on the table. 'Start at the beginning, Jamie. Tell me what's going on.'

Jamie sighed again and said, 'Just before I went to live in London with Roy, I met this bloke who said he was looking for premises for his boys to fight. A sort of boxing club. He told me he kept lads off the streets by teaching them to box.' Vinnie nodded his head and Jamie tipped his chair back into an upright position. 'I said I knew of a place he could rent off me.'

'You haven't got any property to rent to anyone.'

'That was my first mistake, Dad. I thought as I was up in the Smoke, I could rent out Roy's old brothel in Forton Road. Roy hasn't been near the place for years and though he said he'd do the house up, he's never got around to it. I saw leasing it out as a way to make a bit of pin money ...'

'Chancing your luck, weren't you? What if Roy found out?'

'You know what would have happened, he'd have me skinned alive.'

'Roy took you into his firm to keep you out of bleedin' trouble.'

'You think I don't know that? That's why I'm confiding in you now.'

'Carry on,' said Vinnie. Jamie hadn't often been honest with him in the past but he wanted to believe his son, his own flesh and blood, was now telling the truth.

'I just forgot all about it and collected the rent money from him,' Jamie insisted. 'I didn't even need to come down to Gosport to do this. I gave him a post office account number and he paid it in regularly.'

'So how does this tie in with the boys?'

'I came down to Gosport to see Mum and she tells me this boy's body has been found near Walpole Creek. The lad had been beaten up. Is that right?'

'Yes, and the rest of it,' said Vinnie.

'Then Mum tells me some friend of Vera's has a lad what's had the shit kicked out of him but he won't say nothing. And the woman who helps Mum down the White Swan found her kiddie had hanged himself, So I went down to Forton Road and discovered there's a huge cage in the old living room of Chestnut House. I reckon that bastard what rents the place is using the boys for illegal fighting. Making the boys set about each other in the locked cage until one of them drops.'

Vinnie watched as Jamie raised his hand to his mouth as if to stop any more words coming out. This time it was Vinnie who sat back in his rickety chair. For a long time he watched his son. Was he telling the truth? What other reason would there be to confide in him?

'Fucking hell!' No wonder these kids were covered in bruises and of course that would explain the deaths. 'Is Roy involved?'

Jamie shook his head. 'And if he suspects I've dirtied his name, I'll be dead.'

He believed his boy that Roy was completely in the dark about this. Vinnie knew Roy hated cruelty to kids in any form.

'So,' he said. 'What do you want from me?'

'I've turned over a new leaf, Dad. I like working for Roy, it's money for old rope. I just don't want him knowing I was involved in any way. That's why I've come to you. The man that's encouraging these boys to fight must be stopped before another kiddie dies.'

Vinnie stared at his boy. He could see what was being asked of him. That if he kept Jamie's name out of this sad business, Jamie would tell him all he knew.

'What if this bloke talks?'

'It's possible he might. Then Roy would know how stupid I've been. But you could sort it with Roy, Dad. Especially if I tell you I know when the next bout of fights are takin' place. I'll do anything to help, Dad, but I'm doing good with Roy and I want to build on it. Not fall foul of him for simply offering this bloke a place for his sordid goings-on. I didn't know what was really happening at Chestnut House. Now I do, I'm fuckin' appalled. Them poor little kids …'

Vinnie reached across the table and covered his son's hand.

He suddenly realised he'd not touched his boy in years. Jamie stared at him. There were tears in his son's eyes.

'Let me think about this.'

Vinnie turned his head briefly towards the juke box where a lad of about seventeen was hunched over looking at the titles. Already Kool and the Gang were using their vocal chords and the lad was tapping his foot to the sounds.

Vinnie thought of the lack of progress he'd made so far on the case.

He'd visited Vera's mate in Old Road and had talked to young Paulie, who was definitely hiding something.

He'd spoken to Nora Hartington, Derek's mother, while she was behind the bar at the White Swan. Her boy had obviously hanged himself because he was scared stiff. And this kid who'd run from his mother's dead body, where was he?

It was because of information from Daisy and Vera that he'd discovered the fate of Derek, and seen Paulie's injuries. But he was sure they'd not disclosed all they knew. Was it really nothing to do with Roy Kemp?

Jamie got up from the table.

'I'm going to take a slash,' he said.

Vinnie watched his son walk across the room to the door marked Gents. He wanted to believe his boy had got into something that had spiralled beyond his control. He wanted to believe Jamie had taken no part in whatever was happening in Chestnut House.

Jamie didn't have to confide in him. Perhaps being with Roy, in London, really was the making of him.

What if a quiet word with Roy helped to smooth over any possible bad feeling between the big man and Jamie?

He thought of all the times he'd twisted evidence to prevent Roy Kemp's name from being sullied. And he'd gratefully accepted the higher-ranking posts that Roy had manoeuvred. It was a dog-eat-dog world, wasn't it?

Of course, he could keep Jamie's name out of any nastiness that resulted in police prosecution. What kind of father would he be if he didn't give Jamie all the help he could?

Jamie opened the door of his mother's house in Western Way.

'It's only me, Mum.'

'Jamie, Jamie, Jamie,' sang out Gyp as she ran to greet him, her tangle of curls bouncing about her face. He picked her up and cuddled her close.

'I missed you,' he said. She smelled of talcum powder and crayons.

'I missed you as well,' she warbled.

'We're in here,' shouted his mother. As he walked up the parquet-floored hall towards the kitchen, he wanted to believe his father had been taken in by his sob story of being completely in the dark about the use of Chestnut House. If everything went well, all he'd get was a bollocking from Roy. He thought of the missing top of his finger. He might even lose another fingertip, a small price to pay when he could be starting a prison term instead.

And if Heinz decided to split on him who'd take any notice? Jamie knew how much the cons and coppers hated paedophiles. He also knew coppers stuck together, especially where backhanders from their own kind were passed and taken. Roy and his father had so much murky water flowing beneath their bridges. But the one person they both cared about was his mother. They'd keep his name out of the case to protect her.

His mother kissed him on the cheek and pulled out a chair so he could sit around the table with the others. It looked like a family get-together that Jamie hadn't been invited to.

'Eddie's getting married on the Tuesday after Easter,' Daisy said.

'Congratulations, I didn't think you'd take the plunge so quick.' His eyes were on Summer who was dressed in a short-skirted suit and white boots. She looked good enough to eat, he thought.

'Couldn't marry 'em over Easter,' said Vera. 'Fareham registry office is all booked solid.' She looked drawn and ill, thought Jamie. The worry of her forthcoming operation must be doing her head in.

'Do I get an invite?'

'Of course,' said Daisy. Eddie didn't look too pleased but he'd go along with his mother's wishes.

'Eddie's spending Easter Monday goin' out on the piss with his mates. Stag night to remember, eh?' laughed Summer's father. Jamie looked at Eddie, who drew his fingers through his dark hair and said, 'No, you don't get an invite to that. You don't know any of my mates.'

Jamie saw his mother frown. He grinned at Bri. 'I take it old codgers ain't goin' neither?'

Roy jumped in with, 'Not so much of the *old*. Remember who pays your wages. But you're right, I can't keep up with the young'uns no more.'

'Well, I won't be goin' to no stag do,' said Bri. 'I'm off to Littlehampton; there's a book fair on and I need to restock the shop, I'll be gone all day. And as I'm an old codger, all I'll want when I get back is me bed.'

Everyone laughed, his mother the loudest. She looked pretty, sitting next to Roy, who kept stealing glances at her.

'Want to get down.' Gyp was wriggling on Jamie's lap. He held her beneath her arms and stood her on the floor.

'All right, sweetheart?' he asked. Gyp scrambled over to

Summer, who promptly picked her up and sat her on her own lap where the little girl started fingering Summer's dangly earrings.

'I'd better go an' buy some confetti,' Jamie said.

'You can tell 'im about me, if you like.' Vera's eyes were red-rimmed. It looked as though she'd been crying.

'Vera's going into Haslar Hospital on Wednesday and having the operation on the same day.'

Stay positive, he thought. 'That's good news, Auntie Vera. It'll soon be over and done with.'

Vera gave him a weak smile. Jamie knew she'd sooner cut her throat than make the kitchen full of people all gloomy.

'Tea, that's what we need,' Vera said. 'A nice cup of tea to celebrate.'

CHAPTER 27

Roy stared at Vinnie Endersby, then narrowed his eyes as he downed his whisky in one gulp.

'Give us two more, love. Make 'em large ones.'

The red-haired girl behind the bar of the Star grabbed two glasses and set first one then the other beneath the optic. Vinnie picked up the jug of water and poured a little into his whisky then hovered the jug over Roy's glass. Roy waved him away.

The fug in the bar was getting to Roy, and the music, he thought, was too loud. He wondered if he was getting too old for all this.

'So, something's going on down at my place in Forton Road and Jamie, always bloody Jamie, is caught up in it?'

Vinnie nodded. 'There's a fight on Saturday night. I need more than Jamie's confession and Vera and Daisy's suppositions to make arrests.'

'What do you want from me?'

'It's your place. I thought you'd like to be in on it.'

'You think I give a fuck what goes on in a derelict house I just happen to own?'

'You do when it's Daisy's son – and you do when kids are getting hurt. Also, I don't think you won't want the publicity: "Respected Roy Kemp owning a house where kids fight to the death …"'

'You're not pinning those deaths on me.'

'Never said I was, and I'll make sure your name goes unsullied.'

Roy threw back his drink and gave the barmaid, who just happened to be staring at him, a wink. She put down her nail file and sashayed towards him with a broad grin on her red lips. Still got it, ol' boy, he thought.

'Same again?'

'And two packets of peanuts as well, love.'

He pushed a twenty-pound note across the beer-splattered bar. 'Keep the change, love.' She gave him a killer smile. Roy turned to Vinnie.

'And to keep my name out of it, you want what? As if I didn't know.'

'Jamie's not involved.'

'Saturday night?'

'Saturday night. Meet me near the Railway Tavern early.'

Roy drove to the top of Portsdown Hill and parked. He remembered the times he and Daisy had sat in his old Humber, drinking brandy and lime. He felt sad. He wound the car's window down and breathed in the cold, clear night air. Portsmouth lay below him, a panorama of twinkling lights.

He'd had enough. He wanted peace.

Charles had told him that morning that he and Violet had bought a bungalow near the sea at Littlehampton, just a small place but plenty big enough for the two of them. So that was that. Charles and his mother out in the sticks, holding hands near the sailing club or having picnics on the beach. And good luck to them.

But what did *he* want?

He wanted Daisy Lane. That little blonde cow had got

beneath his skin years ago and he couldn't scratch her out of his system.

He sighed and his whole body moved.

Eddie should take his manor and make what he could of it. He should let the younger man make his mark on the underworld. Eddie's father would have wanted it. Besides, he owed it to Daisy's son.

When Eddie Lane had carved out a piece of Roy's manor, Roy had to retaliate. Or become a laughing stock. Even Daisy had eventually accepted the judgement of wrongs righted, even though Eddie's father had died for his stupidity.

Roy hadn't envisaged falling in love with Daisy nor becoming her son's mentor. He loved the child, the boy who was so like his father to look at it hurt. All these years he'd worked with one aim: to present to Eddie what had been denied to his father.

But Eddie didn't want the business. The silly sod wanted to climb the ladder without help.

Oh, he could understand the logic in that. He knew Eddie was tagged 'Roy Kemp's blue-eyed boy'. Yes, he could understand Eddie's reluctance. Didn't mean he had to agree with it, though – especially when he'd just opened up a doorway to a fine little drug-trafficking game in Benidorm. Nice little earner, that one, but it needed someone to run it out there who wasn't afraid of dishing out a bit of violence here and there.

Roy pursed his lips.

He would ask Daisy to marry him one last time. Tell her he wanted to be with Gyp, and be a proper family. Not pop in and out of Daisy's life like a bleedin' jack in the box.

He would *beg* Daisy. Surely the woman knew he'd do *anything* for her?

CHAPTER 28

'You got enough room, mate?' Roy asked. 'If you ain't, it must be because of your bloody big feet, copper!'

Behind him, hidden in the overhanging vines, was Vinnie. The earth smelled damp and mouldy after the rain. The night was as black as pitch but he had a good view of the room and the cage.

'If they put something up against the windows, we won't see a bloody thing,' Vinnie moaned.

'Shut up grumbling,' Roy shot back.

Roy knew they couldn't be spotted from the path. If anyone walked up to the front door of Chestnut House, Vinnie and him were well and truly hidden by the enormous chestnut tree.

'If they cover the windows, then we'll simply break our way in and catch the buggers at what they're up to,' Vinnie said.

'If the bastards make a run for it, they'll be caught by my blokes,' said Roy. 'There's a couple of heavies out the back, near the White Swan, and another three guarding the front, hidden in the bushes over on the St Vincent playing field.'

'So you got it all worked out, have you?' Vinnie was quiet for a moment, listening and watching. 'Don't worry, my blokes are around as well.'

'Remember, Vinnie, don't you do the bleedin' dirty on me.

You promised if we kept your boy Jamie out of it, this house and the fact I own it won't become general knowledge to the rozzers. You got my promise that as soon as you've enough evidence on what these bastards are up to, this house will be gutted. I was goin' to turn it into flats, anyway. Of course the police recommendations you'll get for sorting out this little lot and hopefully finding that youngster's murderer won't be nothin' to be sneezed at, neither.'

Roy knew Vinnie didn't like being told what to do. After all, his rank was that of DCI.

'Have I ever gone back on my word to you? This ain't just my boy; Jamie's also Daisy's son. I'll always have feelings for her, no matter what you think of me. And I admire her for being loyal and speaking to you first about the two boys Vera saw sitting on the step of this place. Daisy didn't want you directly involved before you had a chance to clear yourself. She loves you, that woman does. My God, Daisy Lane's got enough on her plate worrying about Vera and the operation.'

'Daisy's son or not, he deserves to be chastised for this,' Roy said. His voice had fallen to a whisper. More men had knocked on the door of Chestnut House and been admitted.

'He didn't know what he was getting into …'

'Believe that and you'll believe the Solent's made of orangeade,' Roy said. 'But that's my problem, not yours, now he's working for me.'

Roy heard Vinnie sigh. After a while he said, 'Getting a bit noisy in there, isn't it?'

'Yeah, that bugger Heinz can't lose. Getting the punters to pay an entrance fee and then gambling on the kids. How old do you reckon them little sods are?' Roy asked. Already his stomach was on the turn. It had started earlier when he'd seen the cage.

'Eleven, twelve.' Vinnie shrugged. 'There's a fair few blokes in there, women as well. What kind of woman goes to a bloodbath like this?'

'Same kind of woman as likes fights and wrestling, I suppose.' Roy thought carefully. 'No, I take that back. The women what like boxing and wrestling probably like the blokes in shorts. Sweaty flesh gets some of 'em going.'

'That orange-haired little bugger looks a right bruiser, doesn't he?'

'Yeah,' Roy whispered. 'By the state of him, he's probably done this before.' He watched the boy climb the steps and heard the cheer at his entrance. 'Must be the favourite,' said Roy.

'Ain't that the boy from Old Road?'

Roy watched the underweight boy ascend the steps that only seconds before the red-haired boy had run up with ease. There was no spring in this lad's steps. Roy could almost feel the boy's misery.

'We know he's definitely one of the fighters,' said Vinnie when the front door had been pulled to. 'Poor little bastard, ruining himself for money, or a bike or an Atari set.'

'No,' said Roy, his heart heavy. 'This is the kiddie trying to keep his nan alive by buying her treats.'

Paulie walked over to Heinz, who was by himself, checking figures in a book and with his elbows propped on the mantelpiece. Paulie had been crying and he didn't care if it showed. Out of the corner of his eye he could see Earl sitting on the stairs, naked except for the old overcoat slung around him. He couldn't even be bothered to smile at his mate. Earl saw him and looked away.

'I needs the money you owes me, Mr Heinz.' Paulie hated the stench in this room. Sometimes he smelled it in his dreams.

'You'll get it after your fight.' Heinz didn't even bother to look up.

Paulie took a deep breath. 'I don't want to fight any more. I only ever started it because I wanted to buy stuff for me nan.'

'Don't give me your sob stories because you've got a headache or something. Go and get yourself ready, you little runt.' Heinz turned his head to stare at him and Paulie saw his eyes were like chips of ice.

Paulie didn't have a headache but he did have double vision. When he went to touch something, like the door handle just now, he'd tried for the one that wasn't there. But even this wasn't the reason he didn't want to fight.

'My nan died today,' he said.

Heinz studied his face for a few moments and then said, 'You'll need to fight tonight, then, to buy her a few flowers for her grave.'

Paulie stared at the man he hated. He knew when he was beaten. He'd asked for his back pay because he wanted to buy Nan a bunch of daffodils. He wanted to go to the undertakers and put the flowers on her coffin. And now he knew what he'd feared all along – that the only way of getting his wages was to do what Heinz wanted.

Paulie wandered over to the stairs and sat down beside Earl.

'Me nan's dead,' he said, and began to cry. Then he told him he wouldn't have come to Chestnut House tonight if Heinz hadn't owed him money.

'Look, Paulie,' said Earl. 'We're on first. You can't sit next to me crying your eyes out. If you want to get your back wages, you'd better get in the cage when he calls you.'

'What d'yer mean, *we're* on first?'

'We're fightin' each other.'

'But you're my mate.' Paulie felt his world crashing down around him. He saw the tears glisten in Earl's eyes.

'It's none of my doin'. You know what a bastard Heinz is.'

Paulie nodded. Defeated, he began undressing.

The crowd's noise hid Paulie's cries of pain and Earl didn't have to punch hard to get Paulie whimpering against the bars of the cage.

Earl was pummelling Paulie but stopped when the doors at the front and the back of the house crashed open.

Paulie fell to the floor. Everything was swimming inside his head. As though in a faraway dream he heard, through the screaming of the women and the shouting of the men trying to escape, Heinz say, 'What the fuck's goin' on?'

'You're going down for this, scum,' said the man Paulie thought looked like a plain-clothes copper. Paulie had seen plenty of coppers like him down Mayfield and Old Road. Now the man was slipping cuffs on Heinz's wrists. Earl was sitting on the floor watching the proceedings. He looked at Paulie and mouthed, 'I'm sorry.'

A big man with slatey-coloured eyes that looked like they had tears in them was unlocking the cage door.

Paulie's eyes closed.

In the bar of the White Swan, Eddie was relaying the events to an excited Daisy. It was near closing time and the bar was still busy. Chatting and pulling pints, Eddie thought his mother looked in her element.

'What I can't understand is that Chestnut House is just around the corner and I never suspected a thing like that was going on,' said Daisy. She was pouring lemonade into a half a pint of lager for the young bloke at the bar.

'Why didn't you come round and get me? I'd have loved to have seen that Heinz bloke in handcuffs,' she said.

'Mum, it wasn't no TV show!'

Daisy took the man's money and walked over to the till and deftly slipped it inside. Then she returned to Eddie.

'Want another whisky?'

'No, Ma. I didn't come in here to drink. That Heinz didn't broadcast the fights, it was all word of mouth as to when they were going to be held. The kids, poor little buggers, just got in too deep.'

'Vinnie came in earlier, took Derek's mum through to the back and told her all about it.'

Eddie nodded.

'Well, Vinnie told her and me. He said after fighting for months, her son finally earned his bike. Heinz stole it when the lad said he didn't want to fight any more. Derek was desolate and so scared of being made to fight again and terrified of what everyone would think about him that he hanged himself.'

Eddie felt sick as he looked around the bar for Derek's mother. When he'd asked her to hold the fort recently so he could talk to his mother, she'd done it willingly. Nora was a nice woman who'd been dealt a terrible blow. He hoped now she knew the full story of why her son took his life, she'd eventually be able to look forward.

'I made her go home, if that's who you're looking for. Phoned for her sister to come and sit with her.'

'Good idea,' said Eddie. He was getting edgy. In a while it would be last orders and then he'd never get his mother to himself. But he owed it to Daisy to let her know what had really happened at Chestnut House.

'Vera's gone to see her mate at Old Road. Paulie's in hospital and he's likely to be there for some time. That kid's taken a hell of a lot of punishment, Mum.'

Daisy sighed and went to serve Old Jack his tot of Navy Rum. Eddie watched his mother and the old seaman. Wearing black jeans and a black polo-necked jumper she didn't look more than a girl herself. Until you got up close to her and saw the pain in her eyes.

Daisy returned to her son and asked, 'Who's with my Gyp then? Vera's supposed to be in charge.'

'Jamie's with her. When I left, he was telling her all about a one-eyed giant ...'

'Jesus Christ, she'll be 'aving nightmares.'

'I'm not sure Jamie was telling the truth when he said he was unaware of what was going on in that place,' Eddie said quietly.

Daisy glared at him. 'Whether he knew or not, if it hadn't been for him, the coppers might not have found them kids today. I think you should give him the benefit of the doubt.'

Eddie shrugged.

'And the boys?' Daisy asked.

'They've taken them to hospital to keep them in for observation. That boy Earl is the one Vinnie's been searching for. He's the runaway from Portsmouth whose father's been looking for him for a long time.'

'What about the dead kiddie found down Walpole Creek?'

'He's been named already by Heinz. Poor little sod was another runaway, from Berkshire.'

Daisy moved down the other end of the bar to another customer and Eddie was left once more standing at the counter. He could see why the little pub had wormed its way into his mother's heart. It was full of locals and laughter and gossip about the night's happenings. Yes, he could see his mother was

227

happy here. Eddie felt for the envelope in his inside pocket.

Daisy had come back to take up her polishing duties.

'Just stop still for a little while, Mum. I've been wanting to talk to you ever since I got home but there's always been obstacles in the way.'

'So getting' ready to marry Summer is an obstacle, is it? You wait until I tell her ...'

Eddie ignored her banter and took a deep breath. 'I've had the details about the money you left to mature for me. I understand why you felt the need to make me feel secure with the trust fund and I love you for it.' His mother was concentrating on his words, her face serious. He'd got her full attention this time. 'The truth is, I don't want the money. Before you start shouting, I've bought property with it. What I really wanted to do was to give the cash to you but you're so cantankerous, I know you wouldn't take it. I know how proud you are and how bloody independent.'

His mother was shaking her head and looking perplexed. 'But it's money for you, for your future. Why don't you want it?'

'I don't *need* it, Ma.'

Eddie fished in his inside pocket and handed her the letter she'd stopped Vera from steaming open.

'Go on, take it out.'

Daisy's hands trembled as she extracted the letter and read the contents. Eddie saw her read the letter a second time.

'But I don't understand,' she said.

'It's quite simple. I don't want you going out in the cold to markets and car boots to sell stuff any more, having to get up at three or four o'clock in the morning to make a living. You're doing two jobs, running this place as well. You like being behind the bar here. So I bought you the pub.'

CHAPTER 29

Paulie opened his eyes. There were curtains all around his bed. He took a deep breath of the disinfectant tang. He could smell dinner. He liked the meals here in Haslar Hospital; they weren't huge but it seemed as though the trolley was being wheeled around with food every five minutes.

The nurses were very kind to him. Especially the dumpy one with the frizzy hair, she was lovely. He'd had an operation. A lady doctor had visited after it was all over and explained what they'd done and how he'd soon be fit and well. He couldn't remember the exact terms they'd used. The operation must have worked because he could hear better and he felt so much happier. They'd shaved his hair and he had bandages round his head. He'd touched his head and decided he might look a bit like a mummy that came from Egypt.

His mum was holding his hand when he came out of the anaesthetic. He wanted to talk about Nan and she let him. She also told him the council had approved a move to a new house at Bridgemary. He'd have a room of his own and a new school to attend. He told her he'd like that. She'd got a book for him about a man called Biggles who flew aeroplanes. He'd nearly read it all. When she came today he'd ask her if she could get him another one.

He could hear the squeak of the food trolley. He wondered if there was jam roly-poly and custard. He liked that.

Earl looked at the man with wonder. So this was his dad? He didn't know his dad was so tall and good-looking. Earl stared around the room that was full of cupboards with half-open doors with folders in and a woman called Mrs Denver sitting behind a big desk. That pretty lady from the shop with the blue sofas who smelled of poppies had talked for a long time with his dad outside in the corridor.

'We live in the country,' his dad said. 'It's a big house and there's a meadow for the horses. We'll soon get you riding. Would you like that?'

Mrs Denver was writing in a notebook.

Earl felt shy but he nodded anyway. The woman sitting with his dad was small and round and had a smiley face. She smelled like cake.

'I'm never going to take your mum's place, Earl, but I want us to be friends. My name's Cally.' She put out her hand and touched his fingers. He didn't draw away and he could feel her skin was soft. 'We've been deciding for some time now about buying a dog, a puppy. I'd like you to come along with us to choose. Think about it, Earl.'

She didn't look as though she took drugs. Earl smiled back at her.

Daisy sat back on the sofa and laughed. She'd washed the sofa covers and they were sweet-smelling and clean. Her feet were in a bowl of warm water. Vera sat next to her eating a square of Cadbury's milk chocolate. Vera's feet were also in a bucket of warm water.

'This *Shine On Harvey Moon* is good, ain't it, Dais?' For a second or two they continued watching the television.

Daisy wondered how much time she and Vera had left together. Vera had lost a lot of weight she couldn't afford to lose. Her face was gaunt and thin.

She offered a piece of chocolate and Daisy declined.

'Who'd 'ave thought you'd 'ave a pub, Dais? You don't know how happy I am for you.' Vera popped the last bit of chocolate in her mouth and was looking for somewhere to deposit the silver paper. Daisy put out her hand.

'Give it here,' she said, putting the screwed-up wrapper on the arm of the sofa. 'Well, strictly it's owned by Eddie but it'll have my name as proprietor above the door. He wanted me to 'ave the White Swan lock, stock and barrel but I said I'd rather his name stayed on the papers. I rather like the idea of working for me son.'

'But you'll be runnin' it and makin' all the decisions, won't you?'

'Oh, yeah. An' the first thing I'm doing is shutting it down for a few days. We'll get the wedding over and then have a go at a bit of cleanin' and decoratin' down there.'

Vera nodded. Daisy didn't want to talk about her going into hospital and the operation.

'Eddie's turned out a good boy, Dais.'

'Yes, his dad would be proud of him. Mind you, my Jamie showed his true colours, giving Vinnie and Roy the lowdown on that pond scum using them kiddies as punch bags.'

'So he did,' said Vera.

Daisy guessed by the tone of her voice that Vera knew Jamie was only looking after number one. She decided not to carry on that conversation. She wasn't stupid; Jamie had probably been in on that awful scam right up to his bleedin' neck.

'I'd 'ave thought Eddie would prefer a big church do.'

'That surprised me an' all, Vera. But he wants the registry office. So does Summer. Then it's up the Thorngate for a bit of a knees-up. I offered to lay on a spread but he said they got "outside caterers", would you bloody believe it!'

'But the honeymoon is goin' to be right flash, ain't it, Dais?'

'When they goes. So you bloody better come out of that operation with a bleedin' smile on your face because they ain't goin' nowhere until they knows what's happened to you.'

'I'm not stopping them goin' on honeymoon to Africa.'

'Quite true but they bloody love you so much they wouldn't be 'appy knowing you've died on 'em, would they?'

'Daisy Lane, you can be really 'orrible and cruel at times!'

'That's what Roy said, when I told him I didn't want him to stop here tonight. I told him this was a girls' night in.'

'You and him ...' Vera trailed off and then started on another bar of chocolate. This time it was fruit and nut.

'We'll be all right, Vera, me and him. How could we not be after living in each other's pockets all these years?'

'He loves you, Dais.'

'I know, and I love him. But at this moment –' Dais took out a wet, wrinkled-looking foot, lifted it and examined her corn – 'I 'appen to love you more, you silly old tart. Or I would do if you was to break me off a bit of chocolate. Of course, there's no way I'm letting Roy Kemp off me 'ook this time.'

'What you got up your sleeve, Daisy?'

'That's for me to know and you to wonder at, our Vera.'

Summer carefully carried the wicker cat basket up the stairs to the flat.

'You got such a funny little meow,' she said. 'And you're far too little for this big box.' Scrabbling sounds came from inside the basket.

She put a piece of newspaper on the kitchen table and lifted the basket on top of it. 'Now,' she said, 'let me look at you.'

Summer undid the leather straps and put her hand inside. The kitten's claws in the sides of the wicker basket were like Velcro as she tried to prise the little creature free.

'You didn't want to go in and now you don't want to come out.'

Eventually the white ball of fluff stood shaking and mewing. Summer picked the kitten up and hugged it to herself.

'I know a lady called Vera who's going to love you.' The kitten started to purr, a full-throated sound that almost filled the room.

With the kitten stuck to the front of her red coat, Summer went in search of an old feather pillow to tuck inside the basket for her charge to sleep on. Then she put the makeshift bed in the corner of the kitchen near the warm boiler. Next she set down milk in a saucer and a pilchard from a tin in another saucer and a small glass dish of water in case the kitten preferred it. All the while, the kitten clung to her, alternately mewing softly and purring loudly until Summer unhooked it and set it down in front of the food.

'There you are,' she said.

Summer wasn't going to let herself think about the cancer and how much it might really have spread inside Vera. Vera and Daisy had been in her life for as long as she could remember. They were better than the mother she'd had. When her mother died of a drug overdose, Summer had been found by Vera, shut in a wardrobe. Summer reckoned she owed her life to those two women.

Summer took off her coat and threw it over the back of the

chair, eased off her high heels and set the kettle on to boil for tea.

Tomorrow she'd become Mrs Summer Lane, Eddie's wife. She felt so excited.

She'd been up early this morning to cook a fried breakfast for her father. He'd be away all day. She knew after he'd visited the book fair at Littlehampton he'd carry on to Brighton. In The Lanes was a bookshop belonging to a friend of his who specialised in rare books. He also bought popular novels, cowboy books and sets of Agatha Christie novels that came as job lots from house clearances. He then sold these on to Summer's dad because they were in great demand in the Gosport area. He said it spoiled his credibility if a serious buyer discovered a popular detective novel on his shelves.

Afterwards, her dad would drive down to Chichester to see what he could pick up there. Summer didn't expect her father back until darkness fell.

Meanwhile, she had her work cut out packing for the honeymoon and trying on her dress for the umpteenth time. Since she wasn't walking up any church aisle, she'd decided on a cream woollen tight-skirted little number that showed off her curves but was well buttoned to the neck. A cream mock-fur bolero was to cover the top of her dress. If tomorrow was anything like today, she'd be glad of the extra layer.

Then she would clean the flat and tidy downstairs in the shop, which was closed for the next couple of days.

'Guess what else I got for you?' The kitten was lapping at the milk. Summer went to the cupboard beneath the sink and took out a red plastic cat tray. She half filled it with grey cat litter, set it on the floor then picked up the kitten and sat him in it. He promptly jumped out. 'Didn't think much of that, did you?' She frowned. 'Let's hope you like it better later.'

The kettle whistled as she set about making tea. She switched on the radio. 'Tainted Love' came blaring out at her and she promptly turned the volume down so she wouldn't be deafened by Soft Cell. A small smile lifted her lips. Her dad was complaining lately that he wasn't hearing so good. She knew that was a lie. He simply liked loud music so he could jig about to it when he thought no one was watching.

Summer wondered where Eddie was. She hoped his mates wouldn't do anything stupid and tie him naked to a lamp post somewhere. In her bedroom was his wedding gear. There was a new dark suit hanging on the back of the door, a silk shirt and Italian hand-made shoes. He'd also left his leather holdall, packed with stuff he'd need on the honeymoon – if they got that far. If Vera's operation didn't go well, they would stay at Daisy's until things were sorted out. On the bedside table was Eddie's wallet and his father's flick knife, which normally he carried at all times, but stressed he didn't think he'd need today.

'Tyrone's me best man. He's supposed to be looking after me,' he'd said. Tyrone was coming round in the morning to pick up Eddie's clothes. 'Vera reckons it's bad luck to see each other until the actual wedding,' Eddie had said.

There had been times lately when he'd kissed her that she'd wanted more than the kisses. He was the right man for her, and Summer knew when they did have sex together it would be just as perfect as she'd always imagined it would be. Of course she'd petted with other fellers before Eddie, in her experimental stage, but she'd never gone all the way. Her best friend Sue had said, 'You don't know what you're missing, girl.'

Summer had replied, 'I want to be a virgin until the right man comes along.'

Eddie *was* the right man. He was the love of her life. It didn't matter to her that he had had a great many women. He loved her, would always love her.

She didn't want to change him. She didn't want to try to stop him working for Roy, even though she knew some of the work Roy expected of Eddie was frequently on the wrong side of the law. And she knew Eddie wouldn't worry her with what he was up to when it involved crime. The less she knew, the better. But she trusted him never to implicate her in any way.

There'd been talk of Eddie taking over Roy's empire. Would it worry her? No, because Eddie's sense of fairness would ensure he ran the organisation a different way. His way. With the Krays in prison, the old gangland way of life was being replaced by businessmen who already had money but were willing to take a chance to make more. There was no room now for the petty criminals. Organisational skills were a priority and her Eddie knew exactly what he was doing.

Summer picked up her tea and tasted it.

The kitten, which Eddie and she hoped to smuggle into the hospital, was still tackling the pilchard.

Her hand shook and tea sploshed down the front of her sweater when Summer heard the bookshop door open downstairs and the bell clamped, silenced before it could complete its chimes. Then the door clicked shut and the bolt was drawn. Summer cursed herself. The excitement of bringing home the kitten had made her careless. She'd shut the door but not locked it.

Her heart was pounding. Footsteps were soft on the stair carpet, and coming closer. She could smell cologne. Not her father's Brut, nor Eddie's more pricey subtle musk. A sickly smell that turned her stomach, especially when she saw her unwanted visitor.

'Hello, sweetie,' said Jamie. 'All alone?' He walked over to her. She automatically shrank back. The kitten cried and he looked down by his feet. 'So this is the reason you've been visiting the pet shop?' For one awful moment Summer thought he was going to stamp on it. She knew Jamie was guilty of the most merciless crimes.

'What d'you want?' He towered over her. Stand your ground, girl, she told herself. Don't let him see you're afraid of him.

'You know what I want.'

She'd been aware of him following her, spying on her, but she hadn't wanted to tell Eddie. Daisy wanted peace between her boys. Telling Eddie about Jamie would only upset Daisy and cause ructions.

Did Jamie frighten her? Of course he did. She'd spent a lifetime keeping out of his way.

'Why are you always following me?'

He laughed. 'Why do you think?'

He moved closer, resting one hand on her shoulder. He was carefully watching her face. There was something strange in his blue eyes and she felt uneasy. She was never certain how Jamie would react in any situation. Her cup slipped from her fingers and fell to the floor, smashing into pieces. The kitten ran for cover.

'Clumsy,' said Jamie.

She stayed quite still. His hand on her shoulder began caressing the back of her neck. Summer tried to stop trembling. She knew what he wanted from her. What he had always wanted.

The bastard had taken his chance, knowing her father was out until nightfall and Eddie was on the stag day with his mates.

'I could take you now,' said Jamie. 'But you'll just let me

get on with it. I don't want to fuck you like that, I'd like a bit of action on your part.'

'Go fuck yourself,' Summer replied.

'Not while you're here,' Jamie said. His grip on her tightened. She could almost taste his warm breath on her face.

'Get your hands off me!' she cried. She upped her knee, kicking him in the groin. He fell away from her to the floor.

'Didn't expect that,' he gasped. She could see the pain in his face and took the chance to kick out again, this time making contact with his mouth. A thin trickle of blood oozed then dripped from the corner of his lip. Summer wished she hadn't removed her high heels; she could have inflicted more damage.

His hand snaked out and grabbed her ankle. She crashed to the floor and tried to yell out but his other hand trapped her mouth.

He was lying against the side of her. She could feel his hardness growing.

Dear God, she thought, I don't want this. Sweat and fear dripped from her.

It took every ounce of her strength to roll from him and, using the chair, she lifted herself to an upright position. Once standing, Summer ran for her bedroom but he was close behind her. She tried slamming the door on him but he lunged after her and threw her onto the bed. And then he was on top of her. He leered at her after snatching at her flailing arms, pinning them above her head.

'Bitch,' he said, the spit hanging from his mouth.

Summer bit his face. She didn't let go until he hit her across the side of her head and the pain set in. He grabbed her hair and his hand that had held her wrists was now at her throat. She heard the tearing of her blouse. Felt his hand grope for her tits, pulling her bra up around her neck. She heaved herself sideways and was almost in a sitting position, but she was gasping for breath.

'Please ...'

Her pleading went unanswered as he slammed her back down on the bed, catching her shoulder against the bedside table.

Fresh pain shot through her back. Then she remembered what was hidden beneath Eddie's wallet on the small table.

Jamie's hand had found her waistband, and with a rip, her skirt came away. Her thin panties were torn aside with the skirt. He was fumbling at his jeans when her hand met the cold metal.

Think fast, she told herself. The button locked the blade open. Coinciding with the sound of his zip being pulled down, it went unnoticed by him. Summer felt his hard flesh on her bare thigh.

With as much strength as she could summon, she pushed the blade into the part of his body nearest to her. She was amazed that the knife buried itself almost to the hilt.

'Fuck you!' Jamie cried. The sudden pain had stopped him. His body relaxed against her and she said, with more calmness than she thought possible, 'I'll take it out, shall I?'

Summer pulled the knife from the top of his arm. The blood spurted like a fountain. Jamie tried to cover the wound with his hand.

'Help me,' he said. She could smell the blood and its strange metallic odour.

'As I said before, go fuck yourself.' Summer got off the bed. She held the knife in front of her, the blade pointed at him. 'Now get out of this flat. You got wheels, so drive yourself to the hospital.'

'I need something to tie around it.' He had an agonised look on his face.

'Use your fucking shirt. But get down them stairs and out of here *now*!'

Summer suddenly felt very much in charge of things. She wasn't hurt, just shaken, and she was no longer scared, even though her clothes were in shreds around her body. She simply wanted him away from her, away from the flat.

With his arm hanging limply by his side, Jamie leaned against the bedroom door jamb. Blood ran down his arm and dripped on the floor. One handed, he did up his flies.

She still held the knife.

'That's Eddie's,' he said, looking at the knife.

'And I'm Eddie's. Don't you ever forget it.'

She watched him use the wall as a prop as he manoeuvred himself down the stairs. Saw him fumble at the door.

'Fuckin' bitch,' he shot back, turning and staring at her. His face was grey.

'Yes, and I'm Eddie's fuckin' bitch, not yours. Don't forget to be at the registry office tomorrow. Eddie will expect to see you there. You fail to turn up and I'll tell him what happened. He'll kill you, not let you off with a stab wound.'

When she was sure he'd gone, Summer went down and locked the shop door. She leaned against the back of it and felt as though her entire body was made of jelly. When she'd calmed, she took deep breaths then staggered back up the stairs.

Her father wouldn't be able to use his key to enter but she doubted whether she'd sleep before he came home.

Eddie's knife was cleaned and replaced beneath his wallet. The bed was stripped and the washing machine switched on. The bits to the broken cup were picked up and thrown away.

The floors and furniture were polished until there was no cleaning left to do. Jamie's presence *would* be erased.

At last, Summer bundled up her torn clothes, threw them in the pedal bin and scrubbed her skin in the shower.

She wouldn't make a fuss. She didn't want Jamie's death on her conscience if she told Eddie what had happened. She would put the attack from her mind.

Tomorrow was her wedding day.

CHAPTER 30

Easter Monday today, and tomorrow was Eddie's wedding day and there was no fuckin' parking spaces, even at six am, in Curtain Road. The vans used by the traders selling goods at the special bank holiday market were parked bumper to bumper. Petticoat Lane was heaving.

'Fuckin' 'ell.' Tyrone smoothed back his wiry hair. 'This is ridiculous.'

'Go round again.' Eddie could sense Tyrone's unease and he knew he had to keep control. 'And for fuck's sake, keep calm. Remember, we need to be as close to that telephone box as possible. And close to the entrance of Safety Services.'

'Keep faffing about like this and someone's gonna fuckin' guess this van ain't nothin' like the proper Safety Services vans.' Tyrone crunched the gears and Eddie frowned. Jet was the designated driver, not Tyrone, but Jet was at present hiding beyond the outer wall of Safety Services. Jet's driving skills were reserved for when they got away from Curtain Road.

'Quick, get in there!' Eddie motioned to a car backing out.

Tyrone manoeuvred the vehicle into the parking space.

'Thank Christ for that,' said Eddie.

'What if something goes wrong?' Tyrone had a tremble to his voice.

'How the fuck can it? I've been planning this robbery all

243

the time I was in the nick. I got everything sorted from tools to safe houses and routes away from here. No one'll get hurt. The tasers'll make sure of that. Anything we take in, we bring out. Leave nothing for the bastard cops to nail us with. No fuckin' clues means we're home and dry.'

'I'm glad we're finally doin' the job.' Eddie hoped Ty was going to stop moaning. 'For weeks we've been watching this place and discussing it round that table at your mum's house.'

'Had to make sure you dozy lot understood, didn't I? We've got a map of the inside, mate, including the positions of the security cameras. How can we possibly slip up?'

Eddie thought about the men – Clive, Big Col and Jet – who should by now have shimmied over the high wall and secreted themselves about the outside of the Safety Services depot, avoiding the cameras. Now the trick was to get them, him and Tyrone right inside the building. Suddenly, Eddie froze.

'What's the matter with you?' Tyrone was looking at him like he'd cracked up. Eddie wiped away the condensation on the inside of the window.

Across the street, double parked, was Jamie's red car. He blinked to make sure he wasn't seeing things. When Jamie wound the window down and gave him the thumbs-up sign, Eddie thought his worst nightmare had come true. He was furious.

'See that cunt!'

'What?' Tyrone used his sleeve to wipe a circle in the steamed-up window. 'That who I think it is?'

'Too fuckin' right it's Jamie.' Eddie grabbed for the door handle but by the time his feet touched the icy ground, his brother was gone. He climbed back in. He was shaking.

'Dunno what to make of that.' Ty gave him a strange look.

Eddie hadn't told any of them about Jamie's demand for part of the money because no way was he going to give in to the little shit. 'Actually, I do know what it's about, Ty, but there ain't no need for you to worry. I got it all under control.'

But what other surprises did Jamie have in store for him? He shook his head. He had to show Ty he wasn't rattled. He settled himself more comfortably in the passenger seat.

'Let's run through things once more.' Eddie nodded towards the building. 'There is only one man on duty after the night shift leaves an' the day shift arrives. He's goin' to collect his pint of milk to make tea and to get that milk, he comes to the outside area where the milkman has left it in the cubby hole on the road. After he's collected the pint, that's when our blokes hiding around the inside walls can grab hold of him to get him to use his keys to let them right inside the building. When they're in, we're in. Jet'll phone that box's number –' he pointed to the telephone box '– when the perimeter alarms are off.'

He thought of the risks they were taking and how he couldn't be certain Jamie wouldn't fuck things up. I mustn't show fear, he thought. 'Remember, that's when it's okay for us two to drive into the Safety Services building.'

'What'll happen then?'

'We lie low. There'll be employees coming in to work at the depot and later vans will be arriving with their cargoes of cash. Other vehicles will be coming in for fresh supplies of money to replenish local businesses. Of course, the vans with money aboard them will be held by us, with their drivers and guards then locked in at Safety Services.'

'I'm not sure about all the waitin' about . . .'

'For fuck's sake, Ty, it's a waiting game. I've explained this time and time again. Waiting for the bleedin' employees to come to work to co-operate with keys and passwords. Waiting for time-locks on the doors to expire so we can get into the vaults.'

'You sure this is gonna work?'

'I *know* it will work.'

'It's a cheeky crime.'

'That's the beauty of it. I've spent months working on plans, weeks watching the employees and you lot are handpicked because I know you're up to the job. I trust you.'

Jamie was the only fly in the ointment. Eddie never knew what the bugger would come up with next. He wished he could spirit the bastard away. Out of his life, if not for ever, for a bloody long time.

Eddie glanced at the telephone box and hoped it didn't look suspicious that the van was parked next to it with its window rolled down on such a cold day.

'I fuckin' hate all this hangin' about.' Ty moved to make himself more comfortable 'You been so busy goin' over what we got to do when we gets inside Security Services you never told us how you came up with this idea.'

Eddie reckoned it might help to pass the time. 'I was celled in Winchester with a mush who became a good mate.' Eddie thought of Ginge and wished him well. 'He was a forger. One of his clients made the mistake of sharing information.

'Why didn't the client do the job?'

'Good question, Ty. Ginge thought he might have, but the bloke was shot by one of Ronnie Kray's henchmen shortly after he was let out.'

'Fair enough. What I don't understand, is how you got these fuckin' plans? If you ain't never stepped inside the place, how come you knows where everything is and all the bleedin' dimensions?'

'I don't feel proud of meself for the way I went about things. But it's important to me, Tyrone, to do one really big job, bigger than anything Roy Kemp's ever attempted.'

'Why?' Ty leaned back in his seat.

'Inside, I spent a lot of time fightin' off blaggers who referred to me as Roy Kemp's blue-eyed boy.'

'Well, ain't you?'

'See what I mean? I'm fuckin' tagged.'

'Well I wouldn't mind ...'

'Yes, you fuckin' well would if it meant you didn't have an identity of your own. And if you'd taken as much shit in your life as I have.'

There was silence, broken only by the noise from the stream of traffic outside. Eddie wound up the window. 'My feet are fuckin' frozen.'

'Open the window! How we gonna hear the bleedin' phone?'

Eddie glared at Tyrone but wound down the window again.

'You gonna carry on and tell me about how you got the plans of this place?'

'I hung about the exit watching the comings and goings until I spotted who I guessed might be a talker.' He'd got Tyrone's full attention. 'She was wheeling her bike up the road towards the market. I did a quick bit of footwork and got in front of her by way of the stalls and purposely knocked into her.'

'Why?' Ty looked puzzled. 'You got Summer ...'

'Nothin' to do with wanting the bint, dozy. Anyway, after I dusted her off I could see her appraising the goods, like, and I suggested a coffee. It all started from there. It took a week or so to get into her knickers an' you know what Vera says, "The head that shares the pillow shares the secrets."'

Eddie looked at Ty then shifted uncomfortably. He hadn't

liked stringing the woman along. Annie was a nice little thing. She wheeled messages and sometimes cash from one sealed unit to another.

'She'd worked there five years so there wasn't much she didn't know about the place.'

'You was lucky you picked a winner first go. Supposing you picked on a charlady.'

'Charladies know what's goin' on, you dimwit. An' no, I wasn't so lucky when a couple of weeks later we was in this caff an' her boyfriend came up an' walloped me so hard I thought me nose was broke.' He paused and thought of Annie, a pixie of a girl, screaming for her man to stop punishing him. 'Anyway, that all ended happily because afterwards the bozo put a ring on her finger and made her a stay-at-home wife.'

'Did she know what you was up to?'

'Are you fuckin' daft? She thought I was a salesman down here on business. Which I was in a way, only it was me own business. An' before you says anything, she meant nothin' to me. She was a means to an end. I took her nice places and bought her pretty gifts to sweeten her.'

'In return for information about Security Services?'

'When I asked her questions, I got answers. The layout of the place, the hidden cameras, which bloke did what job, how the whole fucking system worked, everything, and she believed I was just being interested in her job. I'd spent all that time inside learning how to draw plans and I wasn't goin' to let it go to waste, was I?'

'Listen!' Eddie heard the jangling sound. He didn't need to answer it. Col wouldn't expect him to. The phone stopped ringing then, after a few seconds, started up again. Two rings meant everything so far had gone to plan.

'Drive her in, Ty.'

The gates opened and allowed them to enter. Tyrone drove the van into the premises of Safety Services and parked in the loading area where Jet was waiting, dressed in a navy boiler suit and plastic mask. The gates behind them had already closed again.

'Put your mask and gloves on,' whispered Eddie. 'And remember, no names.'

'Fuckin' good idea for us all to look identical. But what if Margaret Thatcher's face pops up on an outside camera?' Ty grinned.

'I bleedin' hope the cameras have been disabled,' said Eddie. 'We're all after the big pot.'

In the vault were ten safes each filled with money, and cash-filled vans would arrive throughout the morning.

Eddie jumped from the van. Was it his imagination? The air felt like it was charged with electricity. Was this the 'kick' blokes said they got when on a job?

A tired and scared-looking employee, wearing a light blue suit with the logo SS entwined on the breast pocket, was being held at taserpoint by one of his men. Eddie had to admit their disguises were pretty good; even he had to remember it was Clive holding the taser.

'Alarms disconnected?' Eddie knew his bad attempt at an Irish accent was no better than his clipped south of England voice. But he had to ask; the last thing they needed was a bleedin' mechanical device squealing away. Clive nodded. Eddie turned to the man. 'Do as I say and you'll not get hurt. We don't intend to harm any of you so just make sure you tell the plods we was all nice men.'

Eddie knew all about an alarm that would automatically go off when the vault was opened.

'It's off.'

'Time locks?'

'No.'

'Why hasn't your bastard mate sorted it?' Jesus, he was scared. He didn't like the waste of time, the uncertainty.

'He's on to it now,' said another employee, with his hands tied behind him.

They were now standing in the airtight space between the vault and counting room. Eddie waved his stun gun. 'I wouldn't like you to lie.'

Furious head-shaking was his answer. Eddie walked back towards the doorway. 'We can't be fucked with waiting for time locks when we're walking backwards and forwards collecting the loot,' he said to Clive. 'Blindfold these two again and take them back with the others.'

He knew the vault was linked to the counting room and another airtight space connected that to the office. A steel cage enabled trolleys to be wheeled through and into the vault via the series of time-locked areas. Eventually, the outside shutters would be electronically raised for van loading, or unloading. Their van was parked in the loading bay, ready.

'Where are the rest of the guards and employees?'

'Don't worry, boss,' said Big Col, 'they're all tucked up safe and sound where you wanted 'em.' They were locked in a smaller office off the main one.

'No violence?'

'No violence. Except I had a lairy guard who—'

'You blast him?'

Col nodded.

'He okay now?'

The nod came again. Relief flooded through Eddie. But he still couldn't forget the image of Jamie waving to him from the car's window.

'Fortunate it wasn't a revolver you had in your hand, then, wasn't it? Or we'd have a murder charge hanging over our heads.'

'Sorry, boss.'

Suddenly the rumbling noise started. The time locks had been disabled, and he could hear the sound of trolleys trundling on the wooden floor. He smiled to himself. His men were working with as little dialogue as possible. Wouldn't do for some bright spark to recognise voices.

Eddie walked through into the smaller office designated to confine the guards and employees. Several men and three women were tied up, with duct tape sealing their mouths and eyes. He satisfied himself they were all unharmed.

'Soon be over,' he said to them, with a smile he realised they'd not see behind his rigid mask and their duct tape.

It took until lunchtime to waylay employees of Safety Services, use them to play their parts, either at the switchboard, telephone, electronic keypads or manual locks, and then to confine them.

It was imperative Safety Services had to be seen to be working normally.

Deliveries of cash were accepted by Safety Services usual staff, who had been 'persuaded' to co-operate by Eddie's men. Drivers and staff were then imprisoned. No cash would leave Safety Services. Irate phone calls were admirably dealt with by Safety Services personnel; again with the help of Eddie's men and their tasers.

Eddie walked through the cage and into the vault. From the open safes, a feast of banknotes met his eyes. He could smell the money. His men were filling trolleys and pushing them towards the exit. He let the corners of his mouth raise themselves to a contented smile.

'No one must suspect a robbery's in progress.'

'This part's the easy part, boss,' Col said.

'Nearly done?'

'Nearly done,' said Col. Eddie walked down through the cage and waited for his men to finish loading.

'You know where we're going?' Eddie was talking to Jet. A further feeling of euphoria stole over Eddie, looking in the back of his van at boxes filled with more money than he'd ever dreamed of. Jet nodded and climbed in the driving seat, ready to fire the engine as soon as the shutters were raised for him to drive the van out of the yard and into Curtain Road.

Eddie approached the office where the prisoners were and spoke to a lanky employee. Then he tore the duct tape from his eyes and mouth.

'Ouch!'

'Sorry, mate.' The man stared fearfully at Eddie's taser. 'You press the button for the manual shutter to lift so we can get out of here. Do it right and no one gets hurt. You got the code?' Lanky nodded. Eddie pulled the duct tape from his wrists. The man dialled numbers on a large keypad handed to him. 'Right, now all we need is for you to sit here while I tape you up again. Nice and easy, no violence.'

Eddie bound the man's hands and mouth.

'I'll leave your eyes, mate. That tape's a bugger with your eyebrows.'

Once the shutters rolled up, Eddie gave the signal and they piled into the van.

He held his breath; sweat trickled down his back. Would Jamie have alerted the cops?

There was a hush in the vehicle until they passed though the main gate and into busy Curtain Road.

Then the noise started. The pent-up emotions of them all

overflowing into handshaking, laughter and talk of the job they'd just accomplished.

Eddie's heart was banging away like a drum. He thought of the next step in the operation. Everything except the actual money would be burned when they reached their destination.

'We need to get to Hampshire as soon as possible. No breaking the speed limits and for God's sake take off them twatting masks; all these Margaret Thatcher lookalikes are beginning to unnerve me.'

'How soon d'you reckon them employees'll be found?' asked Clive.

'Soon as someone twigs the excuses being given out over the telephone about Safety Services having van trouble this morning isn't viable.'

'Things'll go fuckin' apeshit,' said Big Col.

Again, laughter filled the van.

'How d'you feel, Eddie Boy?' asked Tyrone.

'Fuckin' marvellous,' he said. His heart was still beating a tattoo inside his chest. Now he could give Summer and his mother everything they'd ever wanted and at last he was his own man. 'Best stag party ever!'

'How much further, boss?'

Eddie glanced at Wickham Square with its old world charm. The place attracted visitors for being one of the prettiest villages in Hampshire.

'Not much further, Jet. There's a turning on the road to Fareham.'

Soon the van was pulling into the yard of the farmhouse from the single track road. Eddie, courtesy of Jamie, half expected blue-uniformed coppers to jump from behind every bush.

'Get this van in that barn, Jet.' He pointed to a clapped-out building. 'We unload first, straight into the house; there's a connecting door so we won't be seen. Don't worry about nosy neighbours – there aren't any. But I've been coming here in a van similar to this irregularly, soon after I rented the place, so if someone does notice the van, they won't think it's out of place.' He looked at the ramshackle buildings and the farm in need of love and attention. It was a pretty place, in the middle of nowhere.

'How did you get hold of this?'

'Bloody nosy, ain't you, Col? I rented it through an agency under a false name; did all the paperwork by phone and fake credit card.'

'Well, I wouldn't fancy livin' here, Eddie.'

'You don't 'ave to.' Eddie turned the key in the lock and the door opened to reveal dusty bits of wooden furniture, a worn wooden floor and the smell of must and decay everywhere.

'We'll unload first.' Eddie passed through the scullery and unlocked the door that led in from the barn. A couple of collared doves made him jump.

'Jesus Christ, I could do with a beer,' said Tyrone, so close behind him he was almost his shadow.

'That fridge.' He pointed to a large old-fashioned, curved Frigidaire in the corner, chugging away. 'It's stocked with beers and there's enough food to feed an army.'

'A real stag party, then?' Tyrone was already pulling open the door to admit the van.

Eddie laughed. 'Yeah, but for God's sake get me to Fareham registry office in the morning, Ty.'

It wasn't long before the men's high spirits were getting the better of them, so Eddie shouted, 'Unloading first, then counting. Before we so much as take a top off a bottle, okay?' Murmurs of assent could be heard amidst the grumbling.

It wasn't until the evening that their chore was complete.

'Whew.' Eddie couldn't believe the total. The room was full of cigarette smoke.

'Seven fuckin' million pounds,' Tyrone said. 'Got to be the largest cash robbery ever.'

'D'you realise how much that is each?' Col was dumfounded at Tyrone's words.

'Wait a bit.' Eddie didn't want things to get out of control. 'You get the money when we leave here. But don't fuckin' spend it yet. We've talked about this.' There were a couple of groans but he carried on. 'If any of us starts flashin' unusual amounts of readies about, the coppers'll want to know where the money's coming from.' He got up and went out to the fridge.

Tucked between two beer bottles was an envelope. Eddie tore it open.

WELL DONE, BRUV. I'M LOOKING FORWARD TO MY SHARE.

'What the fuck!' How had Jamie found out about this place? When had he been here? Eddie was shaking.

'Where's them bleedin' beers?' Jet was shouting.

Eddie screwed up the note and stuffed it in his pocket. He went into the room with his arms full of beers and began passing them around.

Jet took a bottle and shucked off the cap with the opener then passed it on to Col, who asked, 'Where we gettin' rid of the van? Can't leave it here.'

'Torching it Portsmouth way.' Eddie was still handing out beers. He couldn't stop himself from looking at the banknotes in their ordered piles. It was an impressive sight. 'All this crap can be fired too.' He kicked at a mountain of papers, wrappers and cheques. Then he took a great swig of beer and licked his lips with satisfaction.

'Fuckin' 'ell, Eddie, you thought of everything,' Clive said, finishing his beer.

'Been planning it long enough.' Eddie passed him another bottle from the few left on the table. 'There's plenty more beers outside,' he said.

'Can I ask how we're going to get home without transport?' Clive narrowed his eyes.

'In my car. It's in the other barn. But you gotta remember the alibis. You're all with me today because tomorrow I'm getting wed. I choose not to drink any more.' He waved the bottle he was holding. 'An' this first beer is me last, because I need a clear head for tomorrow. Our alibis are we've been visiting the fleshpots of Roy Kemp's bars and clip joints where you've made pigs of yourselves sampling the delights of his girls. I'll stay sober only because I don't want to get picked up for drink-driving. That's our story. Remember, we started celebrating early.'

'Who's goin' to believe you never 'ad a drink on your stag night?' Col laughed and threw his bottle in the corner of the room.

Eddie's mates jeered and laughed and Eddie laughed with them.

But then he looked at each of them in turn.

'We left nothing at Security Services to incriminate us. When we leave here, I expect the food to be eaten, the drink to be drunk and the place to be left exactly as you found it. No fingermarks, no fuckin' mess. There's even some grade A snow in that fridge. Help yourselves. We divide the money, we clean up, and we go fire the van, right?'

'You're the boss.' Tyrone winked at Eddie. 'What you gonna do with your share?'

'Not sure.' His portion meant he could buy the land abroad and share his fortune with his new wife. The hotel he'd have built at Nyali on the sunny coast of Kenya would only be the first of many. Travel agencies were already looking for suitable accommodation for holidaymakers. They'd be happy to fill his hotels with paying guests. Money would make money. And Summer would have a free hand in the designing of their own house, their swimming pool and the décor for the hotels. God, how he loved that woman! Gypsy, his mother, and his wife would want for nothing as long as he lived. Giving his mother the deeds to the White Swan was a safety measure, just in case something happened to him.

He pushed away the thought. Nothing bad was going to happen to him.

And best of all, he'd not trodden on Roy's toes, proving he was his own man.

But was he going to give half his money to Jamie? Was he, fuck!

He looked at his mates, eating, drinking and acting like kids. And why not? They had just pulled off the biggest heist in history.

CHAPTER 31

Eddie was gazing at Summer as if she'd just fallen from heaven and straight into his arms.

Jamie's jaw tightened. Bitch, he thought. Conniving fucking bitch. He watched as Eddie's hand squeezed her shoulder and Summer winced, but quickly reinstated her beaming smile.

Serve the bitch right, thought Jamie. That was the shoulder she'd knocked against the bedside table just before she'd pierced his arm with the knife.

And now here she was as though nothing had happened, having her photograph taken in the hall of the registry office with the air thick with the smell of flowers and perfume and polish from the sturdy wooden furniture.

Jamie brushed against his mother and moaned.

'What's the matter, love?' she asked.

'I had an altercation with my car door yesterday and the door won.'

His mother laughed.

Daisy looked good today, wearing a black suit with a hat to rival Vera's. Vera looked pale, and even the red suit she'd bought especially for the wedding hung on her frame and brought no colour to her face.

Jamie thought back to yesterday. How he'd made it to the War Memorial Hospital he'd never know. He'd told them the truth that it was a knife wound but an accident. He said he and a mate were simply knife-throwing at a fence and when he'd gone to retrieve his knife he'd stepped into the path of his mate's blade.

He supposed they believed him, the nurse didn't question him further.

'You shouldn't have pulled the knife from your arm,' the little blonde with the rustling light blue skirt had said. 'That's why it's bled so much.'

Jamie wanted to tell her he knew that, but the girl he was trying to rape at the time had pulled out the knife vindictively for maximum pain to him.

After they'd X-rayed, stitched and bandaged his arm, he'd been sent away with painkillers and a white cotton sling. The sling had been abandoned for the wedding because it would have caused too many questions. But he *had* turned up at the registry office. To not do so would have caused family bother from his mother and Vera.

Roy had provided cars for the guests, and the next item on the agenda was the party at Thorngate Hall. Jamie would go, he'd drink, see if he could pull a bird and then, much later, go back to his mother's to sleep it off.

The happy couple were staying at a hotel in Lee on the Solent overnight and tomorrow meeting his mother, Gyp and Roy for the vigil at Haslar Hospital. Vera was expected to be at the hospital very early because they were operating in the late afternoon.

Eddie was as proud as a peacock, standing there in his new suit, with his new bride. Everything brand spanking new for his brother. It was so obvious Eddie loved her.

Jamie had no idea what it was like to love someone who wasn't a relation. He loved his mother, he loved Gyp, but if any of the others were on fire, he wouldn't cross the street to piss on them. He cared about Vera, too. She'd always been all right with him.

'Group photo next.' He tried to shrink behind Vera but the photographer was insistent. The man was short, dark and in a shiny suit, and Jamie wondered if he wore the same suit to every function. His mother, one hand in Gypsy's, pulled him along and positioned him next to her.

'Give me Gypsy,' he said, and hoisted the excited little girl on his shoulders. The pain shot along his arm. To the groom, he whispered, 'Went off all right then, yesterday. I'll be in the money soon.' And then he was jostled away by people around him.

'Smile, Gyp,' he said through gritted teeth.

'That's it, folks,' said the photographer.

Jamie stole a glance at Summer. The bitch smiled at him! Actually fucking smiled at him. He didn't return the smile. She was showing off her 'something borrowed', a garter from Vera, 'something blue', a necklace with a dainty blue stone, 'something old', an antique bracelet Daisy had brought her, and 'something new', her wedding ring.

It was as if she felt Jamie's eyes boring into her for she looked across at him.

'You wait, you cunt, I'll make you sorry,' he mouthed at her.

Summer's dress and bolero, chosen with loving care, lay on the floor of the hotel bedroom in a crumpled heap. Eddie's clothes were spread around as though he had needed to cover the room with them.

Summer began to stir in the bed's cocoon of blankets she'd made for herself. He held his breath as she moved.

Last night, he'd been amazed by the great force of her lovemaking, there was so much to find out about her, despite them knowing each other all their lives.

And now he was hard and bursting against her soft body. He touched her beautiful mouth, her closed eyelids and allowed his fingers to ripple her flame-coloured hair.

Her eyes opened and her body arched towards him.

'Hello.' Her voice seemed like honey to him.

'Will you always follow me?'

She nodded her head. 'Anywhere, everywhere.'

He moved on top of her, feeling her yielding and opening especially for him. She was moving, pressing him deeper and deeper inside herself until he heard her muffled cries. He had waited for her and now his increasing hunger gave way to a rhythm until he, too, cried out her name, shuddered and was spent.

'I love you so much,' she whispered.

They sat close together, eating breakfast and trying not to talk about Vera. But Eddie couldn't close his mind to the possible outcome.

Summer asked, 'I wonder where we'll be in five years time?'

'Watching our children playing safely in a pool in the garden of our house.'

Eddie had no qualms now about not being his own man. No longer was he in Roy's shadow. He'd killed a man in prison to prove he could look after himself, and he knew he'd have nightmares about that for the rest of his life. Without encroaching on Roy's territory, he'd masterminded a crime that could go down in history. But inside, in his heart, he was still his mother's child and Summer's husband. He doubted whether he'd ever walk on the wrong side of the law again. Or would he? Bloody Jamie hanging on to his shirt-tails for the rest of his life was not a happy thought.

Ideas had been rolling around in his brain while Summer had slept.

Roy had already suggested Eddie go out to Benidorm to run the new venture. Eddie had politely refused; he had his own plans which he outlined to Roy. Besides, the business in Spain needed a man who could be calm in an emergency but ruthless enough to kill on demand. Eddie knew he was too soft for that kind of business. He wouldn't mind heading up the operation but he didn't want to be physically involved.

Yet the more Eddie thought about taking over Roy's manor, the more it appealed to him. He certainly wouldn't need to abandon his African plans. But would Roy react favourably to him wanting to run the business *his* way?

Eddie took another piece of golden toast and spread it with orange marmalade. One bite and he abandoned it in favour of *The Daily Sketch*.

He'd made the headlines!

The paper was full of the daring raid that had netted the largest cash amount ever stolen. It also mentioned the 'concern' the thieves had taken when imprisoning their guards. Even the tasered man was proud that he'd been singled out by such a gentlemanly crew! There was a big picture of him smiling for the camera.

'Is that what Roy was talking about last night at the Thorngate?'

Eddie nodded and passed her the paper so she could stop trying to read it over his shoulder.

'In five years' time,' Eddie began as Summer put down the paper and sat back on the chair to listen to him, 'we'll be either visiting or living in Kenya. My plan is to buy land and build a hotel close to the beach. People want more than a trip to Spain nowadays. I'll give it to them. Safaris as well. Visiting the Masai Mara and the Great Rift Valley. I'll give them holidays to remember.'

'That'll cost money,' she said. 'It'll make money but you'll need plenty enough to start building.'

Eddie smiled at her. 'I can sort it.'

'Where'll you get that kind of money?' He loved the tiny frown that creased her forehead and relaxed immediately when he whispered, 'Leave that to me.'

Daisy and Roy were sitting in the kitchen at Western Way. She watched him as he held the sleeping Gyp to his chest, matching his breathing to his daughter's, fearful of waking her.

'Drink this,' she commanded, pushing his tea across the table. His eyes met hers and Daisy wondered why she always felt she was being swallowed up whole when Roy looked at her. She went to the cupboard and took out a present she'd bought for Vera. It was wrapped in red tissue paper.

'I want you to put this in your inside pocket. I know it's bulky but it'll fold small enough not to be too noticeable.'

'Why can't you carry it?'

Daisy opened the bag and drew out the contents. 'If I take it in to the hospital, the nosy bat will spot it immediately and say, "What you got there, Daisy?"'

Roy nodded. He looked at the garment. 'Nice, very nice. 'But what if—'

'What if is precisely why I want you to have it in your pocket. I can't very well give this to her if the doctor gives me bad news, can I?'

'Of course not.' He somehow managed to refold the garment and put it back in the bag without waking Gyp.

264

'Last night, Roy, I was holding Vera in me arms until she slept and I never seen no one cry so much in all me bleedin' life. Worst of it was, while I was trying to calm her down, I really wanted to cry with her. An' leaving her there this morning nearly killed me.'

After a decent silence, he asked, 'So, do you want me out of the way or can I stay until you find out whether the operation's over and she's awake?'

'I want you 'ere, Roy. I want you to drive me to the hospital. I need you with me when Eddie and Summer turn up at the hospital. I want to be by Vera's bed when she opens her eyes.'

'What about Gyp?'

'Jamie's coming round before lunchtime to take her out. Reckons he's taking her to Bognor Regis to that holiday camp there. Apparently you can buy tickets that allow you to enter for the day. She'll love it. Children can go on all the rides. He'll take her on the beach, as well . . .'

Daisy caught sight of the horror on Roy's face.

'For God's sake, she couldn't be in safer hands,' she said. 'Jamie would kill for that kiddie, you know he would.'

Gyp woke then and struggled free just as the front door opened and Summer and Eddie swept in.

'That's a nice hotel we stayed at, we had a lovely time.' Summer realised what she'd said and blushed.

Daisy pushed her down into a chair and said, 'I'm sure you did. And did everything come up to your expectations?'

'Leave the girl alone, Daisy, her face is cherry red!' Roy laughed.

'Chastising me now, eh, Roy Kemp?'

'You bloody needs it, sometimes.' Roy looked at her and smiled.

'Eddie, Eddie, Eddie,' sang out Gypsy. Daisy always marvelled that the child could be fast asleep one minute and full of beans the next. 'Come an' play in the garden with me.'

'I don't want to go out there. You go and play.' Eddie had an expensive suit on. Daisy guessed he didn't want to mess it up the first day of his life as a married man. Gyp was already pulling on her red wellingtons.

'You ain't goin' out without a coat.' Daisy helped her into her red mac with the wool lining. 'Nice and warm, eh, Gyp?' The kitchen door to the garden slammed. Gyp was gone.

Loud banging filled the air. Who the hell could it be at her front door? Everyone she loved had a key. She walked through the parquet-floored hall and opened the door.

'Hello, stranger.' Vinnie stood on the step with an enormous bunch of flowers in his hands. He had his police mac on over a light grey suit and looked sheepish.

'I've come for news of Vera. All I know is she went into Haslar this morning, am I right?'

Daisy's heart melted. 'Come in. We're waiting now to hear something. I've been told to phone them.' She stepped back to let him walk inside. He put the flowers on the hall table. At once the blooms filled the air with sweetness. 'I gather they're not for me?'

He gave a half smile and shook his head.

'Go on through then. You want me to take your coat?'

He slipped out of his mac and Daisy folded it over the bottom stair rail.

Her kitchen seemed full of people wanting to know how Vera was.

She watched as Roy and Vinnie politely shook hands. But it wasn't really a greeting between Roy and Vinnie, more a symbol that secrets kept would go on being just that: secrets.

She was making her way to the sink top to plug in the kettle when she heard the front door slam.

The cold air rushed in and brought Jamie with it. His sweet-smelling cologne filled the kitchen.

'Hello, Mum.' He kissed the top of her head then turned to Eddie. 'Wotcher, Eddie.' Eddie just glared.

'What you got on?' Daisy asked. 'It don't 'alf pong!'

Roy looked over. 'That some of that stuff fell off the back of a lorry last week?' Then he laughed. 'You'd think that I paid him enough to buy decent cologne, wouldn't you?'

Jamie took off his coat and slung it over the back of a chair. She saw him grin at Summer then go and stand directly in front of Eddie.

'Got anything for me, brother dear?'

Eddie didn't so much as blink. 'If you don't get out of my fuckin' way, you'll get a bunch of fives.'

Daisy had heard enough.

'For fuck's sake! Vera's in 'ospital an all you two can do is fuckin' bicker! I'm fed up with it. Fuckin' fed up to the teeth with your fighting and squabbling. Don't you know you're bleedin' men, not boys!'

There was an uneasy silence.

In an effort to change the subject, Jamie asked, 'Where's Gyp?'

'Out in the garden,' she replied. She watched Jamie stomp out of the kitchen door.

A moment later, Jamie cried out, 'Mum, Mum!'

His tone sent shivers down her back.

Just as she reached it, the back door was kicked in and Jamie shouted, 'Make some fuckin' room on the floor!'

In his arms he held a soaking-wet child. Her eyes were closed, her hair dripping like rats tails, her skin waxen.

267

'Where's my fuckin' coat?'

Summer held out Jamie's wool coat and Daisy watched while he stripped the small limp body of her daughter, throwing her heavy wet red mac to the floor closely followed by the rest of her clothes until she was down to her white knickers and vest.

Daisy looked into Roy's face. White as a sheet, he stared grimly at the scene before him.

'What ... What ... ?' Daisy was kneeling down beside the lifeless form.

'That fuckin' pond!' Jamie flipped the little girl on to her back and with his coat helping to give warmth to the small form, he began kneading her ribcage and blowing into her mouth.

'Phone for the doctor, Summer. His number's on the pad.' Daisy's voice was curt.

Jamie kneaded, pleading, in between breaths, 'Come on, my angel.'

Then once more his mouth was on hers, trying to breathe life into Gypsy.

Daisy thought how small her daughter looked, swamped in the coat and the parquet flooring all discoloured where the pond water had seeped in. And still Jamie breathed into her.

'Want me to take over?' Eddie bent down to Jamie.

'Fuck off!'

Daisy saw as Eddie got to his feet that he was biting back his tongue.

And then Gyp choked and up came pond water and she struggled to a sitting position and brought up more liquid. She looked utterly dazed.

'There's a good girl.' Jamie rubbed her back. 'Let it all come up.'

'She's fine. Well done, young man.' Doctor Dillinger, who attended to Vera's girls, was one in a million, even if he was struck off by the medical council. He thanked Daisy profusely for his two bottles of whisky and waddled downstairs one step at a time. Daisy heard the front door slam.

'Don't know what we'd do without that drunken ol' bugger.'

She smiled lovingly at Gyp, tucked up in bed with her favourite teddy by her side.

'And thank you, Jamie.' She put a hand on the shoulder of her son, who was sitting on a chair at the side of the bed.

'If you don't mind, Mum, I won't come to the hospital. I'll stay with Gyp. I can read to her,' he said, opening a book.

'No!' Gyp could be forceful when she wanted. 'I want the story about the boy who goes to the haunted house where the axe man chops up . . .'

'I think we'd better leave 'em to it, Dais.' Roy moved towards the door. 'She's as bad as him when it comes to stories.'

'If you scare her to death, you'll 'ave me to answer to,' Daisy said.

Downstairs, Summer had made sandwiches and tea.

'Thanks, love.' She looked at the clock.

'You've got time to eat, Mum.' Eddie was selecting sandwiches and putting them on a plate for her. 'Vera might even still be in the operating theatre.'

Vinnie sat down on one of the pine benches. He'd been remarkably quiet during the time Jamie was saving Gyp's life. Almost as though he couldn't believe it was really his son taking charge.

'I'll fix that netting,' Roy said.

At his remark, Daisy bit her tongue. It was on the tip of it to say, 'That's what you promised before, only you found your-self a bit of skirt.' But instead she leaned across and squeezed his hand. He too had had a bloody awful shock. Gypsy meant the world to him.

'Thank you, Roy.' She'd had enough bad feeling in the house. What she wanted now was peace.

She looked at Eddie. 'You're quiet.'

'I was going to say thank God Jamie went into the garden. Don't know what we'd have done without him.'

Silence reigned as Daisy sipped at her tea.

Eddie would never know how she valued the words he'd just uttered.

After a while, she put down the cup and saucer and an-nounced, 'I'm phoning the hospital. But no word of what happened to Gyp is to reach Vera's ears. She's got enough on her plate.'

CHAPTER 32

The blue-flowered curtains were pulled around the bed. Daisy gulped back a tear, seeing Vera so small beneath the bedspread. Her face was as white as the starched sheets. With no make-up and without her false eyelashes, Daisy could almost believe it was a pale stranger lying there.

Daisy breathed in the bleach smell of the hospital. It wasn't right, she thought. This wasn't Vera's smell. Vera smelled of red poppies on a hot summer's day, not this awful disinfectant rubbish.

As quietly as she could, she pulled across the padded blue chair and sat down close to her friend.

Vera's left arm was on top of the bedspread. Daisy leaned across and felt for her hand; it was cold. She hoped the heat from her own body might give Vera warmth.

Vera's roots needed doing. There was a line of grey almost an inch wide close to the scalp before the jet-black hair appeared. Daisy had heard that hair and nails went on growing after death. She wondered if it was true.

The nurse had been very kind, had even offered Daisy a cup of tea before she allowed her to sit with Vera. There was a plate of Rich Tea biscuits. Vera didn't like Rich Tea, her favourites were the dark chocolate Bourbons. And remembering this had made Daisy want to cry.

On the floor beneath the metal bed were Vera's new slippers. She had refused to wear them when Daisy had presented them to her as a gift.

'I want to wear me own furry high-heeled mules, not them Granny things,' Vera had said.

'Well, you can't. The nurse said you have to have slippers that support the backs of your heels. The hospital ain't goin' to be responsible if you slips and breaks your bloody neck!'

Daisy had left the new ones, pink, with bobbles on the front, and taken Vera's mules home. She'd put them beneath the kitchen table, but she kept staring at them, thinking about Vera's small feet in them and her red-painted toenails peeping out. Eventually she'd taken the mules upstairs and left them on Vera's bed and shut the door.

It was just the same with Vera's nighties.

The nurse had confiscated her bits of lace and net and brought back two blue cotton wraps that tied up at the back. More respectable, the nurse had said. Vera had sulked. Daisy had taken Vera's nightwear home, along with the mules.

Vera's bed was in the oncology ward. There were seven other beds, all filled with women. When they'd arrived early that morning, Vera had complained, 'I thought I was goin' in a mixed ward.'

'Sorry about that,' the young nurse had said.

'Not as much as I am,' Vera had answered.

Daisy had left her friend propped up on pillows nattering to the woman in the next bed. She might have looked calm but Daisy knew how fearful Vera really was.

'I'll come back,' she'd said. Vera had her jab on the back of her hand and Daisy had been allowed to stay until Vera started to drift off.

She'd put her arms around Vera's small body then turned away and walked quickly from the ward.

And now it was over.

And the surgeon would be along to tell Vera and Daisy exactly what had happened during the operation. And she'd find out what the tubes were poking from beneath Vera's right arm.

Vera's eyelids fluttered. Daisy's heart was in her mouth. Vera's eyes opened and tried to focus and settled on Daisy's face.

'Hello,' said Daisy.

The sound that escaped Vera's lips could have been a hello.

'Thirsty?' Vera's lips were white and cracked, so Daisy picked up the sippy cup half full of water and held it to Vera's lips. Vera gurgled away, taking the liquid, then, as though she'd realised it was like a child's spouted cup, pushed it away fiercely with her chin.

'I can see you're gettin' better,' muttered Daisy, setting the sippy cup back down. Vera lay looking at her. Then she tried to raise her right arm and obviously found the effort too difficult. Tears filled her eyes.

'Any pain?'

Vera shook her head. 'Nothin' to it.'

The curtain swished back and a nurse poked her head in.

'You're awake then?'

Vera glared at her.

The nurse gave her a grin and whispered to Daisy, 'The surgeon who performed the op is on her way.'

Daisy smoothed Vera's forehead, pushing back the hair. Vera's left hand was quite still on the bed covers. Daisy thought how peculiar it was to see Vera without her blood-red nail varnish. She also remembered Vera creating blue murder when a nurse brought her some polish remover and suggested she take it off.

The curtain was swept back again to admit a very pretty, middle-aged woman, and two young women with clipboards. The young ones were obviously students.

'You're her next of kin, Daisy Lane?'

Daisy nodded. She wasn't really Vera's next of kin but she'd said she was and she felt like she was.

The woman sat on the bed. Daisy thought it was a very strange thing for a doctor to do, sit on the bed. But it was also intimate and restored Daisy's confidence. There were times when certain rules needed to be swept away and a patient's feelings considered.

She smiled first at Vera then at Daisy.

'Are you happy for my learners to be present?'

'Yes,' Daisy replied. Vera gave a sort of croak.

'Well, Vera, you've had some of the lymph nodes beneath your arm removed. We need to check the cancer hasn't spread. I'm pretty sure it hasn't. We'll get the results of that back soon. We've removed a cancerous growth where we'd pinpointed it from the previous tests, and below that was a small unidentified mass that looked like a suspect deposit so we took that away just in case. You've had what we call a lumpectomy. Which means you've had two pieces of your lower breast on the right side removed. The rest of that breast we've left.'

'Am I going to die?' croaked Vera.

The doctor smiled at her.

'Probably, when you're about ninety years old. You were lucky to have this taken away in its early stages. Later, when you're home, we'll arrange for radiography and you'll be on medication for five years.'

'So I'm not going to die?'

'I hope not; I've used some of my best stitch work on you.'

Daisy asked, 'What are the tubes for?'

'Drainage. You can't go home, Vera, until the drainage stops.'

Vera swallowed and her left hand crept towards the doctor's hands.

'Thank you for saving my life.'

'Not a problem. I'm glad to do it.'

Daisy saw Vera's grip on the doctor's hand tighten.

'How much of the breast is gone?'

For a moment Daisy wanted to snap, 'You should be bloody glad you're going to live.' But she knew how important looking nice meant to Vera.

The doctor enclosed Vera's hand in her own and said, 'Only a small part.' Then she began to laugh. 'But, my dear, *you* can easily afford to lose it. I guarantee with a decent sexy bra, no one'll ever notice!'

Vera started laughing.

'We'll soon have you doing exercises to get the movement going in your arm. You'll be right as rain in no time, and with regular check-ups, we'll be able to make sure hopefully nothing like this happens to you again. Now, if there's anything else you need to know, don't hesitate to ask.' She released Vera's hands and stood up.

'Thank you,' said Vera again. 'Thank you for my life.'

The curtain was swept back. As it fell into place, Daisy looked at Vera then suddenly bent over and snuggled herself in her friend's warm neck.

'I'm so bleedin' 'appy,' Daisy said, sniffing.

The little nurse in the blue uniform came in and asked, 'Would you like your curtains pulled back?'

'Yes, please,' said Vera. Daisy thought Vera had dropped

ten years in ten minutes and Daisy was so happy she got up from her chair and whisked the nurse round and round. 'She's going to be all right, she's going to be all right . . .'

Then Daisy remembered about Gypsy and the pond and her heart plummeted, but instead she said, 'The family's downstairs. Can I go and get them?'

'Sure.' The nurse consulted the watch pinned to her bosom. 'It's almost visiting time and tea time. Cups of tea all round?'

Five minutes later, Daisy had rounded up her family. The tea trolley was trundling along the ward and stopping at each bed to dole out drinks and cake. Daisy was gasping for a cup and knew Vera would be as well, even if she had to take it from that sippy cup.

Summer was first at the bed in a cloud of peachy perfume, putting her arms around Vera, careful of the tubes and bandages.

Vinnie presented her with his flowers and was obviously delighted at the huge smile she gave him.

Eddie sheepishly followed his new wife and was trying hard to disguise the large newspaper-wrapped basket he was carrying. Much scratching and mewing was in evidence. Roy, with the biggest bunch of flowers Daisy had ever seen, followed him.

'What's that?' Vera nodded at the basket. Her voice and her senses seemed to be getting clearer by the second.

'Shhhh!' Daisy said. 'Don't start it off bleedin' yowling! Remember it ain't supposed to be in here.'

Eddie stood the basket on Vera's bed. Then he tore a piece of paper from the cage door. A white face was staring out at Vera.

'Ahhh . . .' Vera's face had creased to a million laughter lines.

The kitten stood its ground, looking at Vera, as if weighing her up.

'It's a tiny cat! Is it mine?'

'Well I don't want the bleedin' moggie on *my* bed,' said Daisy.

'Do you like him?' Summer looked worried.

''Course I likes him.' Vera was trying to poke the fingers of her left hand through the bars. 'What's his name?'

'He hasn't got one yet. You got to give him a name,' said Summer.

'It was all Summer's idea,' said Eddie. 'She knows how you love cats.'

Vera's eyes were full of tears.

'I wish I could do more than touch his fur through the wire,' said Vera.

'That's you all over, ain't it? Got to touch things. You knows you can't let it out on the ward. Supposing it escapes? Or pees under a bed?'

Vera nodded. 'I'm going to hurry up and get better,' she said. 'Boy. His name's Boy. He's my Boy.'

Vera seemed pleased with herself.

'That's a good name,' said Roy, leaning over and kissing her on the forehead. He put the bouquet of flowers on the bedside table.

'Flowers from a gangster,' said Vera happily. 'I bet no one else in 'ere has flowers from a gangster. And flowers from a copper, all on the same day.'

'Daisy's got another present for you as well,' said Roy. 'She made me carry it in me pocket an' I'll be glad to get rid of it, spoiling the line of me Savile Row—'

'Give it to her then,' interrupted Daisy. 'I'll unwrap it for you.'

And from the tissue paper, Daisy took the red lace basque.

She shook it to take away the creases. Vera's eyes were as bright as buttons.

It had detachable straps, a bra to die for and sassy suspenders. Lace flowed like confetti.

'Oh, Daisy,' Vera said. Her eyes fell on the large cup size.

Again, silence descended on the little group, broken only by the kitten's purring.

'Don't worry,' Vera said. 'I got more'n enough left to fill those cups!'

CHAPTER 33

'We need to talk, you and I.' Eddie had driven Vinnie back to Western Way to collect his car. In the kitchen, he poured the detective a measure of whisky and took one for himself. For once, he wasn't worried about Jamie overhearing. He'd gone upstairs to find Gyp and Jamie asleep, surrounded by toys.

'Do we?' Vinnie sat down at the table and twisted his glass around in his hand.

'I don't want to fanny about so let's get down to business.'

'You got something to say, you say it.' Vinnie stared at him.

Eddie swallowed a mouthful of drink. 'I don't think it would do your standing in the police force much good if it comes out that Jamie was instrumental in the deaths of those boys. I happen to know a spot of promotion is headed your way and that could throw a spanner in the works, couldn't it?'

Vinnie narrowed his eyes.

'Roy and I have already worked out a plan. And how d'you know about the promotion?'

Eddie tapped the side of his nose. He watched Vinnie swirling his drink. 'Do you want a splash of water in that?'

Vinnie nodded and Eddie took the glass and held it beneath the tap for the smallest dribble, then he passed it back to Vinnie.

'Whatever plans you made with Roy is no concern of mine. I'm running his manor *my way*. The old way is gone and it's time we had a new regime. Once again, any finger of suspicion pointed towards your son has been, profitably for you, turned away …'

'What the fuck! I told you it's bloody sorted.'

'Vinnie, Vinnie, don't lose your temper with me. I'm just pointing out you've not come to any arrangement with *me*.'

'What are you talking about, boy?' Vinnie threw back his whisky and set the glass down hard on the table.

Eddie gave him a small smile. 'Calm down, and don't "Boy" me. Not now or ever. You see, I've taken over Roy's patch and with that comes all the aggro, and the benefits, and all the past dirty little secrets about burials of boxers in Stanley Park. They never did find the body of Valentine Waite, did they?'

Vinnie was silent for a moment, then, 'You'd find it hard to prove.'

'Does the pet grave marked Jock mean anything? They'll dig up bones, Vinnie, but they won't be bleedin' dog bones. Oh, Vinnie, I could go on for a long while about the arrangements you had with Roy Kemp for keeping both your noses clean. But I won't. *My* one bit of aggro is the Security Services robbery and any evidence that might turn up.'

It was almost as if Vinnie had stopped breathing. He stared at Eddie for a long while. Then he said, 'That was you? Well, I'll be fucked. I never thought you had it in you!' Eddie thought the look on Vinnie's face was laughable.

'See, Vinnie, you never knew what I was capable of, did you?'

Eddie didn't wait for an answer but downed the rest of his drink and refilled for both of them. Once again, he crossed to the tap and dropped a smidgen of water in for Vinnie. As he slid the drink across the table he said, 'I want you to think very carefully about any answer you give me.'

It seemed to Eddie the seconds ticked by like hours.

He didn't dislike Vinnie. He didn't much like him for the way he'd never been a proper father to Jamie, though. Eddie took a swallow of whisky and stared again at Vinnie. Then he stood in front of the seated man.

'All I can say to you about the robbery' – Vinnie looked up at him and lifted one eyebrow – 'is it was too well thought out and cleverly executed for the police to find enough to go on, and will remain that way. You know as well as I do that if a crime isn't solved in the first few days, it possibly doesn't ever get solved.'

'So I say, robbery, and you say, what robbery?'

'If you like.' Vinnie sighed, then threw back his drink.

'So, just as you've got used to "helping" Roy, now you're going to "help" me.'

'You're blackmailing me because I want to keep my son in the clear?'

'Got it in one, Vinnie.'

Eddie sat himself down opposite Vinnie. He was still a good-looking bloke, he thought. No wonder he'd turned his mother's head all those years ago.

Eddie spoke softly, 'It shall be termed atonement.'

'Atonement? For what?'

'For never being there when Jamie needed you as a kid.'

'I ... I ...'

'Come on, admit it. You've always put promotion first. Couldn't stay with Mum because she was from the wrong side of the tracks, not good enough for you. It's your fault Jamie's screwed up.'

'No, fuck you, you're not pinning his psycho ways on me ...' Vinnie made to get up.

'You can't even sit and discuss this, which shows how guilty you feel about him. Well, I'll tell you something, Vinnie Endersby, today I saw a new side to Jamie and I know you did. You were fuckin' gobsmacked when he saved our Gyp's life, and so was I. But when he was a kid, he idolised you. And you never gave a flying fuck! I've often wondered how he would have turned out if you'd been in his life more. Yet you let him down, time and time again, you bastard. And now when he gets his wires crossed, all you do is haul him out of trouble, hoping he thinks you care about him.'

'I don't have to take this shit.'

'Yes, you do. And you'll do what I want you to from now on else you'll never climb to the top of the tree in the force. Atonement, Vinnie. You make sure my name stays clear and I'll make sure *I* look after your son. He'll be happy in Spain, you know.'

Vinnie sat looking into his empty glass for a long time. Then he pulled the bottle of whisky across the table, refilled both drinks and handed Eddie his glass. He clinked Eddie's glass with his.

'Atonement.'

Vera sat on a kitchen chair at the table with the kitten asleep on her lap.

Daisy looked at her fondly, but not so fondly at the white hairs that drifted to the floor at each of Vera's strokes to the cat's fur. She took a deep breath of the heavenly smell that was coming from the oven and competing with Californian Poppy. Daisy smiled to herself.

'Thank goodness you're home, our Vera,' said Daisy, as she bustled about putting knives and forks on the table. She always liked laying the table for a crowd.

'I'm not sayin' it wasn't nice in Haslar, because the nurses and doctors were kindness itself, but there's nothin' like sleeping in yer own bleedin' bed.'

Vera had a crooked false eyelash that Daisy longed to straighten but she didn't want to draw attention to it. She was happy to see Vera had put on weight. Gone was that scraggy look she'd taken into hospital with her.

Daisy looked down at her black wool dress that was speckled in white.

'If I didn't like your Boy, I'd wring his bleedin' neck. I opened me wardrobe door and the little bugger was asleep in the bottom on me dress. I know I put this frock on a hanger; he must have clawed it down.'

'He loves you, Dais.'

Daisy narrowed her eyes and pursed her lips.

Jamie was sprawled on a chair, flicking through car magazines with Gyp asleep and draped over him like a second skin.

Daisy's eyes flew to Eddie, who was helping Summer with the lunch. Several times earlier that morning she'd heard Jamie whisper to him, 'Where's my fuckin' money, bruv?'

Each time, Eddie had ignored him. Daisy wasn't going to interfere. It was their business. They thought she didn't know what it was all about. There ain't no secrets in her family, she thought, nor should there be. Just as long as they didn't start another fight. If they did, she'd bang their bleedin' 'eads together.

'I'll 'ave to go down to Heavenly Bodies, make sure Lol's all right.'

'Vera, you ain't goin' nowhere yet. Use the bloody telephone! That'll tell you she's all right. Which she was when I phoned her an hour ago. She sends her love and says she'll come out here to see you when it ain't so busy. P'raps bring a couple of the girls. They all miss you.' Daisy glared at her.

'You better get used to doin' as you're told because you ain't doin' nothin' too strenuous until you finishes the course of radiography.'

'I keep telling you, Dais, just lying on a bed an' bein' zapped with a strong X-ray thing don't hurt at all.'

'You reckon this is enough carrots, Mum?' asked Eddie.

Daisy went over and lifted the lid off the freshly cut vegetables he'd prepared.

'You got enough there to feed a bleedin' army. What's Summer cooking?'

'Shepherd's pie.'

'Summer!' Daisy's voice must have carried into the garden because Summer came in with damp washing piled in a basket.

'I thought I'd bring this in before the rain comes down. What's the matter?'

'You're too good to my Eddie. He's not used to all this home cooking. Didn't anyone ever tell you you're a bloody lovely cook?'

Summer hauled out the wooden clothes horse and began arranging the washing over it. She turned to Daisy.

'It's no good you bein' nice to me. That bread pudding in the oven what's got your tastebuds goin' ain't nowhere near ready, yet!'

'Ohh!'

'Look, Mum, since you've told Vera she can't go back to the massage parlour yet as she needs to get her strength back, I hope you're not thinking of sneaking off to the White Swan, as soon as we've left for our honeymoon?'

'Will you quit worrying? I'm goin' nowhere near the place, Eddie, until the renovations is finished. Be nice to have proper flushes on the toilets.'

Daisy tried to ignore the fruity smell wafting though the

kitchen. She went over and sat on the arm of the big chair nearest the old-fashioned Welsh dresser.

'Are you asleep, Roy?' She bent down close and whispered in his ear.

He was dressed in jeans and a light blue shirt with the sleeves rolled up. He jolted awake. 'No, I was just resting my eyes.' He rubbed an eye with the back of his hand.

Daisy started laughing.

He traced her cheek with his other hand. 'What's tickled your fancy?'

'Just you, Roy. Thinking about this morning in bed an' you a big tough London gangster putting dolly clothes on Gyp's Sindy doll ...'

'She asked me to.' He sounded indignant.

'That child wraps you round her little finger.'

He grabbed hold of Daisy and pulled her on to his lap where she fitted exactly right.

'So do you.'

Daisy looked down at her man's smiling face. Then she bent her head and kissed him.

'Shall we tell, 'em?' she asked.

'You do it,' he said.

'Me an' Roy's goin' to be married.'

''Bout bloody time,' Jamie spoke in a whisper so as not to wake Gyp.

Vera had her mouth open. Then she closed it and opened it again to say, 'You can't keep running backwards and forwards to London even if you are wed. But I think it's lovely, Dais, an' I'm so happy for you.'

'I'm not going to live in London any more,' said Roy.

'Where you goin' then, Roy? Daisy won't live anywhere but Gosport.'

Roy smiled at her.

'I shall have to live here, then.'

Vera looked happy but Daisy knew she was worried that she'd be in the way. Daisy didn't want Vera to decide she had to move out. Daisy wanted Roy and her friend living in this big house and she didn't see why she couldn't have what she wanted.

'Don't say nuffin', Vera. You ain't goin' nowhere! I can read your mind like a bleedin' book.'

'An' I quite like seeing two lots of frillies hanging in the bathroom!'

Vera blushed. Daisy knew she didn't mind Roy's saucy words.

'Summer and me are goin' to live in London in Roy's house. I can keep an eye on things better in London.' Eddie looked pleased with himself.

'Eddie's taking over Roy's manor,' said Daisy.

Again, Vera's mouth was agape.

'Fuckin' blue-eyed boy!' muttered Jamie.

'Don't you swear like that with my daughter on your lap!' said Daisy angrily.

'Be quiet, the pair of you!' Both Jamie and Daisy looked up at Eddie's authoritative tone. Was this really her boy taking charge of the situation?

'You, Jamie, have done nothing but ask me for money. I'm going to give you the chance to earn it.'

Daisy looked at Jamie's scowling face.

'I'm sending you to Benidorm to take charge of the clubs and other businesses we got opening up in Spain. Roy reckons you're just the bloke to run things and so do I. You'll put the fear of God into anyone who tries to cream off a bit of my assets. An' I'll put the fuckin' fear of God into you if you double-cross me.'

Jamie, for once in his life, was speechless. Then, 'Am I to be my own boss with blokes beneath me?'

Eddie nodded. 'At the end of the day, you'll be answerable to me. But only if I find you're not doing your job. It's tough over there. But you choose your own team and all the time the money's rolling *my* way, you get to do things *your* way.' Daisy could see Jamie was over the moon. 'And stop asking me for fuckin' money! You'll be doing so well you'll be shitting money! Deal?'

Eddie walked over to Jamie, put out his hand and waited for Jamie to shake on it.

'Deal.'

'Thanks be to God! I never thought I'd see the day my two boys shook hands on anything!' Daisy felt the tears rise.

'What are you goin' to do, Roy?' Vera leaned back in her chair while the small cat stretched. 'You been a busy bloke all your life, I can't see you taking things easy.'

'I got clubs in Portsmouth—'

'No more shady deals, though,' broke in Daisy. 'An' *no drugs!*'

'I made a promise to you, Daisy, and I'll keep it. That fighting down at Chestnut House has set me thinking. What I'd really like to do is open a gym where boys can learn to fight properly. Me, Reg and Ronnie went to a gym when we was kids an' it taught us how to handle ourselves.' He looked at Daisy. 'Yeah, I'd really like that, get a few trainers in ...'

'Well, I think that's an excellent idea.' Vera was nodding her head enthusiastically.

'There is one thing, Eddie,' said Daisy. 'I'm pleased you're taking over Roy's business, you know I am. But you'll be on the wrong side of the law. I couldn't bear it if you went back inside. I'm sure Summer'll agree with me.' Daisy looked at her daughter-in-law for confirmation and got it.

'Mum, I told the truth when I said I'll not go back in prison again. Roy's way of handling the business is different to mine. Neither me nor Jamie will see the inside of a prison, that I can promise you.'

Daisy gave a sigh of relief then. 'But you can't be sure ...'

'Oh, but I think I am, Mum.'

His assurance made her happy and she trusted him. She turned her head and bent and gave Roy a kiss on his head.

'Ain't that bread pudding ready yet?' she asked after a little while.

Summer grinned at her. 'No.'

Daisy looked around the kitchen at her family. She was happier than she'd been in a long time. She smiled into Roy's face. All her life she'd thought she was an independent bitch, that she no longer wanted a man permanently in her life. Then, the timing just hadn't been right, but it was now.

Daisy sighed happily. 'I guess that's that, then.'

About the Author

June Hampson was born in Gosport, Hampshire, where she still lives. She has had a variety of jobs including: waitress, fruit picker, barmaid, shop assistant and market trader selling second-hand books. June has had many short stories published in women's magazines. *Fighting Dirty* is her sixth novel in the Daisy Lane series.